WHEN CHAOS REIGNS

A POLITICAL THRILLER

SCOTT COTTRELL

Publish Authority

When Chaos Reigns

Editor: Nancy Laning
Cover Design Lead: Raeghan Rebstock

ISBN 978-1-954000-58-2 (Paperback)
ISBN 978-1-954000-59-9 (eBook)

Published 2023 by Publish Authority,
300 Colonial Center Parkway, Suite 100
Roswell, GA USA
PublishAuthority.com

Printed in the United States of America

IN PRAISE OF "WHEN CHAOS REIGNS"

"An informative and compelling story. Given current events, When Chaos Reigns is a read of the plausible danger facing America."

– – ROBERT T. BUCKNER

"*When Chaos Reigns* is a novel of contemporary interest as we see both Chinese forces maneuvering against US forces in the Pacific and Russia wreaking havoc in Europe. Perhaps the work is predictive of what we should expect to see in the near future. Read it to find out!."

– KENN RIORDAN , JR, FORMER OSD STAFF OFFICER FOR MISSILE AND CHEM / BIO COUNTER-PROLIFERATION

"Drawing on his experience as commander of US Army Kwajalein Atoll / Kwajalein Missile Range, as a West Point & US Naval War College graduate, retired Colonel Scott Cottrell provides a fascinating tale of global intrigue and political tensions intertwined with well-researched historical facts in *When Chaos Reigns*. With the recently heightened tensions in US-China relations, this book may soon be all too real."

– DOUG NICHOL

"Buckle Up! From the beginning, *When Chaos Reigns* is a gripping page-turner for sure. A history lesson steeped in suspense, with a storyline of world events plausible enough to take your breath. A must-read for ALL wishing to know how tomorrow's headlines could read. This stuff could really happen!"

– DAVID BISHOP, GRADUATE OF THE CITADEL

"*When Chaos Reigns* leaves your head swirling as you consider its possibilities. The plot line makes you feel like you're reading the unnerving news reports of a parallel world that could easily become those of our own."

– JOHN CLEVELAND

"*When Chaos Reigns* centers on a real-life Pacific scenario that kept me spellbound with every turn of the page. It is not the end of current world headlines but the beginning of the chaos wrought by a dominating evil empire that must be recurringly reigned in. Or chaos will reign."

– STAN PARKER, SGT MAJ, (RET)
U. S. ARMY SPECIAL FORCES.

"I totally enjoyed [*When Chaos Reigns*]. Once I started reading it, I couldn't put it down. ... This author puts a spellbinding grip on his readers, far better than nearly everyone else of a similar bent I've read. He writes like John le Carré.

– JOHN WOODWARD

To Peggy, my wife and my best friend,

FOREWORD

Kwajalein Atoll? Am I the only one with no idea what or where the Kwajalein Atoll is? It is hardly a household term. However, now, perhaps it should be. The atoll, known as Kwajalein, lies in the Marshall Islands in the west-central Pacific Ocean, 2,400 miles from Honolulu, Hawaii, consists of 97 islands and islets with a total land area of six square miles, and has a long militarily strategic history. Today, Kwajalein is a part of the Ronald Reagan Ballistic Missile Defense Test Site and is integral to the defense of the United States. Who doesn't use the Global Positioning System (GPS) on occasion? Kwajalein is one of the five ground stations used to control GPS. This U.S. Army facility and Washington, D.C., are two settings for the novel. Colonel Scott Cottrell, US ARMY (Ret) knows more than a little about the facility. One of his prestigious assignments was Commander of the U.S. Army Kwajalein Atoll/Kwajalein Missile Range. For the reader, that is looking through the lens of actual experience and expertise.

When Chaos Reigns is loaded with twists and turns of political intrigue and military strategy. Here again, Scott Cottrell's education at the U.S. Military Academy at West Point, his graduate studies and military assignments add a depth of knowledge not often seen in works of fiction. A credible contemplation of a current-day war with China would demand that level of knowledge.

What about Scott's novel, *When Chaos Reigns*? "Outstanding" would describe it. So would stating that it is captivating, historically pertinent, and an enjoyable read. Scott has managed to intertwine a compelling fictional story with contemporary history, both military and political. I was taken by how a seemingly simple, personal event can lead to circumstances of utmost global importance. If one has the slightest curiosity concerning the intricacies of the political motivations and decisions that have guided or misguided America's foreign and domestic policies since World War II, this novel will not disappoint.

J.M. Patton, author of *A full Measure* trilogy

PROLOGUE

This fictional story takes place in the present day central and western Pacific and several other places around the globe. It is a blend of history, historical and current-day facts, and fiction. There is a group of atolls and islands called the Marshall Islands in the central Pacific, and the US Army has a world-class missile range in Kwajalein Atoll of the Marshall Islands called the Reagan Test Site. There was a significant operation in Kwajalein Atoll during World War II called Operation Flintlock, and the US conducted hydrogen bomb testing in the Marshall Islands in the 1950s.

The South China Sea, including the island groups of the Paracels, the Spratly Islands, and Scarborough Shoals, is a contested area in the western Pacific, with known oil reserves and even more extensive but unproven oil and gas reserves near the Philippines. The US has a mutual defense treaty with the Philippines, one of several countries, including China, contesting for control of portions of the South China Sea and its island groups. The Philippines claim Scarborough Shoals as its own. Taiwan also has vital economic interests in the South China Sea and is at its northern end.

However, the storyline is fictional. Any similarities of the fictional characters to any actual person, except where noted, are incidental. Some actions and comments have been attributed to several historical figures to facilitate the storyline but are not intended to enhance or diminish their character.

Please note the President of the US (POTUS) in this story is fictional and is not listed as either Democrat or Republican. There is no intent to disparage any individual or entity of the US government. The primary purpose of this fictional work is to highlight constitutional issues currently practiced by our government, specifically as they relate to the military. The story also highlights how faith can play a significant role in the military and our everyday lives.

The maps (included) portray the location of the Marshall Islands, specifically Kwajalein Atoll, in relation to the central Pacific Ocean and the South China Sea.

Chapter end notes are used after selected passages to give credit for information gleaned while researching this fictional story. The author also uses experiences from his four years at the United States Military Academy (USMA) at West Point and twenty-nine years on active duty in the US Army. This experience includes two years on Kwajalein as the Commander and almost ten years in County Public Works agencies to add color and background to the storyline.

NOTE: Named characters and military and other abbreviations are provided in the Glossary at the back of this book, following the chapters' Endnotes.

The Marshall Islands in the Central Pacific

Marshall Islands

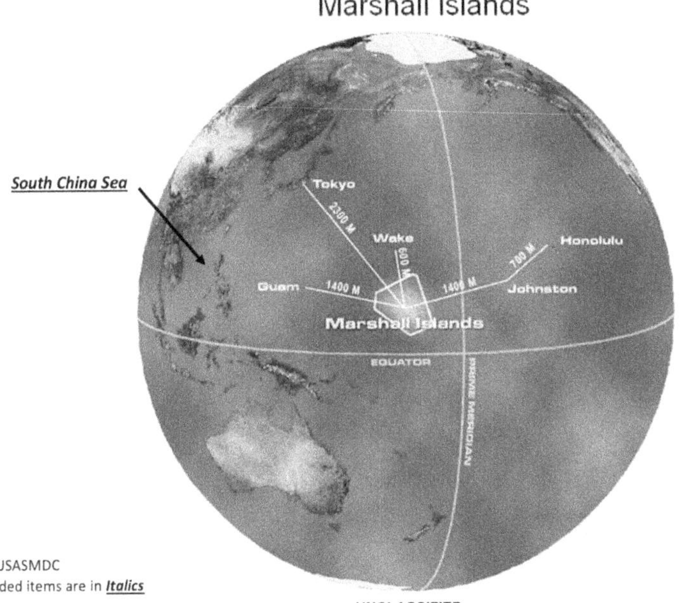

UNCLASSIFIED

INTRODUCTION

President Roland Justice was in no mood for a recalcitrant and blustery Senate bent on finding him guilty of high crimes and misdemeanors. Just who did they think they were? He, Roland, was the elected President of the United States—the POTUS, the most powerful man on the face of the earth, leading the most powerful nation in the history of mankind.

As he took the podium in the Rose Garden that morning for the hastily called press conference, most reporters and onlookers expected to hear his formal resignation or some sort of remorse on his part.

Were they ever in for a surprise!

PART I

THE STORY BEFORE THE STORY

CHAPTER 1

THE MARSHALL ISLANDS— HISTORY, FACTS, AND FICTION

Pokak Atoll, Marshall Islands, August 21, 1526

THE HEAT AND HUMIDITY WERE BRUTAL. CAPTAIN ALONSO DE Salazar thought he was hallucinating when he caught a glimpse of the tiny, flat coral atoll, literally in the middle of nowhere, halfway between the Hawaiian Islands and Australia, neither of which the Spaniard was even aware. His planned circumnavigation of the globe, a la Magellan, had been fraught with problems. In fact, his was the last ship remaining in the troubled convoy that started with seven ships under Garcia Jofre de Loaisa in 1525 from Spain.[1] Not wanting to waste any more time, de Salazar dutifully recorded his observation of this dry, low-lying, and apparently unoccupied atoll for posterity. He continued slowly west along the inter-tropical convergence zone—the doldrums in the vernacular or the *capa caida* in his native Spanish. *La zona de las calmas ecuatoriales* for those who had the time to spell it out. Little did he know of the existence of the other atolls and islands to the southwest of this atoll and the role this group of atolls and islands would play in the future.

Amata watched the Spanish galleon disappear in the

distance. Uncertain of its intent, he quickly completed his fishing and gathering on Pokak Atoll (a.k.a. Taongi) in the Ratak (eastern or sunrise) Chain of atolls and islands. Boarding his out-rigger canoe, he headed for the larger Kwajalein Atoll in the Ralik (western or sunset) Chain.[2] An unusual site in other parts of the world, this small boat had one out-rigger, a central mast with a triangular sail made of coconut palm fronds, and a simple rudder for steering fast and close to the wind. Most unusual was the map Amata now used to return to Kwajalein. It wasn't a map at all— it was some sort of stick chart used by the Micronesians for navigating the waters in that part of the world. The shape and alignment of the sticks showed the various waves, swells, and oceanic streams as they hit and rebounded off the islands. These actions remained constant enough for the trained eye and allowed navigation over long distances in and around the Ralik and Ratak chains of atolls and islands where Amata lived. Amata's great-grandfather claimed that their ancestors used the stick charts when they left Palau, Papua, and other parts of the western Pacific seeking new homes to the east—in the Marshall Islands. The folks in Panape, Kosrae, Truk, Yap, and Kwajalein all had their own stick charts. Perhaps the strange ship that passed by had one too!

Kwajalein Atoll, Marshall Islands, June 25–30, 1788

Captain John Marshall piloted his ship, the *HMS Scarborough*, through the shallow waters of the multitude of small coral atolls and islands, sweating in the 89-degree heat and 95 percent humidity. He and Captain Thomas Gilbert of the *HMS Charlotte* had been transporting convicts from Great Britain to Botany Bay in Australia while also seeking a new route to China.[3] Captain Marshall was aware of this group of islands from sailors' tales and logs of the numerous European ships that had passed that way since the 1500s. He had heard about Alonso de Salazar's visit. But this was the first time he had cruised the crystal-clear waters, visited the coral islands and deep-water lagoons, and met with their curious people. Captain Marshall noted the plentiful coconut palm trees, the abundant fishing, and the vibrant reefs. Had he more time to spend, he might have enjoyed a brief respite on the white sandy beaches shadowed by the brilliant, green, tall coconut palm trees—all lit up by the bright sun in a dark blue and cloudless sky. But he had business to attend to. So, Marshall mapped the islands and atolls and named them after himself, as only an 18th Century British Naval Captain of His Majesty's Royal Navy could do.

Amata watched intently as the two English ships set sail. He was amazed at the double-deck, triple-masted ships of war with their large white sails and iron cannon. Over the years, his father and grandfather had regaled him with tales of these ships and the fair-skinned sailors and Marines they held. Several of these erstwhile sailors had been shipwrecked or cast out of their ships over the years and taken up with some local women—a few fair-skinned, blue-eyed Marshallese children on Ebeye and Kwajalein were a testament to that. Amata was also aware of a Catholic priest in Kwajalein Atoll and another on Majuro Atoll to the southeast. Their strange God, His Son Jesus, and the Virgin Mary were contrary to Amata's notion of the world. But a number of his friends seemed to respond to their message. He was certainly not about to add a picture of a cross to his heavily tattooed body.

———

Kwajalein Atoll, Marshall Islands, February 28, 1889

Hans Wilhelm hated his job, the islands he had to live on, and the people he had to work with. Since the Kaiser had officially taken possession of these god-forsaken coral atolls, there had been trouble for Hans and those like him. Few fruits and vegetables grew in the Marshall Islands, at least not in the thin layer of soil, and most not naturally. The coconuts and coconut milk were tasty once you got them open, but that was about it, except for maybe the coconut crabs, whose giant claw was delicious compared to his smaller one. The breadfruit tasted like dry wood chips, the bananas were small and dry, and the rat population was ever-expanding as European ships had been divesting themselves of these ugly stowaways for centuries. The chickens the Spaniards had shipped in since the mid-1500s, and the ones the Germans brought were scrawny at best. However, the copra was a different matter altogether. A product of the coconut, the copra, or coconut meat, was a valuable source of coconut oil for the European markets.

As early as the 1860s, German companies had been setting up shop in the central Pacific, especially in the Marshall Islands. Hans worked for one of the largest companies, Jaluit Gesellschaft, which had been turning a nice profit for years. But once Germany bought the Marshall Islands from Spain in 1884 with simultaneous increased taxation and control by the Kaiser's government,[4] the margins had been dwindling, and so had the perks that people like Hans had come to expect. Adding to his displeasure of the Marshall Islands, American missionaries from Hawaii and the mainland United States were constantly harassing him about safe working conditions and twisting his arm to allow their "converts" to have Sundays off! *Maybe it was time to try another profession,* Hans mused to himself as he told Amata to tighten the rope that secured the shipment of copra bound for Europe.

————

Kwajalein Atoll, Marshall Islands, November 17, 1914

World War I had been going on for months with no end in sight. Ensign Fujiyama of the Imperial Japanese Navy was less than thrilled to be in the Marshall Islands, in the middle of nowhere, and on seemingly insignificant spits of land. *What good could ever come from this place*? Fujiyama wondered what the Germans, the Spaniards, or even American missionaries had ever seen in these atolls and islands. Copra was becoming a thing of the past, whether for its oil or the cattle fodder it became, as natural oil pumped from the ground rapidly replaced it in Europe and elsewhere. These little islands and their native inhabitants were useless, in his opinion. The people were lazy, and the lands had no natural resources to speak of that might serve Japanese interests. However, those were thoughts that would never cross Fujiyama's lips aloud. One did not question His Imperial Highness or the Admiralty who worked for Him.

Following Japan's takeover of the Marshall Islands from Germany after the onset of World War I[5]—the Great War, the War to End All Wars, as it was called—Ensign Fujiyama continued with his assigned mission to consolidate control of Kwajalein Atoll. He began planning for the future fortification of the major islands such as Kwajalein, Roi, Namur, Meck, and Ebeye.

————

Washington, DC, October 1923

Lieutenant Colonel Pete Ellis, United State Marine Corps, was a military and naval planner par excellence. He understood the importance of the Philippines to the US Government and their strategic position in the western Pacific from whence the US could influence developments in China, Japan, and the East Indies. Subic Bay Naval Base and Clark Army Airfield in the Philippines were vital national assets that had to be protected. He also understood lines of communication in military terms and the importance of keeping them open. It was evident to Lieutenant Colonel Ellis that any fortified position which sat astride the lines of communication (and resupply) between the Hawaiian Islands and the Philippines was a potential threat to that strategic position. Pete Ellis was nobody's fool. He could read the tea leaves. He understood power projection, the value of the Navy's new aircraft carriers, their steaming radius, and the legs of the aircraft they carried. He saw the need for something in the middle of the Pacific Ocean to use as a base of operations and resupply if the US ever had to retake the Philippines. It was as obvious to him as the nose on his face—the Marshall Islands met every criterion and therefore had to be secured in case the Philippines ever fell.[6]

———

Kwajalein Atoll, Marshall Islands, October 1935

It had been over two years since Japan notified the world that she planned to withdraw from the League of Nations. This notice included a covenant for no fortification in the former German possessions in the Pacific, including the Marshall Islands. Furthermore, their withdrawal from the League did not negate the provisions of the 1922 Naval Limitations Treaty she had signed with the USA, United Kingdom (UK), France, and Italy. Nor did it "unbind" her from the prohibition against fortifying those islands. Captain Hidemi Yoshida of the Imperial Japanese Navy was one of the leaders of the efforts to improve the Marshall Islands' navigational infrastructure, ostensibly for purely peaceful and economic purposes.[7] It may have started that way, but the improvements changed in nature somewhere along the line.

The general concept of fortifications was to build reinforced concrete pillboxes on the larger islands, facing outward toward the ocean rather than toward the interior lagoon, as few passes in the coral reef could handle large warships. The pillboxes housed large cannon/howitzers and were positioned to ensure interlocking fires and mutual support in most areas.

One of the more peculiar aspects of this construction effort was the makeup of the concrete used in the pillboxes and all the concrete produced on the islands. Rather than ship gravel thousands of miles across the Pacific for the concrete mixture, they used coral debris. At low tide, they blew up portions of the reef immediately adjacent to the islands on the ocean side and crushed the resulting coral debris for rock, leaving scars that would remain for centuries.

Freshwater was also a scarce commodity in the Marshall Islands. What water they could capture from the rains or pump from the shallow lens wells was guarded, with a passion, by the Japanese sailors and soldiers and not used for concrete. Hence, they used salt water for the concrete mix. While this might sound like an innovative idea to the uninformed, this was the next thing to being sacrilegious to a civil engineer. The salt in the water would weaken the cementitious property of the cement and could quickly erode the metal reinforcing bars (rebar) that gave the pillboxes most of their tensile strength holding the massive concrete structures together—it just wasn't done. Fortunately for Japan (or unfortunately, as the case might be), Captain Yoshida was not a great civil engineer, so saltwater concrete was the soup du jour. It worked amazingly well!

Amata did not have the foggiest notion whether saltwater from the lagoon or freshwater from the lens wells was better for concrete. He was more than thrilled when the Japanese decided to use salt water. Life was hard enough under the Japanese military occupation. While the Germans had been brutal to deal with, at least they paid the locals for their land (sometimes) and paid nominal wages for their hard work harvesting the copra. The Japanese simply took the land, impressed the men and teenage boys as workers, and used the women poorly. Life was not good in Kwajalein in the 1930s. The same was true on the atoll's other major islands, as the Japanese Navy made life miserable for all concerned. But at least the locals still had access to freshwater using their own lens wells and the rainwater they captured in wooden barrels and other catchment systems—until the Japanese found them.

A freshwater lens was a shallow and thin layer of captured rainwater about five to twenty feet below the surface, depending on the island's elevation at that point, and maybe ten to twenty feet thick, depending on several geologic, meteorological, and usage factors. Near the center of the larger islands, where subsurface structure permitted it, rainwater would seep through the soil and remain there in limestone strata as a freshwater lens. The natives learned soon after they arrived in the Marshall Islands to dig down to these lenses for their freshwater, ergo, a lens well. Good to know in dry times.

———

Paracel Islands, South China Sea, July 31, 1940

Isao Akisao was thanking his lucky stars as he exited the plane and stepped onto the short runway in the Paracel Islands after spending the last two months in the South China Sea on Scarborough Shoals. He was headed back to Tokyo. To the eighteen-year-old engineering student intern for the Japanese government, it had been an opportunity of a lifetime to work with the people studying the oil and natural gas reserves suspected in and around the South China Sea.

The island groups of the Paracels, the Spratly Islands, and Scarborough Shoals occupied the shallow South China Sea, for which control was contested by China, Viet Nam, the Commonwealth of the Philippines, Japan, and others.[8] As a natural trading route among the nations of the area, it was alive with trading vessels of every sort imaginable, from the Chinese junks to steam-driven cargo ships, to the more modern oil-burning Japanese cruisers.

It had not taken long for Isao to make a name for himself with the Japanese Military Commander defending the drilling platform near the Scarborough Shoals, the tiny coral reef atoll nearest the Philippines. He was up before anyone else on the platform in these shallow waters, reviewing the drilling logs from the previous day's activities and talking with the Japanese soldiers. He pestered the scientists with questions about their drilling techniques and analysis of the sludge, sand, and coral samples brought to the surface, generally making a large nuisance of himself. It had been hot work as temperatures soared during the day with little shade, but rewarding for the bright engineering student from Tokyo.

Isao knew the work in the South China Sea was of vital national importance to the Japanese Empire due to the tightening of oil supplies and increased prices of oil that the

Americans were charging his homeland. How dare they do that? Didn't they know that the western Pacific was a Japanese area of influence? Only Japanese hegemony in the western Pacific would allow his country to prosper and compete on the world stage. They would show the rest of the world that it was not just Caucasian nations that could manage success but Asian peoples (and a particular Asian island empire with the Rising Sun on its flag) as well. The Greater East Asia Co-Prosperity Sphere,[9] he had heard it called. The western Pacific from Japan to Manchuria, to Indochina and the Dutch East Indies, then to New Guinea, and the island groups as far to the east as the Gilberts and Marshalls were led by the Japanese Empire! In time, it would challenge Europe and the United States for economic prosperity in the region, indeed, in the world!

CHAPTER 2
OPERATION FLINTLOCK

Scarborough Shoals, South China Sea, October 31, 1943

THINGS HAD CHANGED DRAMATICALLY FOR ISAO. JAPAN BOMBED Pearl Harbor on December 7, 1941, and then proceeded to attack and take over large parts of the western Pacific, including the Philippines, seemingly making real their dream of the Greater East Asia Co-Prosperity Sphere. As a recent geological engineering graduate of the University of Tokyo, he had been sent back to the South China Sea. He was to assist in the renewed effort to identify and extract oil and gas from the area to support the Japanese Empire's forces as they defended the western Pacific against the American, British, Australian, and New Zealand forces. Now, he was again by the Scarborough Shoals, back on a new mobile platform, drilling in new areas to the west of the Magalawa Island of the Philippines and just east of the Scarborough Shoals.

Isao had been reviewing drilling logs from the past three years and the most recent logs developed in the last few months. He noticed the evidence of unusually large seams of oil and sometimes gas, suspended or trapped in the geologic structure beneath the floor of the shallow waters near Scarborough Shoals. After reviewing logs from drilling rigs in the Spratly Islands, close to the Paracel Islands, he also noticed similar deposits near them. However, the largest deposits by far, and what appeared to rival Saudi Arabia in their extent, were those just east of the Scarborough Shoals.

Unfortunately, these deposits were unlike those found in parts of the Dutch East Indies, Texas, and Oklahoma, or places like Saudi Arabia in the Middle East or Venezuela in South America. Those deposits were more consolidated and easier to extract with the technology of the day. Isao was sure that the technology and equipment to extract the oil and gas near Scarborough Shoals did not exist. And if it did, it would be too expensive to extract, given the current price for a barrel of oil. It wasn't even close. As clearly as he could determine, the best way to obtain the oil under the South China Sea would be to crack somehow or fracture the geologic structure so that the oil and natural gas would be free to pool or consolidate. Then it could be forced out under pressure using water or air. But, as Isao knew, this was impossible in 1943 Japan.

Isao tried in vain to convince the Japanese leadership on the Scarborough Shoals platform of the vast potential of his theory, but they were only interested in what they could extract now. So, he completed his dissertation on the future of oil and gas extraction in the South China Sea and put it in his footlocker for possible future use when he could work on his master's degree in Tokyo. But that would have to wait until after Japan had kicked the Americans out of the western Pacific.

Scarborough Shoals, South China Sea, November 9, 1943

It was another beautiful sunny day on the platform when Isao went to get his weekly mail drop. And now his world was about to be turned upside down! The orders were clear and unequivocal: Reserve Corporal (CPL) Isao Akisao was to report to the 6th Base Force on Kwajalein Atoll in the Marshall Islands. The orders were signed by rear Admiral Monzo Akiyama, Commanding Officer. Isao gathered his meager belongings, stuffed them in his footlocker, and boarded the seaplane leaving the Scarborough Shoals. He and several other active and reserve soldiers were headed to Kwajalein Island, the southernmost island of the almost one hundred islets surrounding the world's largest lagoon in the middle of the Kwajalein Atoll, part of the Ralik Chain of the Marshall Islands. *What are the Marshall Islands, and why am I going there?* Mused Isao as he barfed for the third time on the large seaplane that was transporting him across several thousand miles of open ocean. The next day, he landed near Ebeye Island and then barfed a fourth time as his seaplane drifted toward the ramp on the lagoon side. A few hours later, after a short landing craft ride, he disembarked on Kwajalein Island, his new home away from home.

Kwajalein Atoll, Marshall Islands, November 15, 1943

Rear Admiral Akiyama surveyed his command, his military mission, and the terrain he called home. If there was ever a more beautiful spot on earth, Akiyama could not imagine where it would be or what it would be like. He had been to Fujiyama's summit and seen pictures of the Grand Canyon in America and the Pyramids in Egypt. But none of these could compare in simple beauty to the clear, warm, and sparkling water that rose and fell inside the lagoon with the tides like a giant commode, or the dark green palm fronds of the lush coconut trees, all set against the bluest sky he had ever seen.

So much for creation; he had a job to do, and that was to

firm up the fortifications of Kwajalein Atoll and prepare to support the Japanese Naval Forces as they countered the expected American push across the Pacific. Improvements to the runway on the western end of the island were behind schedule, and his workforce of Korean and Marshallese laborers was becoming increasingly inefficient. Perhaps a little more whip and a little less food would motivate them correctly. He had more to think about than just Kwajalein Atoll, as his 6th Base Force provided support to all the Marshall Islands. The Marshall Islands had been key to the Empire's plans since the war started—as the submarines that took part in the attack on Pearl Harbor were anchored in the Kwajalein lagoon. Now it was a major resupply, communications, and intelligence center for the Japanese Combined Fleet at Truk, a little over 1000 miles to the southwest.[1]

There were forty pillboxes on Kwajalein Island at the southern end of the atoll. Fifty-two pillboxes and similar emplacements were on Roi and Namur Islands (Roi and Namur had once been two distinct islands but had recently been joined by a causeway) in the northeast corner. In addition, there were massive concrete block houses, gun emplacements, and modern airfields on both Kwajalein Island and Roi-Namur. With a force of eight thousand men split between Kwajalein and Roi-Namur, Akiyama had a capable, albeit small, force.[2] He also had local knowledge of the islands, the atoll, and the reef surrounding it, which gave him an advantage if the atoll were ever attacked. But that was highly unlikely in his estimation.

Yes, in a pathetic attempt to show the American people that they were still in control of the situation, Admiral Halsey's US Naval forces had bombed Kwajalein Atoll on February 1, 1942, but it had been relatively quiet since.[3] That raid had been like a sweat bee sting—a little irritating but harmless overall.

Kwajalein and Roi-Namur Islands, Kwajalein Atoll, Marshall Islands, December 5, 1943

Rear Admiral Mongo Akiyama was more than a little worried now, and so was Rear Admiral Michiyuki Yamada, Commander of the 4th Combined Air Group aviation assets on Roi-Namur.[4] The Empire had lost the Battle of Tarawa just a couple of weeks before when the American Marines would simply not give up, inflicting a horrendous loss on Japan in the face of staggering American losses. In central Pacific terms, the Gilbert Islands were not that far southeast of the Marshall Islands, so it would only be a matter of time before the Americans turned their attention to the Marshalls.

The air raids began suddenly as 246 carrier-launched American bombers began attacking Kwajalein Atoll. The effects were devastating to Japanese ships and aircraft alike, but the destruction was not total. What neither admiral knew, but both suspected, was that there would be more air raids. And they were correct. During the rest of December and January, Kwajalein and other atolls in the Marshalls were under frequent attack. Another major carrier strike occurred on January 29, 1944, and then again on January 30, 1944, as more than four hundred sorties were combined with naval bombardment to soften up Kwajalein and Roi-Namur.[5] American planners would not make the mistakes of Tarawa, where the beaches had not been adequately softened before the assault, and the Marines were left unsupported at the height of the battle. American admirals and planners had read Lieutenant Colonel Ellis's paper from 1923 and were unleashing Operation Flintlock on Kwajalein Atoll as they moved west across the Pacific.

Kwajalein Atoll, Marshall Islands, February 1, 1944

Carrier aircraft and naval bombardment had extensively prepared Kwajalein and Roi-Namur for amphibious landings. The previous day, January 31, 1944—D-day for Operation Flintlock—forces from the 7th Infantry Division (Army) and the 4th Marine Division had landed on islets adjacent to Kwajalein and Roi-Namur. Their mission was to ensure they had control of South Pass near Kwajalein and Mellu Pass next to Roi-Namur, respectively. These were two of the few deep-water passes into the Kwajalein lagoon. They also used those islets to stage their divisional artillery to provide even heavier gun support, supplement, and eventually replace the carrier aircraft and naval gunfire once the 7th and 4th were ashore. Both large and small howitzers were used just before the main landing on Kwajalein and Roi-Namur, scheduled for 0930 hours (9:30 a.m.) on February 1. They would also take calls for fire from the Army and Marine commanders on the ground during the battles on Kwajalein and Roi-Namur, respectively.[6]

At sunrise, the massive and final preparatory fires began on Kwajalein as naval gunfire, including broadsides from battleships and cruisers, aircraft bombing runs, and artillery fire unleashed thousands of naval shells, almost 30,000 artillery shells, and several 2000-pound bombs on Kwajalein. Additional aircraft sorties from six carriers also strafed suspected enemy positions.[7]

The men of the 184th Regimental Combat Team (RCT), 7th Infantry Division, had seen limited action against the Japanese in the Aleutian Islands of Alaska, but Kwajalein was an entirely new experience. As they landed on the west end of the island in their tracked amphibian vehicles and assorted landing craft to the left of their sister unit, the 32nd Regimental Combat Team (RCT), the initial enemy response was minimal. But, as the day wore on, it was obvious that the Japanese were still alive and kicking.[8] And while the aerial, naval, and artillery bombardments had been effective to a great degree, this was not going to be a cakewalk. Corporal Ralph Grayson had heard that they expected to clear the island in two days, advancing past the runway on the first day and to the east end of the island by the second day. Apparently, the Japanese had other ideas, as they were tenacious in defending their terrain, conducting night-time banzai raids, and refusing to surrender, almost to a man.

Around 1300 hours (1:00 p.m.) on February 1, Corporal Grayson, and indeed the rest of the 7th Division, heard a low rumble and then a large explosion that sounded like a cross between an earthquake and a large quarry blast. Far to the north, they could see a large black cloud rising a few thousand feet in the air. For days, they would not know that what they heard was a torpedo warehouse on Namur, fifty miles to the north. It exploded after a 4th Marine Division ordnance team had thrown a satchel charge in it, not knowing that it housed the torpedoes for the entire Japanese Navy.[9] The fog of war was on display for all to see until the black cloud finally dissipated, and the Marines recovered their dead.

By the end of February 1, Corporal Grayson was hungry, covered with sweat, disoriented in the dense jungle-like vegetation, and thought he was somewhere near the west end of the runway. The heat remained intense, and the humidity was oppressive. These factors were complicated by the dense and tangled vegetation, at least that part that the American preparatory fires had not obliterated. The 184th Regimental Combat Team had not made their first day's objective. Although Corporal Grayson did not know it, this was what von

Clausewitz called "friction." While a plan may look good on paper, once in motion, many factors, small and large, can delay and disrupt even the best-laid plans. He was often on his belly, listening to bullets whizzing overhead and then to the screams of other soldiers as the Japanese snipers found their marks. His battle buddy died just after dusk when a Japanese sniper in the remains of a tree near the runway had gotten off a lucky shot. Grayson had responded quickly with his M1 Garand rifle, wounding the sniper and then using his flame thrower to seal the deal after the Japanese sniper had fallen to the ground. The sight and odor of the enemy soldier burning to death temporarily satisfied his anger, but it was a sight that would haunt him for the rest of his life. As a believer, he understood the need for governments and armies and God's role in raising them up and bringing them down. He understood that defending his country through service in the military was an honorable thing to do. He recalled that Jesus marveled at a Roman Centurion's faith during his ministry in Israel. But Corporal Grayson could not shake the thought that he had exacted frightening revenge on that Japanese soldier, not just performed his duty. How he wished he was back home in Fort Payne, Alabama—plenty of heat and humidity there, but no jungles and certainly no midnight banzai attacks or snipers to contend with.

Corporal Isao Akisao also saw the Japanese sniper take his shot. He saw the American soldier crumple to the ground as the bullet ripped through his head. Then he froze as the other American soldier standing next to him quickly engaged the Japanese sniper with his rifle, dropped him from the tree, and burned him alive with his flame thrower. He wanted to shoot his fellow Japanese soldier to put him out of his misery; he also wanted to shoot the American soldier who wielded the flame thrower so well, but he feared for his own life. He was a geologic engineer, not a Samurai, and he did not want to die. Not today! He slowly worked his way to the east end of the runway that night, praying to any god who might listen to him that neither the Americans nor the Japanese would hear or see him crawling. But he would never forget the face of the American soldier he saw in the light of the burning corpse.

Kwajalein Island was laced with pillboxes and other reinforced concrete positions for the Japanese's 127mm twin dual-mount guns, a.k.a. Singapore Guns, and 80mm single-mount guns. Fortunately, most of these faced out toward the ocean. But there were also numerous machine gun emplacements throughout the island and even a few antitank ditches just to complicate and delay movement.[10] The 184th Regimental Combat Team had finally taken its portion of the runway by the end of February 2. Still, even with the 32nd Regimental Combat Team, it would require two more days of intense, hand-to-hand combat before clearing the island around 1920 hours (7:20 p.m.) on the evening of February 4.[11] Corporal Grayson and the 184th Regimental Combat Team ended up at Echo Pier on the lagoon side, the western side of the island.

———

Kwajalein Island, Kwajalein Atoll, February 5, 1944

Early in the morning of February 5, as the occasional sporadic fire began to die down, Corporal Grayson's platoon was assigned the task of rounding up the few Japanese soldiers who had not been killed or committed Hari Kari. The 7th Division's G2 Intelligence Section was to interrogate them. As the day wore on, his platoon took few prisoners, and the sounds of Japanese suicides by bayonet, pistol, or hand grenade permeated the island. Grayson tried frantically to capture someone or anyone to provide his lieutenant with someone to march back to the G2, but he was not having much luck. Around 1300 (1:00 p.m.), he stopped for a bite to eat along with the rest of his squad, sat down on a fallen coconut tree trunk, and opened his can of C-rations containing ham and eggs. C-rats, as the soldiers called them, were edible, barely, but more so if you had access to the hood of a running Jeep to warm up the can first. But Grayson was not so lucky. So, he simply used the small handheld P-38 can opener the Army so wisely provided and flicked the top of the can in some nearby bushes at the entrance of what used to be a blockhouse.

Corporal Akisao heard the P-38 blade scraping against the metal can, then listened to the can lid clang against the concrete and turned toward the noise. He recognized the face of Corporal Grayson as he hid in the nearby rubbled blockhouse adjacent to Echo Pier. Fearing the business end of the flame thrower the American still carried, Akisao freaked out and ran to the back entrance of the blockhouse, where another American soldier shot him in the leg. That soldier would have completed the job; however, Grayson stopped him from firing again. Assuming the worst, Akisao waited in terror for the flame thrower to burn him alive. He was stunned when the soldier put his flame thrower down, applied a field dressing to the wound, and escorted him to the G2's collection point. Grayson's platoon leader, the Second Lieutenant "Butter Bar," was delighted! After all, a dead Japanese soldier could provide little intelligence.

After his interrogation, as he and just a handful of other Japanese soldiers were escorted from the G2's collection point to the improvised POW holding area, Akisao noticed Corporal Grayson as one of the escorts. Upon arrival at the holding area, Akisao addressed Grayson in his halting English to thank him for saving his life. He handed Grayson his helmet, which

Grayson assumed was just a gift, spoils of war, a war trophy, so to speak. He looked around to ensure no one was looking and slipped it into his butt pack—something to impress his friends with once he got back to the US. What Grayson did not see was a small envelope well-hidden in the liner of the helmet.

PART II

THE STORY

CHAPTER 3

KWAJALEIN—WHAT'S IN A NAME?

Kwajalein Atoll, Marshall Islands, November 14, Present Day

Colonel Seth Grayson, Commander, US Army Garrison-Kwajalein Atoll, also known as the garrison, surveyed his command and scratched his head. As he understood it, Reagan Test Site, located in the Kwajalein Atoll of the Marshall Islands, was one of the premier missile and radar test facilities in the world.[1] It used to be that the Reagan Test Site was under and reported to the Commander, US Army Garrison-Kwajalein Atoll. It made sense, as the test site needed the garrison for support, and the garrison was the senior command. Just a few years prior, in the fall of 2013, the Army transferred the garrison function from US Army Space and Missile Defense Command to the Pacific Office in Honolulu of the Installation Management Command. The Reagan Test Site was the raison d'etre for the garrison but was now directly under the US Army Space and Missile Defense Command in Huntsville, Alabama, and Washington, DC, instead of the garrison.[2] One of the nine tenets of the US Army's principles of war, its guiding principles for military operations, was "unity of command." Grayson wondered if the previous arrangement of the Reagan Test Site Range Director (Lieutenant Colonel) working directly for the Garrison Commander (Colonel), who in turn worked for the Space and Missile Defense Command Commanding General, was not a better example of "unity of command."

But, the current situation consisted of two separate commands on such a small island. Both were there for the same reason but reported to two different senior commands thousands of miles away. Unity of Command?

As Colonel Grayson studied the history of Kwajalein, he learned a great deal. Beginning in February 1944, Kwajalein had been a US Navy supply installation. It was also used in support of the Korean War. The Army's NIKE-ZEUS anti-missile program's need for a test range saved Kwajalein from closure in 1959, opening a new era and mission. That was followed by the transfer of Kwajalein to the Army in 1964. Since then, it appeared that numerous test programs had used Kwajalein's constantly upgraded facilities and isolation to their advantage for both missile and sensor testing. This included the NIKE-X Project Office and the SPARTAN and SPRINT missile tests in the late 60s.[3] During the '70s and '80s, Kwajalein hosted the Homing Overlay Experiment program and the ultimate interception of an Intercontinental Ballistic Missile (ICBM) from Vandenberg Air Force Base. Then came the Exoatmospheric Re-entry Vehicle Interceptor System tests in the '90s,[4] followed by the National Missile Defense program and Patriot PAC-II missile tests in the late 90s and early 2000s.

Colonel Grayson was surprised to learn that the US Air Force's ICBM readiness program was a consistent client of Kwajalein and the Reagan Test Site. Several times a year, the USAF would pick a missile detachment for a no-notice scramble and launch drill from Vandenberg Air Force Base in California. The dummy warheads were targeted to splash down in the Kwajalein lagoon and then recovered by the small two-man sub that was part of the garrison inventory. More recently, the warheads would land just east of the atoll in the Kwajalein Missile Impact Scoring System area, where an array of hydrophones triangulate their exact touchdown points on the ocean floor. Not bad from more than four thousand miles away!

Seth's history lesson was eye-opening and informative!

Kwajalein Island

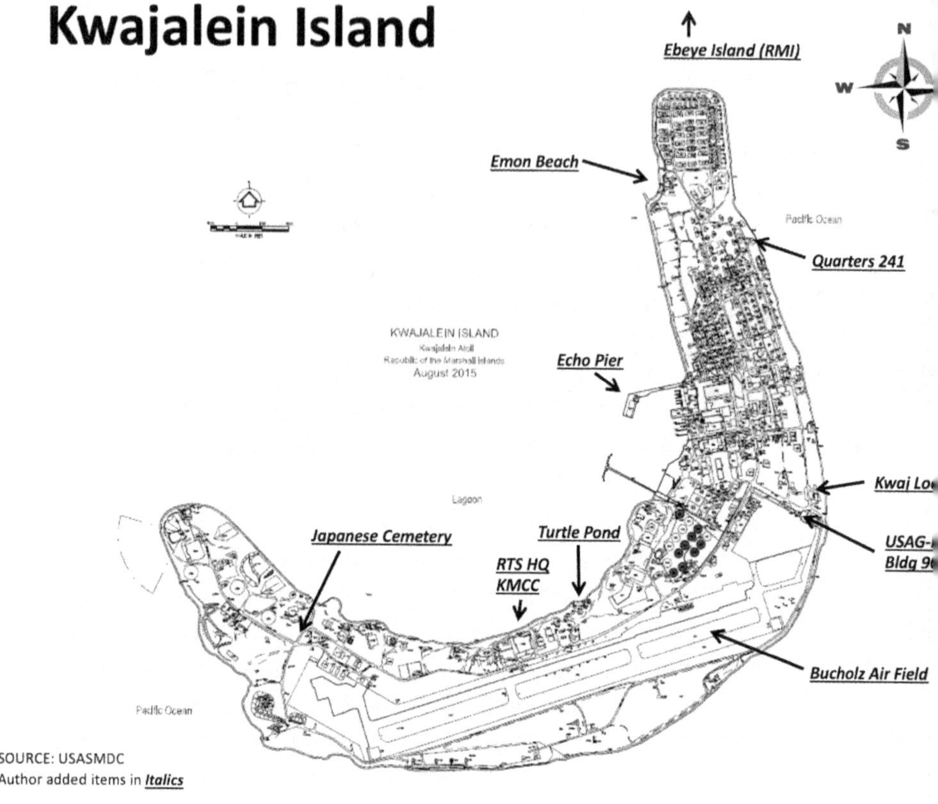

SOURCE: USASMDC
Author added items in *Italics*

Map of Kwajalein Atoll

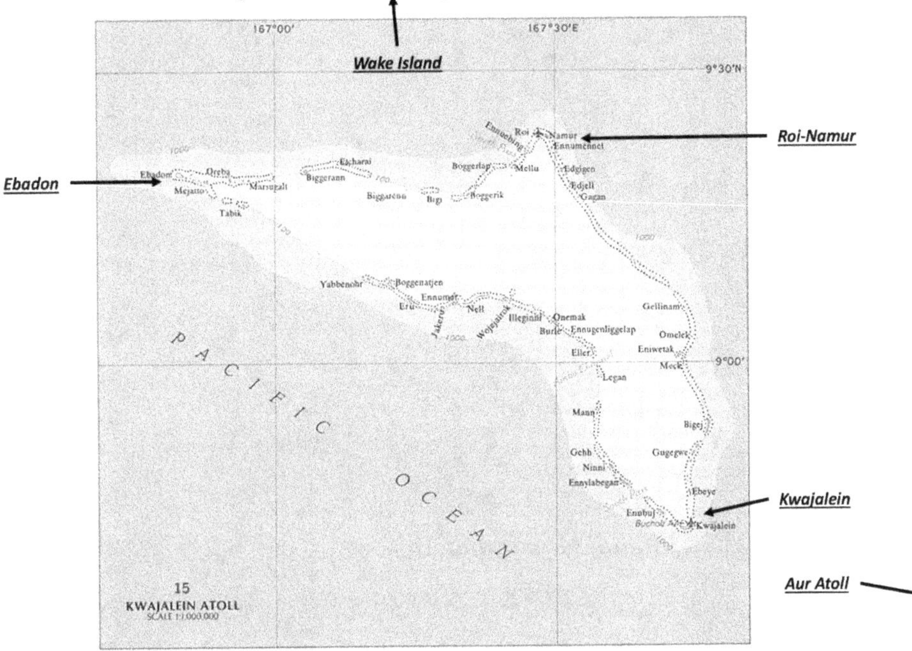

Ebadon

Roi-Namur

Kwajalein

Aur Atoll

SOURCE: US Dept of Interior, Public Domain
Author added items in *Italics*

UNCLASSIFIED

CHAPTER 4
LIFE ON KWAJALEIN

Kwajalein Island, November 15

Colonel Seth Grayson and his wife, Sara, were still getting used to the heat and humidity as well as their bicycles. With such a large number of people working on Kwajalein (more than two thousand Americans consisting of about twenty-five military, sixty Department of the Army civilians, and two thousand contractor personnel and their families) and such a small island, it did not make sense to allow privately owned vehicles on Kwajalein. Additionally, it would be an extra cost to maintain enough gas and diesel to support all those vehicles. Ergo, the approved means of transport for all was the ubiquitous bicycle. They were everywhere, often tricked out with fancy handlebars and banana seats and painted in bright colors. However, all were subject to a highly corrosive environment, about seven times that of Hawaii. With the prevailing trade winds blowing much of the year and the constant salt spray from the waves crashing onto the shore, it did not take much for the winds to pick up the salt spray and carry it across such a small island. Unless protected and frequently hosed off, an average bicycle might last a few months before rusting away. Of course, it could be gone sooner than that if left unsecured at night. It would then be spirited off to an Ebeye chop shop for the metal, spare parts, or just someone else's bike.

Ebeye was a neighboring island in Kwajalein Atoll, inhabited by about 13,000 Marshallese, many of whom found their way there to seek employment on Kwajalein. Unfortunately, the American contractor with the base operations support contract for the garrison only needed about 1200 Marshallese daily on Kwajalein, Roi-Namur, and Meck Island. The security contractor employed few Marshallese, and virtually none were hired by the meteorological support contractor or the range systems contractor who ran the Reagan Test Site. Ebeye had once been known as a Jewel of the Pacific. But it was now an island under severe stress due to the large influx of people from the atoll and neighboring atolls and poor maintenance efforts. There were some paved roads and occasional electricity from a large power generation plant when it was working. There was a large desalinization plant for freshwater, but it was usually down for maintenance, and spare parts were hard to come by in the middle of the Pacific. US Army Garrison-Kwajalein Atoll could provide limited support under the Compact of Free Association between the US government and the Marshallese government.[1] But, more extensive efforts were supposed to be made on a reimbursable basis. That reimbursement was often years in arrears. It was ignored by the Kwajalein Atoll Local Government as much as possible due to the lack of funding from the Marshallese government in Majuro. It was a vicious cycle.

Seth and Sara Grayson had been married for more than twenty years. Seth was a graduate of the United States Military Academy at West Point, NY, or West Point for short. A veteran of Company E-4, United States Corps of Cadets, he had spent most of his time living in the "Lost Fifties" barracks near the old gym. When allowed, he might spend time eating at the old cadet boodler—or snack bar, known as the "Weapons Room." Once, when he was a Plebe (freshman), he lived on the fifth floor of the 55th Division, the top floor, about as far away from the Duty Officer as one could get. It was there he spent hours memorizing his Plebe "poop" (information) from his copy of "Bugle Notes." Worth's Battalion Orders was one of his favorites: "But an officer on duty knows no one…etc., etc., etc." When he was a Firstie (senior), he lived in the 49th Division for a while and got to ride "Otis," the ancient elevator to the seventh floor, every day after classes. That was his special treat, as most of the cadets' barracks had only freight elevators the cadets could not use. Those elevators were for the exclusive use of the BPs, the contracted barracks police—the custodians. A far cry from the Greek fraternity houses on typical college campuses, but you take what you can get.

One of Grayson's more pleasant memories was marching with his regiment of cadets by company formation and emerging from the sally port under Eisenhower Hall onto the parade field. As they passed in review, the smell of perfume from the young ladies who came to watch was a grateful change from the odor of sweat from his classmates at the end of a warm parade.

Grayson was above average academically at the Academy, graduating in the top five percent of his class and earning the coveted stars for his cadet uniform collar—a "Star Man." Grayson remembered his days at West Point well, now that he was an old "grad." He also recalled the Commissioned Officer's oath of office he took when he was commissioned as a Second Lieutenant on graduation day so long ago:

"I, Seth Grayson, having been appointed an officer in the Army of the United States, as indicated above in the grade of

Second Lieutenant, do solemnly swear (or affirm) that I will support and defend the Constitution of the United States against all enemies, foreign and domestic; that I will bear true faith and allegiance to the same; that I take this obligation freely, without any mental reservations or purpose of evasion; and that will well and faithfully discharge the duties of the office upon which I am about to enter. So help me God."

Seth Grayson worked hard as he rose through the ranks from Second Lieutenant to First Lieutenant. Then with some respect shared between him and the more senior non-commissioned officers, he was promoted to captain and gained increased responsibility as a field grade officer—first as a major and then as a lieutenant colonel. Along the way, Seth completed the Army's Command and General Staff College and its very special School of Advanced Military Studies. Yes, he was a "Jedi Knight," as others called them (some say mocked) early on in the program. As a new colonel, he attended the US Army War College at Carlisle Barracks, Pennsylvania, as a geographical bachelor. At the same time, Sara and the kids stayed at their previous "permanent change of station" location for high school continuity purposes.

At Carlisle, Colonel Grayson had time to get into documents and literature dating back to the founding of the United States and even before that. He thoroughly studied the US Constitution, the Bill of Rights, and all the other amendments, and then the *Federalist Papers* penned by Jay, Madison, and Hamilton. The *Federalist Papers* was a collection of articles those men wrote while the proposed Constitution was under review by the states and their citizens for possible acceptance and implementation. They were brilliant men who wrote such a detailed explanation of the rationale behind the Constitution that he wondered why it was not required reading in all high schools and colleges. But he also read other books, such as the

Anti-Federalist Papers written around the same time, which gave the other side of the coin—the arguments against the new Constitution and for sticking with the weak Articles of Confederation. Reading the Constitution through the prism of those two polar documents and the lens of other early documents such as the "Mayflower Compact" gave him a deep appreciation for the Constitution's genius, the men who wrote it, and their faith in providence.

Also of great interest to Seth were other works such as Adam Smith's *The Wealth of Nations*, which outlined how a nation's wealth is created and how free trade can play a part. He also read *Democracy in America* written by the Frenchman D'Toqueville in the 1830s after his trip to the US. It provided an excellent and unbiased discussion of the strengths of the new nation and one of its significant weaknesses—slavery.

Seth knew the Constitution was not perfect. It had within it the seeds of the Civil War, i.e., the provision for slavery to remain. Still, it was the best that was obtainable at the time to ensure the continuance of a viable nation, given the realities of that nation after the War of Independence and the failed Articles of Confederation. The southern colonies would not have joined the northern colonies if slavery was not allowed by the Constitution. Seth firmly believed in the viability of the Constitution and the rule of law. He frequently harkened back to his graduation day from West Point and his oath of office, "... support and defend the Constitution of the United States against all enemies, foreign and domestic, and bear true faith and allegiance to the same," or words to that effect. Seth sometimes wondered what a domestic enemy of the Constitution would look like.

Seth was an Air Defense Artillery officer who was disappointed over his selection for Colonel-level command at Kwajalein instead of one of the Army's premier Air Defense

Artillery brigades or regiments. But a garrison command was better than no command, so he and Sara had packed up their household goods and shipped them to Kwajalein. Their teenage daughter, Callie, traveled with them to Kwaj in the summer before she traveled back to the continental United States for college. During her Christmas and summer visits to Kwajalein, she frequently traveled to Ebeye on one of the water taxi landing crafts, or Landing Craft Mechanized (LCM). That craft primarily transported the 1200 Marshallese workers back and forth but also allowed those Americans who wanted, to visit Ebeye. Callie used her visits to teach English to Marshallese 8th graders in their local schools.

As the Colonel's wife, Sara Grayson was the de facto leader of the Yokwe Yuk Women's Club on Kwajalein. It was an excellent organization that provided friendships for the wives of the military, the Department of the Army civilians, and contractors who were far from home. It also provided a forum for supporting Marshallese women in the atoll, who were largely uneducated, poorly treated in the Marshallese society, and in need of a friend. Each year, this group traveled to the far northwest corner of the atoll, to the isolated island of Ebadon, and brought clothes, food, and medical supplies to a small community that was essentially cut off from the rest of the atoll. This group also visited other isolated Marshallese villages on the islands of Carlos and Majetto. They made numerous trips to Ebeye to work with the ladies there and support them primarily through the several churches on that island.

———

SARA GRAYSON STOOD ABOUT 5'4" and weighed less than 120 pounds, although you would never get her to tell you her weight. Even after two children and following her husband around the world, she maintained her shape through a steady workout routine and watching her diet; her blond hair and blue eyes sparkled. When Sara entered a room, she lit it up like Roman candles with her personality and wit and made everyone feel welcome through her innate gift of compassion. She was the love of Seth's life and vice versa. Together, they formed a team that worked hard to meet the command's mission and take care of their people, all of them. They had not always been so caring, but once they completely surrendered to God and fully accepted who Christ was and what He had done for them, they could only care for others more than themselves. They also cared deeply for their country, which seemed to be slipping further and further away from its Judeo-Christian foundation, if not biblical roots. Together, they had attended Methodist, Pentecostal, Southern Baptist, and nondenominational churches because of their postings in various parts of the US and the world. They learned that it was not their denomination but their faith in Christ alone that gave them hope and secured their eternal life. And they knew that a return to Christ was the only hope for the nation. Seth remembered that it was President Reagan who had been fond of quoting 2nd Chronicles 7:14, "If my people who are called by my name, will humble themselves and pray, and seek my face, and turn from their wicked ways, then will I hear from heaven and will forgive their sin, and will heal their land."

Colonel Grayson had spent the first couple of months of his command learning all he could about the Reagan Test Site mission and its needs. His job as the Kwajalein Atoll (USAG-KA) Garrison Commander demanded he understand what he was supporting. The Reagan Test Site Range Director was Lieutenant Colonel Ron Bakerson, a graduate of the Virginia Military Institute and a member of the Army's Acquisition Corps. Lieutenant Colonel Bakerson and Colonel Grayson forged a "professional friendship" and respect for each other early on. They worked hard to avoid any chain of command issues that could hinder their successes and careers. As they toured the high-tech facilities on the various islands that the garrison and Reagan Test Site used courtesy of the Compact of Free Association, Grayson could not help but be amazed.

The garrison was granted all or portions of eleven islands around the atoll for their sensors, launch facilities, and base support operations by the Compact with the Republic of the Marshall Islands. By now, they were using only eight regularly. Kwajalein Island was the largest—the namesake of the atoll— and the command. Located at the southern end of the world's largest lagoon, Kwajalein was about three miles long and a half-mile wide. The Boeing 767-capable runway of Bucholz Field took up about a third of that. But the island of Kwaj also had some of the sensors and cameras used by the various missile and sensor tests that "rented" the Reagan Test Site facilities. These sensors included the Kwajalein Missile Range Safety Ship, Super RADOT (recording automatic digital optical tracker), and RADOT cameras for high-speed, long-range images of in-bound tests.[2] Kwajalein's suite of sensors also included the huge X-band Phased Array Ground-Based Radar Prototype, built in the late '90s to support national missile defense testing.[3]

In the northeast corner of the atoll, Roi-Namur was the second-largest island. Originally two islands, the gap between them had been bridged by a causeway over the years, initially by the Japanese but then filled in by the Americans. Roi-Namur was home to the KREMS suite of high-tech sensors. The Kiernan Re-entry Measurement System included four state-of-the-art research and development sensors that needed the services (and genius) of MIT/Lincoln Lab to manage them. ALTAIR was the largest sensor, with a diameter of 150', and mounted on a circular rail with electric motors that could spin it at thirteen degrees per second. It could track small objects in space out to 100,000 km through integrated pulses. TRADEX was the earliest large radar in the KREMS complex but continuously updated. It could perform long-range re-entry vehicle tracking and orbital space debris tracking of objects as small as five centimeters. ALCOR could accommodate both beacon tracking and skin tracking. It could also perform imaging for the US Space Force. Finally, the Millimeter-wave (MMW) sensor could provide extremely precise skin tracking and assist in space surveillance.[4] The constantly updated KREMS complex housed the world's most sophisticated suite of sensors available for missile testing, bar none. It was and is a national asset.

Telemetry cameras were positioned on Kwajalein, Roi-Namur, Gagan, and Illeginni. Meck Island housed a rocket launch facility for national missile defense interceptors. Smaller launch facilities were on Roi-Namur, Omelek, and even Wake Island, far to the north, for small target missiles. Of particular note was the Kwajalein Missile Impact Scoring System, located just east of Gagan on the ocean side. The system could triangulate the splashdown site of a test missile or warhead from the noise of impact and then transmit that data to the test owner, who knew where they were aiming. Then the owner could adjust his navigational controls based on the test data. A corresponding land impact area was on Illeginni.[5]

———

COLONEL AND MRS. GRAYSON spent that Sunday morning attending the Protestant Chapel service at the Kwajalein Chapel, an open-sided structure built soon after the US took over the island from Japan. Close to it stood the Richardson

Theater, an outdoor stage where Bob Hope had once entertained the troops during World War II. Nearby was the relatively new Marshallese Cultural Center, built by the US for the Marshallese people to demonstrate their culture up close and personal to the Americans stationed there. It also served to remind the Marshallese of their proud heritage.

Around noon Colonel Grayson boarded one of the five old Huey helicopters that the base operations support contractor operated and flew over several islands under his purview. He hoped to get the newer Blackhawks soon. As he overflew the lagoon, he could see several coral heads just under the water's surface and the sharks circling them in search of food. The pilot flew him to Illeginni Island first, the land impact site. He inspected the remnants of structures from previous tests and the preparations underway for the test scheduled in the next six months. All was going well as he kicked at one of the ever-present rats that infested the island. Next, he flew to Roi-Namur, where he was met by the senior rep from MIT/Lincoln Labs, who took him on his third tour of the KREMS complex. There was a lot to take in and not a lot of time to do it in the face of the upcoming testing schedule.

As he headed back to the Roi runway, he first stopped at the Gimbels store (no relation to Gimbels in New York City) to buy a Coca-Cola. Gimbels was the grocery/convenience store on Roi-Namur for the government civilians and contractor personnel assigned there. He also noticed the 9-hole golf course, including one of the greens with a bush in the middle, and quietly reminded himself that he still needed to try it out. He flew back to Kwajalein on a DASH 7, a fifty-passenger, four-prop aircraft operated by the base operations support contractor. The contractor had three of these aircraft to transport folks who resided on Kwajalein but worked on Roi-Namur. Many flew back and forth daily to augment the 120 who lived and worked on Roi-Namur. As he flew back, the plane passed over one of the two, two-hundred-passenger hi-speed catamaran boats that transported American workers from Kwajalein and Marshallese from Ebeye to Meck and Roi-Namur each day—the Jera and the Jelang-K. Seth was starting to feel a little bit better about his "garrison" command. Considering the fact that he had various barges, two LCUs (landing craft utility), two LSTs (landing ship tank), five LCMs (landing craft mechanized or the water taxis), one safety ship, and one minisub in his mini-Navy—all in addition to his Air Force of five helicopters and three fixed-wing aircraft,[6] Seth was definitely feeling better.

Kwajalein Island, Kwajalein Atoll, November 16

Monday morning, Seth and Sara slept in. It was their day off. Their Monday was Sunday in the US. Being on the other side of the International Date Line from Hawaii, Huntsville, and Washington, DC, Kwajalein's workweek was Tuesday through Saturday to match the Monday through Friday of the others. They had their weekend on Sunday and Monday, Kwaj time. Seth hopped onto his bicycle and pedaled to the 9-hole Holmberg Fairways golf course adjacent to the Kwajalein runway on the island's west end. He picked up his clubs from the locker he rented for the year and met Lieutenant Colonel Ron Bakerson, Range Director, and Lieutenant Colonel Eli Shan, Deputy Commander of US Army Garrison –Kwajalein Atoll, for a round of golf. A high handicapper, Seth nonetheless always enjoyed playing the short course until he got to the 8th and 9th holes, which were directly into the typical 20-knot trade winds, making those two short par-five holes tough. He had already pulled more than a few golf balls onto the runway in the few months he had been there.

When he finally headed back toward Quarters 241, the former Officers Club and now the Commander's home for his tour of duty, Seth ran into Sara on her bicycle at the Ten-Ten convenience store. She had already been to Macy's general store (no relation to the Macy's chain in the US) and the "Surfway" grocery store. Her bike basket was loaded with goods. They pedaled together along Ocean Drive, enjoying the scent of the ocean spray, the blue skies, the aroma from the bougainvillea plants, and the swaying of the dark green palm fronds of the coconut palm trees. Later that day, they headed to the lagoon for a picnic and swim. Avid snorkelers, Seth and Sara, loved the lagoon's warm and clear blue waters, the soft sand of Emon Beach, the multicolored coral reefs, and the even more colorful fish and aquatic life that called the reefs home. Even the sharks that swam curiously by them as they snorkeled were beautiful from a distance. It seemed to Seth that God was showing off when He created Kwajalein. It was a short but needed respite from their busy lives before Seth had to prepare for his temporary duty trip back to the mainland.

"Can you find my dark suit and tie?" Seth hollered to Sara from the front of their quarters to the back, where the master bedroom was. "I assume they will have Grandpa Grayson's funeral service when Ron and I are back in Huntsville for the Space and Missile Defense Command Commanders meeting at Redstone. It is only a short drive to Fort Payne from Redstone. I think the Space and Missile Defense Command Commander understands the role that US Army Garrison-Kwajalein Atoll plays in supporting the test range and how inextricably we are tied together, and that's why I have been invited to their meeting. Ron understands that we are 'two peas in a pod.'"

Grandpa Grayson, Corporal Ralph Grayson, had been an

Infantryman in the 184th Regimental Combat Team, 7th Infantry Division during World War II, serving in both Kiska in the Aleutian Islands and then taking part in the amphibious assault of Kwajalein in February 1944.

Seth and his Grandpa Grayson had spent hours discussing Kwajalein last year when Seth learned of his pending assignment. The smell of the ocean, the smell of burning flesh—a result of the flamethrower he wielded—the rubbled structures, the broken trees, and the relentless trade winds, heat, and humidity with no shade. All this weighed heavily on Grandpa's mind for over seventy years. Kwajalein was not a pretty sight once the 7th Division had cleared it of the Japanese forces stationed there. Corporal (Grandpa) Grayson was lost in the moment as he recalled with horror what he had done to the Japanese sniper; he had hoped that saving the other Japanese soldier would somehow make things right with God. He had prayed that it would, almost every night since that time. He had confessed his aggression to God, not that he had fired on an enemy combatant, but that he had wielded the flamethrower unnecessarily and unmercifully on a disarmed Japanese soldier. He knew God forgave him, but it was difficult to forgive himself.

Grandpa had briefly shown Seth the old helmet a surviving Japanese soldier had given him. A bit of a surprise as most Japanese military men were either killed by the Americans or committed suicide rather than be taken alive. And now, Corporal Ralph Grayson was gone, dead at ninety-five.

"Sara, I have to go. The old DC-8 that the US Air Force's Air Mobility Command sent out this morning will be flying back to Hickam Air Force Base soon, and then I only have a few hours to get over to Honolulu to catch the flight to Huntsville."

Sara jumped in the golf cart parked in the carport next to Quarters 241 and drove her husband to the airfield adjacent to his office. Since this was official business, they used the Army-owned golf cart rather than their bicycles.

As SHE WATCHED the news on Armed Forces Network later that day, Sara was more than dismayed to learn about the thousands of illegal immigrants and drugs flooding across the border with Mexico into the US on a daily basis, with no apparent end in sight. *What is going on here, and what will it lead to?* she thought.

CHAPTER 5

SECRETARY OF STATE AT THE UN

New York City, November 16

Secretary of State James Aranson was ready to discuss the issue with the UN Security Council. Rather than allow the US Ambassador to the UN to take the credit for this new initiative, he would do the talking. After all, it might bode well for a presidential run in the future. If he could influence a new paradigm in the South China Sea to be an integral part of a new and more significant trade agreement with the ChiComs—one that further opened the doors for US businesses in Mainland China and vice versa—he would have a leg up on the future competition. Not to mention he could satisfy the current president's penchant for all things Chinese. And shut up some of the rumblings from the Defense Department, specifically the Joint Chiefs, about getting too close to the People's Republic of China (PRC).

How often did he, Secretary Aranson, have to hear about all the classified information related to the space and missile programs that an earlier administration had given away in the 1990s under the guise of mil-to-mil contacts to improve our trade balance? Or the avionics technology the current administration had traded for export/import concessions that never seemed to materialize?

The other members of the Security Council were taking their seats in the classified briefing room as Secretary Aranson cleared his throat. *Would they ever settle and stop chitchatting?* China, Russia, the United Kingdom (UK), and France were last to quieten down. As permanent members of the Security Council along with the US, they knew their way around the table and the issues. They were not about to let the American Secretary of State rule the roost. The ten rotational members, especially the five that were still relatively new, were ready to go.[1] Having reviewed the US's pre-brief information on the agenda item, most expected that Angola would side with China on this issue. Gabon and Ghana would favor whatever the Russians suggested. Still, Brazil and the United Arab Emirates were circumspect about anything that granted any advantage to China in the South China Sea. After all, they were significant oil producers themselves.

Aranson realized the general alignment of the ten "junior partners" in the room and that of the permanent members as well. While not frequent, it was not unheard of for China (the PRC) and Russia to agree on something which reinforced each other's deepest wants and needs, while France swayed in any direction just to show how independent they were. Go figure. The UK was different. While they may have some liberal leanings at home, they could be hawkish and quite conservative regarding the PRC and Russia. Secretary Aranson would have his hands full, bringing all fifteen nations together unanimously on his proposal or at least getting the requisite nine affirmative votes with no vetoes from the five permanent members. But he was confident of success through the superior nature of his intellect, a little obfuscation of the facts, and some intense behind-the-scenes arm twisting.

CHAPTER 6
MEETING AT THE ARIZONA BORDER

San Miguel Gate, near Sells, Arizona, November 16

SELLS, ARIZONA, WAS A SMALL TOWN NEAR THE US-MEXICAN border. Its claim to fame was the Tohono O'odham Nation of nomadic Native Americans and their annual rodeo. Across the southern border from Sells was the town of El Bajio in the Sonora District of Mexico. There is a little-known border crossing near Sells called the San Miguel Gate. In this place, until recent years, the members of the Tohono O'odham Native American Nation could cross almost freely between the US and Mexico, as their reservation, their lands, and their nation spanned an area that covered portions of southern Arizona and northern Sonora. Only a low fence along the border was a minor hindrance to vehicles but no impediment to those on foot. The Border Patrol staffing level was deficient, and the area they had to cover was large.[1] It was an unusual arrangement indeed, but it had served the nation well, especially at rodeo time in late January, when thousands of people flocked to the area to see the largest Indian rodeo in Arizona, perhaps in all the United States.[2]

So, what interest could a South American drug lord have in

a rodeo? Carlos de Von Heim led the drug cartel with a firm hand—a lethal hand when necessary—to ensure the smooth flow of cocaine from Bolivia and meth chemicals from Mexico into the US. His profit margin was unbelievable, and he wanted to keep it that way.

His grandfather, Johann Von Heim, had fled Germany in 1945 and made his way to La Paz, Bolivia, where he opened a restaurant. Eventually, Johann found his way to Cochabamba in the Central Bolivian Plateau, where he opened his second restaurant, and then on to Santa Cruz in eastern Bolivia, in the heart of the Amazon, where he opened his third. His family flourished in Santa Cruz, a large, growing, and bustling town with curious nonstop airline connections to Miami. Santa Cruz is where his only grandson, Carlos, was raised and where he was introduced to the coca plants of Bolivia. The Santa Cruz to Miami airline connection paid off quickly when Carlos got older. Using the restaurant as a front as his grandfather aged, Carlos hired local college students and some American college students to serve as both waiters and his "mules." They carried cocaine to the US through Miami in their luggage, sewn inside their clothes, or even in plastic bags they swallowed.

Bolivia is one of those South American countries with untold natural resources that can never seem to get their act together long enough to become solvent and flourish without the illegal but profitable reliance on cocaine. Once the world's silver capital, Potosi still produced much silver and tin. Tungsten was also present in large amounts in some parts. Natural gas was abundant in land-locked Bolivia, but sometimes challenging to get to the world market from such remote places as Puerto Linares. And there was always tension with Peru over borders. Therefore, after establishing himself as one of the premier cartel "jefes" in South America, and because the Drug Enforcement Agency had gotten too close to his operations in Santa Cruz, Carlos moved his headquarters from Bolivia to Mexico City. This was a city of more than twenty million people where he and his organization could blend in and hide in plain sight while growing the "business." His new restaurant franchise in Mexico City served as a prominent but legal and usually ignored front for his growing entrepreneurial spirit! With the now porous border with the US, perhaps he could include the fentanyl flowing into Mexico from China, in his menu of illicit drugs he was sending across the border. He smiled at this financially lucrative prospect. Things were looking up for Carlos and his expanding number of "mercantile options" at the almost non-existent border.

Carlos started the meeting in El Bajio around 10:00 a.m. He welcomed his guests and poured them a drink, all except Abdul, who actually believed all that nonsense in the Koran about not imbibing alcohol. Abdul bin Rastafa was a United Arab Emirates national with ties to the Sunni-dominated Al Jihadi Levant (AJL), which was looking for easier ways into the United States— access points that could facilitate the movement of bulkier items. AJL was primarily made up of former ISIS and Al Qaeda fighters. Abdul brought money to the table and a hatred for the Americans that knew no bounds. This was because his older brother had been killed in Iraq by the 30mm chain gun of an American A-10 close air support jet while working for Saddam Hussein in 1990. He had been chewing on that for more than thirty years. The cartel could use that kind of hatred when the time came. Carlos wondered if the rumors about a rapprochement between the AJL and ISIS were true, or was it between the AJL and Iran? Who knew? They were all crazy, in his opinion, but useful.

General Shin Yao from the PRC People's Liberation Army and General Valeri Borzovich from the Russian Strategic Defense Forces had no reservations about consuming the tequila that Carlos served and warmed up to him quickly. One would have thought that Carlos had called the meeting. Yet, actually, China's embassy in Mexico had approached Carlos about the meeting and the recommended location, El Bajio, just across the border from Sells, Arizona, and the San Miguel Gate.

Carlos was not sure what China and Russia would gain from the unholy alliance with his cartel and the AJL, but he guessed America's best interests were not at the center of it. He knew that President Putin of Russia was livid with the West, specifically NATO and the European Union but even more so, the USA. He knew it was the USA's leadership, even if from "behind" where the President of the United States remained, that galvanized the West's resistance to Putin's special military operation into Ukraine. They had provided President Zelensky of Ukraine with the weapons and supplies he needed to hamper Putin's plans.

It could have been resolved even more favorably for Ukraine if the West had been quicker on the draw in supplying Zelensky, but better late than never.

Carlos surmised that Putin intended to take all of Ukraine to "rescue" the Russians living there from the neo-Nazis. Instead, he was left with the Donbas region in southeastern Ukraine (in which he already had a foothold via Russian nationalists and Spetznaz in the area), continued to hold the Crimean Peninsula, and created a land corridor from the Donbas to the Crimea. His plans to take Odesa failed when the Ukraine military sank the Russian cruiser in the Black Sea. It was embarrassing. The West's sanctions of Russian oligarchs and banks and shutting down Russian gas and oil pipelines into Western Europe only enraged him more. He wasn't too thrilled with recent moves by the US to open up Cuba, either.

The PRC's rationale for the alliance was more challenging to figure out. However, Carlos assumed it had something to do with their desire for hegemony in the Pacific. The Philippines' recent overtures to the US about re-establishing and increasing military presence there and the addendum to the 1951 Mutual Defense Treaty that the US signed in 2014 with the Philippines, could not have made them feel good. It was called the Enhanced Defense Cooperation Agreement.[3] Nor could the rapidity with which the CIA and NSA determined that North Korea was behind the recent cyberattacks in the US, which meant it would not be too much longer before they realized the extent to which the PRC had assisted Pyongyang. But specifically, Carlos was still not sure what they were after. The PRC had an enormous bargaining chip that they held over the heads of the insatiable American government. That is, they held over a trillion dollars of the US national debt. Taiwan was always an issue between them and DC, but Congress appeared to be a little more protective of Taiwan than the South China Sea. At least for now. But hey, they were alluding to some actions across the globe that would demand the attention, capital, and forces of the US, thus taking their eyes off the US-Mexican border. Those kinds of things could make for significant distractions from the already porous border and facilitate the expansion of his enterprise. Or maybe he was the distraction for them.

At the end of the meeting, the group walked within a few hundred yards of the San Miguel Gate, surveyed the situation with field glasses from behind a hill, and then General Yap made a quick phone call.

CHAPTER 7
THE PRESIDENT AND RIMPAC

Washington, DC, November 20

President Roland Justice entered the Oval Office, where the others were already gathered. This was the weekly update from his domestic and international department heads, advisors, and staff, followed by his guidance. He would convene a smaller, more focused group when hot issues boiled up. The first to speak was Jack Ruiz, Secretary of Homeland Security.

"Mr. President, as you know, the number of teenage students and even more minor children crossing into the US continues to grow—the perception is that we will not refuse them. Canceling the title 42 COVID restriction will only make it worse, both actual and perceived, as the caravans are growing larger and are nonstop. While we have been deporting record numbers of non-approved immigrants, at least on paper, during your tenure, we are also *not* deporting more based on your guidance after the midterms. That executive action is still in effect, albeit hampered by a lower federal court's injunction, until the re-vamped Supreme Court completes its review of your action. The fact sheet we prepared for release emphasizes a crackdown at the border while allowing us not to deport worthy families. Here is an excerpt from it:

"The President's Immigration Accountability Executive Actions will help secure the border, hold nearly five million undocumented immigrants accountable, and ensure that everyone plays by the same rules. Acting within his legal authority, the President is taking an important step to fix our broken immigration system."

"These executive actions crack down on illegal immigration at the border, prioritize deporting felons, not families, and require certain undocumented immigrants to pass a criminal background check and pay their fair share of taxes as they register to temporarily stay in the US without fear of deportation."[1]

Ruiz continued. "It seems there is a huge rumor mill south of the border, suggesting that your executive action mandates explicitly that anyone under eighteen shall not ever be deported. We know that is not true, but certain parties in Mexico seem to have been promulgating that rumor. On another point, as you are aware, we have closed several border crossings over the years and are upgrading others, such as the large crossing at San Ysidro, south of San Diego.[2] We are also dismantling some of the fencing that was built during the Bush and Trump administrations, per your direction, as it appears too repressive. The governors of Texas, New Mexico, and Arizona have all called to complain, but we have threatened them with lawsuits if they attempt to secure the borders in their states. Texas is ignoring us and actually trying to control the flow since they called up some National Guard and started busing immigrants to New York City and DC. Arizona is threatening to declare an invasion so they can call up all their National Guard and have actually installed empty vans in the gaps in some fencing. But I am pretty sure the next lawsuit we file will pull them back. That is, while the Supreme Court is configured as it is. The recent retirement of the ultraconservative Justice Smith works in our favor on this issue."

"Good," said the President. "I am tired of these state governors thinking they can overrule the federal government's actions. I am responsible for controlling the border and determining who gets in and who stays, not them."

Janey Mills, Secretary of the Interior, spoke next.

"The recent war in Ukraine and the greed of sizeable American petroleum companies continue to keep the price at the pump excessively high. While we showed the voters that we cared by releasing millions of gallons from the strategic reserve and tried to get the Oil Producing and Exporting Countries (OPEC), Venezuela, and even Iran to produce more oil, we knew that wouldn't be enough. Actually, this is working in our favor as we wean Americans off fossil fuels and onto electric cars. We still hear an occasional whine about the Keystone Pipeline, especially now with the gas prices so high. Your move to ostensibly open up some federal lands for more exploration should quiet that down, although we know our permitting process will hamper that.

"And the fracking," said the President. "I would really like to rein that in. Next week, bring me some proposals to review. Maybe Amanda can include them in her work."

Then it was Defense's turn. Sitting in for Secretary of Defense Amanda Carson, who was away at a global climate change conference, an existential threat to the American way of life in the minds of a significant number of the President's donors, the Chairman of the Joint Chiefs of Staff Admiral Halsey Burke began. "Mr. President, the airstrikes on the pop-up remnants of ISIS continue. And now, they have joined forces with the remnants of Al Qaeda to create Al Jihadi Levant or the AJL.

In Syria, the Russians are hitting some of the bad guys some of the time as they continue to push their agenda while tacitly still supporting President Assad. I think the Secretary of State's cease-fire negotiations with them may reap some benefits for the Syrian people, if not the Jihadists. The Kurds are seeing significant success in northern Iraq and even parts of Syria. Tensions between the Kurds and Turkey are almost at the explosion point. The Iraqi Army continues to make improvements. But Libya and Tunisia are seeing increased ISIS, now AJL, activity, as is Egypt. We are seeing a significant increase in chatter and action on the outskirts of Baghdad now that Ramadi has fallen again. The mortars and shelling of the international community's Green Zone are pretty much unabated at this point. I would like to request an increase of 1,500 in the number of our Special Forces advisors on the ground and put in some multiple launch rocket system artillery units near Baghdad as a defensive measure for counter-battery fires."

"Noted," said the President. "What else do you have?"

"Sir, we need to look again at our overall goal, our desired end state, and the strategy for attaining those ends, such as destroying AJL. Then we need to assess the ways we can meet that strategy, the means we have to apply those ways, and see what adjustments we need to make. We need to identify AJL's strategic and operational centers of gravity and apply assets against them in an organized and aggressive way. We are simply marking time under the present arrangement, even as AJL is making strategic partners of groups like Boko Haram, Al Shabab, and Abu Sayyaf. I have planners in the Joint Staff J3 Operations Section and J5 Plans Section looking at this now. They are also working with the Central Command Plans,

Special Operations Command Plans Sections at MacDill Air Force Base in Tampa, and XVIII Airborne Corps G3 planners at Fort Bragg.. Oh, I forgot the new name, Fort Liberty, in Fayetteville. They have shown me a few scenarios that could make great strides relatively quickly. The beheadings must be stopped. We looked weak to our allies and foes in the Middle East a few years ago when an American female aid worker from Iowa was beheaded just because she had been working in a health clinic northeast of Damascus. We did nothing, and they have long memories. She was not a crazy Jihadist bride; she was a legit medical worker in the wrong place at the wrong time."

"I said noted, Admiral," repeated the President. "Look, I have requested an extension of the Authorization for Use of Military Force from Congress that allows some increase in our noncombat forces on the ground and additional funding for three years. The Iraqis need to resecure Baghdad, and my relations with the Ayatollah in Tehran seem to be paying off near Mosul. Now, what else do you have?"

The tension in the air was thick. The Chairman of the Joint Staff squirmed in his seat and paused for what seemed like an eternity before continuing. "Sir, Putin appears to be licking his wounds after his stalemate in Ukraine. He is poised for renewed aggression in other parts of Ukraine and Moldova. Still, intel suggests a couple of years before he can reconstitute his forces sufficiently, given the sanctions in place. And now he is strongly hinting that he may use tactical nukes if his 300,000-reserve call-up fails to get him what he wants. Moving on, as you will recall, the Enhanced Defense Cooperation Agreement to the Mutual Defense Treaty we have with the Philippines includes some specific Maritime Security and Enhanced Awareness provisions we want to exercise."[3]

"Tell me more," said President Justice.

Glad to have finally struck a more receptive cord in the President's nerve bank, Admiral Burke perked up. "As you are aware, the South China Sea and Spratly Islands area has long been a contested part of the world among several nations, the Philippines included. The PRC has been doing a lot of saber-rattling lately about their claims in the area, as have Taiwan and Viet Nam. In fact, the PRC has run several naval shows of force in the South China Sea recently to bully their would-be rivals in the area. You may recall they ran some Philippine soldiers off the Scarborough Shoals a while back, even though the shoals belong to the Philippines. The South China Sea is a fertile fishing ground and has long been rumored to hold significant oil and natural gas deposits—more than are currently developed. Personally, I would be surprised if anything ever comes of that as it is too remote and would be difficult to extract given what I know about the area."

"Continue," said the President with a slight smile on his face.

"Thank you, Mr. President. We see a joint and combined Navy-Air Force-Army exercise lasting about two weeks. This would show our solidarity with the Philippines regarding the protection of their interests around their archipelago, specifically near the Scarborough Shoals area in the South China Sea, which is off their western coast. I say combined because we would also invite the Aussies and Kiwis, as well as Malaysia, Japan, South Korea, and many other friendly nations. I would make it a piece of the RIMPAC (Rim of the Pacific) exercise in the summer. I already have the Joint Staff J3 Operations Section and Pacific Command J5 Plans Section in Hawaii developing the plans. We broached the subject with the Filipinos, and they liked it. The Enhanced Defense Cooperation Agreement specifically allows for exercises like this. And of course, the Philippines' recent overtures to us about closer military ties could reap great benefits for us in the western Pacific, spelled S-U-B-I-C Naval Base and C-L-A-R-K Air Force Base."

"What about the Chinese?" asked the President. "We invited them to the last RIMPAC. You know the old saying, 'Keep your friends close, and keep your enemies closer.'"

"Sir, I am not sure how the Philippines would feel about that."

"Invite the PRC and scale back the Philippine portion of the exercise near the Scarborough Shoals to just a simple US and PRC Navy presence exercise. In talking to the PRC President, he has promised me that their intentions in the South China Sea are honorable for all. They could act as the stabilizing force in the area to ensure that all parties are fairly accommodated. While you are at it, invite the Russians too. I want to gain some influence over their actions slowly."

"Sir, the Enhanced Defense Cooperation Agreement is an executive agreement that you endorsed. The Senate did not contest it for their constitutional approval because both parties liked it and saw it as an extension of the Senate-approved treaty. The underlying 1951 Mutual Defense Treaty we have with the Philippines is a constitutionally approved treaty with strong support in both houses and both parties. That treaty does allow the US to come to the aid, militarily, of the Filipinos if they are attacked in the Pacific Ocean area. We confirmed that area several years ago as including the South China Sea.[4] Given the recent Chinese aggressive actions near Scarborough Shoals aimed at the Philippine Navy personnel, I must again recommend the larger combined and joint exercise with the Philippines and not with the PRC."

"Admiral, lest you forget, you are not in charge of foreign policy. I am. You are not in charge of, nor do you play a role in interpreting our defense treaties. I am, and I do. Your proposed exercise is not the message I am trying to send at the moment. So, unless you have anything further of any real significance, and I doubt that, you will refine the exercise in the South China Sea as I described it, and you will invite the PRC and the Russians to RIMPAC. You are dismissed," said the President.

Admiral Burke was having difficulty restraining himself as he left the room and mused to himself in a barely audible voice, "the Chairman of the Joint Chiefs of Staff does not play a role in interpreting defense treaties?"

After several others spoke, the Director of National Intelligence said terrorist threats from abroad could impact the President's agenda. In passing, he noted that the head of the Russian Strategic Defense Forces and a senior PRC Peoples Liberation Army general were both in Mexico with overlapping visits. One was scheduled to visit Cancun on the Gulf Coast and the other to Acapulco on the Pacific coast. Otherwise, not much else was mentioned.

———

THE ANCHOR on the conservative FTX news, was dominating prime time news, and he knew it. "What is wrong with the President?" he asked rhetorically, facing the camera. "Doesn't he understand the serious nature of our open borders with Mexico? Oh wait, he has never been there and thinks there are more important things to do. Dereliction of duty if you ask me."

CHAPTER 8
THE JAPANESE HELMET

Fort Payne, Alabama, November 21

COLONEL GRAYSON'S MEETING IN HUNTSVILLE WITH THE Commanding General and Deputy Commanding General of Space and Missile Defense Command had been dull and typical. All except for the idea that they may be opening the use of the Reagan Test Site and the Kwajalein Garrison facilities soon to "other" allies. He wondered what that meant. But the Space and Missile Defense Command meeting was followed by his Grandpa Grayson's funeral in Fort Payne, Alabama. As a veteran of World War II, Corporal Ralph Grayson was entitled to military honors at the graveside. In these fiscally constrained times, that usually meant a tape recording of taps and a folded flag. Seth Grayson spoke to the Garrison Commander of Redstone Arsenal, Alabama, about getting the full complement of "honors," so the graveside ceremony was a dignified and respectful service.

The Redstone Garrison Commander and Command Sergeant Major attended, as did a squad of seven soldiers and their squad leader, to carry the coffin from the hearse to the gravesite. Those same soldiers folded the flag and gave it to the

Command Sergeant Major, who presented it to Seth's grandmother, and then those same seven fired three volleys each from their M16A4 rifles for the twenty-one-gun salute. Finally, a member of the Army Material Command Band from Redstone played taps on his bugle. They laid Corporal Ralph Grayson to rest as tears flowed down Seth's cheek.

After the funeral, Grandma Grayson told Seth that his grandpa had left several things for him in the attic. He was despondent as he climbed the stairs to the attic in his grandfather's house in Fort Payne. Seth recalled endless summers visiting his grandpa. More tears rolled down his cheeks as he rifled through several old Army footlockers.

"Your grandfather loved you dearly, Seth," whispered Grandma. "He was so proud of you when you graduated from West Point, and he watched with enormous satisfaction as you were promoted through the ranks to Colonel. He laughed when you were promoted from lieutenant to captain, as he never liked the "Louies," as he called them. Grandpa said they didn't know what they were doing half the time. He was beside himself when he first heard about your assignment to Kwajalein. I know Kwajalein was a difficult time for him, and I know something awful happened there in 1944, but he would never let me in."

Seth knew that Grandpa would not have wanted Grandma to know about the sniper and flamethrower incident, so he let her last comment pass. Grandpa and Grandma had lived in that two-story white frame house for almost seventy years after he returned from the Pacific and married her. She had way more good memories than bad and loved Grandpa with all her heart. Now that he was gone, she should complete her days in that beautiful old house in peace with the magnolias in the front yard, azalea bushes in the back yard, and her wonderful Ralph always on her mind.

The attic in their house was huge and dusty but remarkably free of pests and insects, probably due to the extensive use of cedar flooring and paneling. One single light bulb hung from a rafter in the ceiling, providing just enough light not to trip. Seth found some old combat boots, leggings, and an overseas service cap in one footlocker. The second one was in a dark corner, so he had to use a flashlight Grandma gave him. In that one, Seth found an old US Army helmet and liner, an ancient C-ration box, a small, rusty P38 can opener, and medals from his time in the Pacific Theater, including a Purple Heart and Silver Star, neither of which Seth knew that Grandpa had received. Grandpa had never talked much about the war, except for his time in Kwajalein.

Then he noticed it—another helmet—but nothing like the typical US Army helmet from World War II. As he turned it over in his hand, he realized it was a Japanese soldier's helmet, the one his grandpa had briefly shown him just last year before he and Sara moved to Kwajalein. An old helmet, but well preserved in the dry footlockers and with a Japanese pistol inside it. Bringing home this kind of campaign trinket would get you in trouble these days, but World War II was a different kind of war fought by a different breed of men from a far different nation than it is now. He noticed the corner of a faded piece of paper in a small slit of the helmet's lining. Carefully pulling back the helmet liner, he exposed an envelope with a document handwritten in Japanese block form. Almost perfectly preserved, it would make a great item for the shadow box he planned to create for his grandma, highlighting Grandpa's time in the Army. He put the letter in a new envelope and packed it, the helmet, and several other items in a box that he would ship back to Kwajalein. He would enlist the help of Sara to create the shadow box and maybe find someone to translate the Japanese.

Aboard Flights to Kwajalein, November 22

The flights back to Kwajalein seemed to take forever, as they usually did, but this time, Seth's heart remained heavy from his grandfather's funeral. It was only a few days before Thanksgiving, but he could not get his mind off the funeral nor the Space and Missile Defense Command Commander's comment about "other" allies using Kwajalein. As he read the Huntsville newspaper, his mind wandered until he saw an AP article about the upcoming RIMPAC, including the PRC and Russia. He also noticed that US Army Garrison-Kwajalein Atoll and Reagan Test Site would be within the exercise boundaries. It seemed odd to him that this kind of information was already being released, or even released at all, since it was probably classified. But hey, if a senator or congressman released it for political reasons, it was all A-OK. If someone in the military released it early, they could be facing court-martial charges. Then, he fell asleep as he flew from Huntsville to Atlanta. That was followed by a long flight to Honolulu, then remaining overnight at the VIP suites on Fort Shafter, Honolulu. The next day, he was driven to Hickam Air Force Base, where he caught another DC 8 back to Kwajalein, crossing the international dateline and arriving on November 24. He was dog-tired when Sara collected him and his luggage in the golf cart and drove him back to Quarters 241. Home, sweet home!

Kwajalein Island, Kwajalein Atoll, December 1

There were numerous unusual, if not bizarre, aspects to this US Army garrison command in the central Pacific. First was the number of actual "rocket scientists" he got to meet and work with during the course of the various missile and sensor tests that put Kwajalein's isolation and facilities to good use. They seemed like ordinary people, but they were geniuses, literally. They were good people—hardworking folks who wanted to see every test succeed with flying colors and to ensure their sensors were always up to date. The juxtaposition of their space-age technology against the traditional ways of the Marshallese people was a frequent source of humor and sadness as their exploitation by their own government had held them down in the past. One of Seth's favorite pictures was that of the contrails from dummy warheads of a Minuteman or Peacekeeper test screaming down toward the lagoon over the picture of a Marshallese woman weaving a basket or cracking open a coconut inside her grass-roof-and-dirt-floor house.

He never grew tired of the beauty that he found on Kwajalein: the dark green of the coconut palm fronds against the dark blue skies, the fragrance of the plumeria flowers, orange canna lilies, and white orchids woven into headbands for the ladies, and the crystal-clear waters of the lagoon that made for a snorkeler's paradise. The scuba divers also loved the lagoon for all the World War II equipment, aircraft, and ships that lay on the bottom to explore. And then there was also the *Prinz Eugen*, a German battleship and sister to the *Bismarck*, that ended up in the lagoon, upside down and slowly leaking oil. It was said to have been one of the numerous hulks that were positioned around Bikini and Eniwetok during one of the H-bomb tests to assess the blast effects of the weapon. It was so damaged that it was towed to Kwajalein afterward, where it capsized and remains there today.

The traditional "Jobwe stick dance" the young Marshallese boys performed was another example of the beauty of the Marshall Islands. It was from an age gone by but also the stuff of National Geographic quality. The precision of these preteen boys was phenomenal as they whirled and danced to the incessant beat of the drums and smacked their ornately carved and decorative sticks on the ground or against the sticks of the other dancers. Dressed in their finest attire, including necklaces of coral and shark's teeth with palm frond kilts and bare feet, it was rare actually to see a performance. Marshallese royalty—the Iroijs, the princes of the islands—were the expected audience. As the Commander and First Lady of US Army Garrison—Kwajalein Atoll, Seth and Sara had been honored to witness one. It was terrific, with some dances lasting as long as thirty minutes, nonstop!

On a sadder note, the Kwajalein Hospital, manned by the base operations support contractor, had been used for a number of years to treat old Marshallese from the Bikini and Eniwetok atolls. They were irradiated after the wind shifted just prior to the Bravo Blast Hydrogen bomb test in 1954. The resulting irradiated dust and radioactive fall-out covered Rongelap, where the Marshallese had been moved for safety![1] Ever since then, every six months, they traveled to Kwajalein, where folks from the Department of the Interior worked with the base contractor medical staff to check them out. A sad state of affairs that cost the US government billions of dollars to correct and manage—if managing long-term radiation sickness and the resultant cancer is something one manages.

Equally poignant was the annual ceremony at the Japanese Cemetery on Kwajalein. The US Departments of Defense and

State officially sanctioned the event. Every year about twenty or so (the number was dwindling) Japanese veterans, who had been stationed in the Marshall Islands during World War II, traveled to the Japanese Cemetery on Kwajalein to pay their respects to their friends who fell during Operation Flintlock. Each year, their senior representative made a short speech through an interpreter who traveled with them from Tokyo. Then the Commander of US Army Garrison-Kwajalein Atoll, who was also the US Pacific Command Commander's Representative to the Marshall Islands, would reciprocate with an equally short speech, translated by the same person. Perfunctory gifts were exchanged, and both parties departed for the year.

This year started out the same until one old gentleman in a wheelchair became agitated when Colonel Grayson was introduced. When his talk was over, Colonel Grayson closed with a short benediction. Then he asked the translator if there was anything the elderly man needed and if, perhaps, he should get out of the sun. In his halting English, the old man asked, "You have a relative who served in Kwajalein during the war?" Grayson was stunned. The memories of his grandfather's recent burial came flooding back, and he turned away from the old man to hide his tears. Sara grabbed his arm. Regaining his composure, Seth told the translator, "Yes, my grandfather, Corporal Ralph Grayson, served on Kwajalein and took part in the amphibious landing and capture of Kwajalein in February 1944."

The elderly Japanese man smiled and cried simultaneously and waved his hands furiously. "*Herumetto, herumetto!*" he screamed and clapped his hands. Dressed in a long formal silk robe and sash, with silver hair and dark eyes, he looked like an ancient Samurai warrior—a Samurai warrior in a wheelchair! "*Herumetto, herumetto!*" he shouted louder. The translator calmed him down and told Seth that *herumetto* was Japanese for helmet.

"The gentleman is wondering if your grandfather ever told you about a Japanese soldier's helmet he got while he was in Kwajalein," she said. "He says he gave one to him."

Seth turned pale as he realized he was facing the Japanese soldier that Grandpa Grayson had escorted to the G2 Intelligence Section interrogation after saving his life—the same soldier who had given Corporal Grayson the helmet with the mysterious letter stuck inside the liner more than seventy years ago as a gift for not cremating him with the flamethrower.

As believers, both Seth and Sara realized this moment was not a mere coincidence of life. This was not an accidental meeting but proof to them of just who controlled the universe and the fullness thereof. A "divine appointment," her pastor once called this sort of event. Sara said, "Let's all go to the cool, air-conditioned Louie Zamperini mess hall and have an early lunch. I think we should get to know this gentleman better."

Seth beamed, "Sara, please go with Donna from Public Affairs and this gentleman and the translator and get a table at the mess hall. Donna, call ahead and let them know we're coming. I have to run home and get something. I will meet you all there in a few minutes. Their flight back to Tokyo leaves in a few hours, and we have much to discuss before that happens."

Seth dashed home as fast as the governor-controlled golf cart would take him and found the letter from the helmet. He carried both the helmet and the letter to the mess hall and joined the group. Using young Meiko, the translator, whenever his English failed, the old former Corporal Isao Akisao told Seth and Sara about his time on Kwajalein. He reminisced about watchfully waiting for the Americans to attack, the dreadful bombardments and the screams of his fellow soldiers, and then the day of the amphibious assault. He relayed to Seth just how intense the combat was and how frightened he was. Tears welled up as he recalled watching Seth's grandfather respond to the Japanese sniper's attack with his rifle and flamethrower. But he also told them about the unbelievable mercy Corporal Ralph Grayson had shown to Isao—after he had been shot in the leg—by not burning him to death and not allowing the other American soldier to kill him.

"I gave him my *herumetto*, my helmet, as a gift for not killing me, but it was a Trojan horse gift, a good Trojan horse gift, for inside it was a letter of great importance!"

Seth queried him, "What does the letter say? Grandpa Grayson never mentioned it; apparently, it has been hidden in the liner for over seventy years. As far as my grandmother and I can tell, he never told anyone about the letter, nor had it translated. We are not sure he even knew it was in the liner."

Isao responded guardedly, "It is my findings concerning the estimated quantity, quality, and viability for extracting extensive oil and natural gas deposits in the South China Sea in general, and specifically near the Scarborough Shoals," whispered Isao. "Long suspected but never verified due to changing tectonic plate conditions, volcanic activity and earthquakes, and major storms, it is my opinion that the size of the reserves in that part of the South China Sea is something nations go to war over. The paper is the result of my studies before and during the war before my government sent me to Kwajalein. After the war, I returned to the university to complete my master's degree, but I was never able to return to Scarborough Shoals. As a former Japanese soldier, I was not welcome in the Philippines. After many years, I became involved in the nuclear power plant industry and nearly forgot about my paper, but I could never forget your grandfather's face. It haunted me. But this year, my granddaughter, Meiko, who is also our translator, convinced me to return to Kwajalein.

Meiko and I have had dozens of talks about faith. She is a believer in your Jesus, one of the very few in Japan, and she told me that she was convinced in her heart that I needed to travel to Kwajalein to put my demons to rest. So here we are."

Another divine appointment, thought Sara.

"Yes, we are," said Seth. "But tell me, after all the changing conditions you mentioned, do you still believe the oil reserves exist? And if those reserves are so large, why has no country ever started drilling?"

"Without a doubt, the reserves are still there. While the changing conditions could mask much of what I found, they would not eliminate it. It might make it more difficult to extract or maybe make it simpler. During World War II, fracking was not a viable method for extraction. We knew little about that, which would have been too costly and time-consuming anyway. But with the advancements the United States has made in fracking, Scarborough Shoals could become another Fort Worth, Texas, North Dakota, or both. In 1940, when Japan ruled the western Pacific, I believed Japan should control the South China Sea and everything in it. By 1943, having seen what we did to the Marshallese and finally hearing about what we did to the Chinese people in Nanking in the late 1930s, I believed my paper would be in better hands if the Americans had it. That is where your grandfather came in."

Meiko spent the next two hours translating the document into English, and then she gave Seth the original. She kept a copy of it.

Seth wasn't sure where all this was leading, but one thing was for sure, he would let his chain of command know. He called Lieutenant Colonel Ron Bakerson and Lieutenant Colonel Eli Shan to his office and told them about the elderly Japanese soldier's letter. He then sent a classified email via the secure internet to his boss, the Senior Executive Service government supervisor in the Pacific Region Office on Oahu. He CC'd the three-star general commanding Installation Management Command. He also copied Ron on his email, and Ron sent it to the one-star general in Huntsville and the three-star general commanding Space and Missile Defense Command in Washington, DC.

CHAPTER 9

CLASSIFIED INFO: SHARED OR LEAKED?

Washington, DC, December 8

PRESIDENT JUSTICE WAS SKEPTICAL AND ELATED AT THE SAME TIME. He and Secretary of State James Aranson could not believe their good fortune over the recent information they'd received from the Department of Defense related to expected oil and gas reserves in the eastern South China Sea, near the Philippines. If true, it would add to their planned paradigm shift in the area and further enhance future trading with China. This could be a win-win for the US-PRC relationship. Of course, they would have to smooth things over with the Filipinos, but that could be done. And besides, the Filipinos did not have a viable space and missile program, a military that could reach across the oceans, or aircraft carriers like the ones the PRC has.

"James, contact the Chinese ambassador and bring him up to date on what we recently learned about the gas and oil in the South China Sea near the Scarborough Shoals," said the President. "Please explain how this can increase the value of our trade agreement with them and the proposed paradigm shift in the South China Sea. Tell no one else."

Then the President told his Chief of Staff to call in the Secretary of Defense and Chairman of the Joint Chiefs. Secretary of Defense Amanda Carson, and the Chairman of the Joint Chiefs of Staff Admiral Halsey Burke, entered together. You could not call them friendly toward each other, but they had grown to understand each other's perspectives. Carson had risen through the ranks of the Department of Defense via the federal government employee route. She had never been in the military, neither active, reserve, nor guard, but she had seen a lot of old war movies, as she used to quip. However, having spent her entire thirty-year career in the Department of Defense, and specifically in the Pentagon itself, except for occasional official temporary duty trips, Amanda Carson did know the inner workings of the building well. She also learned how to tickle the bureaucracy, both of which were requisite qualities for a successful Secretary of Defense. She was bright, well-spoken, and very pro-President.

Admiral Halsey Burke was an Annapolis man, a United States Naval Academy graduate. He had seen more war than most Americans had seen of their navels. He was anxious to serve the Secretary of Defense and President well but also had reservations about Secretary of Defense Carson. She spent more time at global climate change conferences than she did developing a serious strategy to defeat terrorist groups or assessing the current situation in Ukraine and what that could mean for the long-term viability of NATO. Additionally, she spent too little time counseling the President on his dangerous flirtations with Iran. Admiral Burke did not care for the President's proposed 250-ship Navy—it was already well under 300. Nor did he cotton to the idea of dropping the number of active Army Divisions to seven—ten was already too low. But what could you do? The President of the United States is the

Commander in Chief, and Admiral Burke was duty and constitutionally bound to follow his direction. In Admiral Burke's mind, unless the President was asking the military to do something illegal, immoral, or unethical or that violated the Constitution, he would follow. The recent guidance from the President regarding RIMPAC and the exercise in the South China Sea was not to his liking but was on the up and up as far as he knew.

"Amanda, Admiral Burke, good to see you both. Amanda, how was the global climate change conference?"

"We made a lot of headway," said Secretary of Defense Carson. "Almost all of the western powers and much of the Far East are on board with the climate change protocol that would require another cut in CO_2 emissions of twenty percent more by 2024. Even the PRC and Russia agreed to this, which is remarkable considering their current records on pollution, especially the Chinese. India, Thailand, and Indonesia are still holding out, but the international pressure is mounting. We are having a follow-on conference in February at Key West. A stable environment is a prerequisite to any lasting peace accord anywhere on the face of the earth. Don't you agree, Admiral?"

Admiral Burke grunted without commitment. The President noticed the Chairman's reluctance but decided to ignore it for now. "Admiral Burke, in a matter related to RIMPAC and my plans to increase mil-to-mil contacts and cooperation with the PRC and Russia, I have promised both their leaders access to the Reagan Test Site in Kwajalein. Do you foresee any problems with that?"

"Sir, I must insist you coordinate these kinds of initiatives with us first. If by access you mean a once-in-a-lifetime visit to Kwaj and an unclassified tour of the facilities, no problem, I guess. If you mean establishing a presence on Kwajalein or anywhere in the Marshalls or conducting missile and sensor tests there, I would have a huge problem with that. The Reagan Test Site is a world-class missile and sensor test range involving unclassified, confidential, secret, and even some top-secret and other activities and tests. It has a direct line into NORAD for certain functions and supports our military space launch program by finding the path of least resistance for each orbit of each craft through the 10,000-plus pieces of space junk out there. It is not a place we want to invite 'new but untested friends.'"

President Justice grew red in the face and spoke with a low growl. "How dare you insinuate that any actions by my administration might harm our national security. Both leaders have pledged their word to me that they only want to see how we manage testing activities so that they can learn from us." He grew louder, "I also told them they could use the Reagan Test Site capabilities for low-level missile tests of their own, which must be completely open to our observers. So, for a meager cost to us, we will reap the goodwill of two important economic competitors and even some concessions from the PRC. It is good for us," he shouted.

"Sir, the Chinese and Russians already do their own sophisticated missile and sensor testing operating at extremely high levels. Why do they need to learn more about our testing? And there is nothing low-level about the KREMS suite of radars, the underwater hydrophone array, or the launch facilities at Meck…"[1]

"Enough, Admiral." The President cut him off. "Your failure to play team ball is becoming tiresome and has been noticed by the Secretary of Defense in addition to others in my administration. We are proposing nothing untoward. I am using our military as a piece of my international economic strategy, that's all. Now, get on board or cast off."

"My apologies, sir. It is just that some of these actions as they relate to the PRC would appear to run counter to our mutual defense treaty with the Philippines, and..." Admiral Burke looked up.

The President stared, not moving a muscle for about thirty seconds before quietly saying, "Admiral, don't you worry about the Philippines. They are our allies, but that 1951 treaty is not worth the paper it is written on since the Philippines invited our military to leave their country in the '90s."

Silence reigned as Burke pondered his career after the military. *How far can the President of the United States go in terms of sharing classified technology, techniques, and methods that set the US military apart? And with whom can he share such information? And can he legally ignore or abrogate a senate-approved treaty with the Philippines in favor of an economic outreach to a former foe?*

Indeed, the PRC was not the same China it was under Chairman Mao, maybe, but neither were they cut from the same cloth as Australia or the UK—well trusted and long-term allies who had shown their metal on more than one occasion. And the bottom-line question was, does the provision in the Constitution that makes the President the Commander in Chief of the military outweigh or override all other aspects of the Constitution?

"Look, Admiral," said the President as he calmed down. "Trust me that I know what I am doing on the foreign policy side. This is way more advantageous to us than to either the PRC or Russia. So please relay my decision to the Secretary of the Army and then to Space and Missile Defense Command. He was already forewarned by the Secretary of Defense. So, let the Commander of Space and Missile Defense Command know he will be contacted by senior military reps from both countries within a few days about the tests they would like to conduct and any facilities or sensor needs they have. Accommodate them. Yes, be suspicious and make sure that the Reagan Test

Site assigns someone to watch their every move, but accommodate them. That, my dear Admiral, is my direct order to you. Follow it, or I will have you replaced."

"Yes, sir," came out of the Admiral's mouth, but several expletives were on his mind.

South China Sea – Competing Claims

Source: UNCLOS, CIA

Author added items are in ***Italics***

UNCLASSIFIED

CHAPTER 10

UN SHIFTS CONTROL OF SOUTH CHINA SEA

New York City, December 15

THE INTERPRETERS AT THE UN WERE A SPECIAL LOT WITH UNIQUE capabilities. Jill Bishop had a BA degree from Boston College and an MA degree from Oberlin in Mandarin Chinese. Her husband worked in the Pentagon on the Joint Staff J3 Operations Section, which provided for interesting dinner table conversations when they could actually talk about their work. Usually, their work was so classified they just talked about the latest news and talk show, which frequently turned out to mirror their work.

Secretary of State James Aranson approached the podium in the UN Security Council's classified briefing room and asked for quiet. After much delay and adjusting of chairs, he began: "Ladies and gentlemen, last month, I broached a subject with you about a new paradigm in the western Pacific, one that would enhance peace and security, and open trade routes for all —a paradigm that would also ensure the proper environmental management of the fish and wildlife in a vulnerable area. Specifically, I am talking about the South China Sea and its various island groups. As I recall from last month, several of you were behind this plan, a few were undecided, and a couple of you seemed to oppose it. Let me spend a little more time explaining the program and its pros and cons.

"We call it the South China Sea Paradigm for Progress. SCSPFP for short. In our concept, the PRC Navy would be responsible for ensuring all waterways and trade routes throughout the South China Sea and among the various island groups in the South China Sea, would remain open to all. Fishing rights for each nation would be protected out to the internationally recognized twelve-mile limit. The PRC would make annual reports to the Security Council on the status of their activities and the growth of commerce within the South China Sea. Any nation who felt another country was hampering its trade or was concerned by the growing pirate activity could request assistance from the PRC Navy, which would respond within forty-eight hours to investigate.

"Nothing in this proposed paradigm shift negates or in any way alters any treaty obligations the US has with any interested parties or nations of the area. In fact, this proposal would enhance the mutual defense treaties we have in the region, as the PRC and the US Navy would be sharing information.

"Now, we have all heard rumors about the unconfirmed reports of some vast, ill-defined gas and oil deposits in the South China Sea. First of all, if that ever did come to fruition, this agreement would protect the exploration and extraction rights of every nation that borders the South China Sea. But I am here to tell you that those unconfirmed reports are just that —unconfirmed reports. We have seen nothing in the last fifty years from our geologists and our friends suggesting there are any enormous deposits of note. On the contrary, what we have seen suggests only the currently developed sites and some minor pockets elsewhere. I am holding a recent USGS report that bears witness to that. Copies are in front of you."

"Fox in the hen house" was a common phrase bantered about for the next few hours. Several parties were painfully aware of the PRC's previous assertion that the South China Sea was a Chinese body of water. They knew how they had bullied several nations over the last few years in various parts of it and how they were actively creating new islands in the South China Sea by dredging the bottom and then depositing the sludge and sand in spots to their liking[1] (to their expansionist and defensive liking). Woody Island in the Paracels had essentially become a Chinese military base with surface-to-air missiles.

Secretary of State Aranson calmly explained the talks he already had with the PRC Ambassador to the UN and their Ambassador to the US. He said, "I have their assurances that the PRC would abide by the proposed new paradigm not to take control of the entire area but to assist in its overall safety, security, and management, thereby enhancing the economic benefit that each nation of the South China Sea would derive."

It was bureaucratic double-speak at its best. But once the PRC ambassador finished his two-hour harangue about fail-safe checks embedded in the agreement and the oversight of the PRC Navy by the US Navy, a few of the holdouts relaxed their stance. As expected, the US, China, Russia, Gabon, and Ghana had signed on immediately. France was not far behind as they were large recipients of gas from Russia and wanted to show their support in exchange for a promised reduction of the threats of renewed violence toward Ukraine.

Brazil yielded when presented with the option of receiving significantly increased funding from the US for the United States Antarctic Program, which uses facilities on the South Island of New Zealand for preparing and launching expeditions to the Antarctic.[2] It seemed Brazil wanted a piece of the Antarctic action, and the US was willing to provide that.

All the members of the UN Security Council were on board

except the UK, one of the five permanent members. They smelled a rat but did not want to say so publicly. A sidebar meeting among the US, the PRC, and the UK ensued for hours. In the final analysis, there were some "happy to glad" edits and rewording of some portions to either clarify (or cloud) some provisions depending on where you sat. There were also additional sidebar conversations (and presumably agreements) related to residual British interests in Hong Kong. But by midnight, an agreement had been reached among all fifteen members of the UN Security Council. It was called the UN Resolution for South China Sea Paradigm for Progress (SCSPFP). It would go into effect on the 4th of July, subject, of course, to each member nation's national government agreeing to it.

THAT NIGHT, Jill Bishop flew back to Washington, DC, for her planned two-week leave. Exhausted from her interpreting session with the UN Security Council, she just wanted to go home and crash. Jill pondered whether this was something she should or could share with her husband, COL Will Bishop, but chose to keep silent for the moment. It was her job. Besides, she could not imagine the US Senate would ever approve such a treaty under their "advise and consent" role in the Constitution.

Washington, DC, January 5

"Idiotic!" shouted the Speaker of the House.

"Troubling, very troubling!" yelled the Senate Majority Leader on their first day back from Christmas break. A political firestorm was brewing. Ever since Secretary Aranson had presented the proposed UN Resolution for SCSPFP to the Senate Foreign Relations Committee, things got heated. Even before that, as leaks from the UN were common, the concern over a proposed UN treaty that would give the PRC "unprecedented" control of the South China Sea, had been growing. Now it was an uproar. This prompted some junior congressmen in the opposition party to quietly look up the process for impeachment of a sitting president.

The President of the Philippines called President Justice several times but could not get through to him. Instead, he was shunted to Secretary Aranson, who tried to smooth his ruffled feathers and assuage his concern for the Philippine Islands' claims in the South China Sea, specifically the Scarborough Shoals. "Mr. President, be reasonable. If you have read the agreement, you know that it requires the PRC to respect and protect the rights of all nations with legitimate claims in the South China Sea, including yours. And the US Navy will overwatch the PRC Navy just as a precaution. Finally, there is always the 1951 Mutual Defense Treaty that the USA and Philippines share. We will not leave you hanging," beamed Secretary Aranson.

"Mr. Secretary, may I remind you of the fall of Saigon in 1975? Your rapid retreat from Beirut after the bombing in 1983, your embarrassment and departure from Somalia in the mid-90s, your most recent unilateral withdrawal from Iraq, and the meaningless red lines you drew in the Syrian sand in 2013. And let's not forget how 'well' you met your commitments to Ukraine under the Budapest Memorandum— your country's pledges in recent history have not been cause for confidence in America. The way America withdrew from Afghanistan has to be the most disgusting and shameful political decision I have ever seen, bar none. Your agreements seem to blow in the prevailing political or media wind. I hope and pray your Senate will not consent to it. And if they somehow fall prey to the pretty language in it, then let's hope you honor our 1951 Mutual Defense Treaty, as I will almost certainly be forced to call upon you when the PRC uses the agreement to its advantage and our disadvantage. Give my regards to the President. I hope he trips over his clubs on the back nine." The President of the Philippines slammed the phone down before Secretary Aranson could remind him that the South China Sea Paradigm for Progress would take effect on the anniversary of Philippines Independence Day, the 4th of July. The irony was delicious!

———

Washington, DC, January 12

The Senate Majority Leader from West Virginia read the results. "Ladies and gentlemen, the final vote on the proposed UN Security Resolution South China Sea Paradigm for Progress is as follows: yeas thirty and nays seventy. The nays have it."

Rather than a raucous cheer or hurrah, the Senate floor breathed a collective sigh of relief as most members of both parties had significant concerns about the proposed treaty, which the Department of State had only superficially vetted with the leadership of the Senate.

"After much review and discussion, and based on the recommendation of the Senate Foreign Relations Committee after questioning an array of political and military witnesses, the United States Senate does not consent to the proposed treaty as stated in the UN Security Council resolution." It was a news bombshell that hit the wires quickly. The major networks covered it, as did the wire services and the few remaining print media. The administration promptly engaged the social networks first and then the Senate Foreign Relations Committee staff, who had already prepared Facebook, Twitter, and Vine announcements. The FTX and CTN networks' talking heads discussed the issue at length that evening. Unfortunately, most Americans were unaware of the problem and the possible ramifications if the Senate had approved the treaty, or they were unaware there had been a treaty up for consideration. Nor were most Americans aware the US Constitution gives final approval authority for any treaty to the US Senate under Article II, Section 2. The Senate is required to advise and consent to any proposed treaty, and it must receive two-thirds of the senators' votes who are present to go forward.[3]

The White House, January 15

It was late Friday evening when the White House released a statement concerning Executive Action # 20XX-1. The terse statement said the President had signed the executive action, which allowed the US government to continue working with the UN Security Council on the refinement and future implementation of the South China Sea Paradigm for Progress. That was it—no details, no explanation of what "continue working with" meant, and it did not include the wording of the actual executive action. On the surface, it seemed innocuous enough; the President can give orders to his department heads and officials under the rubric of an executive order, but those orders must be consistent with the Constitution and laws passed by Congress. Executive Orders are actually published in the Federal Registry. Executive actions are a bit more amorphous and general. They seem to express policy and general guidance.[4] They should comply with the US

Constitution, Laws, and Supreme Court decisions. Definitely, a grey area, as neither executive orders nor executive actions are even mentioned in the Constitution but have been abused by presidents from both major parties.

Somewhere along the line, the people elected to the office of President began to "drink the Kool-Aid" that anoints them as the "most powerful leader on earth." It was never intended that way. The Constitution does use the phrase "executive power" when referring to the position of the President, to wit: "The executive Power shall be vested in the President of the United States of America." (Article II, Section 1). But that's it. That is all the Constitution says about it.

Similarly, the "legislative Power" is given to Congress, and the "judicial Power" is given to the Supreme Court. From the beginning, the position of President was supposed to be one that had to share power with Congress and the Supreme Court and was designed by the framers as one part of the separation of powers with internal checks and balances. It was not supposed to be the most powerful position on the earth. Alexander Hamilton spent much time on this subject before the Constitution was ratified, in the *Federalist Papers*, specifically number 69, which was careful to point out the limitations of the presidency.[5]

The term *executive* means having the power to put laws or decisions into effect—to execute them, not create them. The executive branch is supposed to take the laws that Congress has passed (and the President approved) and implement them through its various departments. But here we are, with most recent presidents issuing several hundred executive orders, each. Of course, some executive orders are more limited in scope than others, but the trend is alarming. George Washington issued 8 in 8 years; Lincoln issued 48 in 4 years; Woodrow Wilson 1803 in 8 years; FDR 3721 in 12 years, Truman

907 in 8 years; Ike 424 in 8 years, JKF 214 in 3 years, LBJ 325 in 5 years; Nixon 346 in 5 years, Reagan 381 in 8 years; Bush the First 166 in 4 years; Clinton 364 in 8 years; and Bush the Second 291 in 8 years.[6] Obama and Trump also used executive orders to excess, and President Justice's count is still underway. Both Democrat and Republican presidents have used them to excess. Executive Action # 20XX-1 was just one more in a long line of presidential overreaches.

Both the FTX and CTN morning news anchors were all over the latest executive action the next day, that seemed to duck the constitutional requirement for senate approval of treaties. But they had different perspectives. To the FTX team, it smelled of the administration cozying up to China for what? Personal gain? Was this the proper way to protect and defend the Constitution? To the CTN team, it was a brilliant piece of statecraft, bringing us closer to China and her millions of potential customers while ensuring low labor costs for American businesses. The FTX pundit reiterated her earlier concerns about following the Constitution.

Seth and Sara looked at each other in disbelief over what they had just heard on the news.

CHAPTER 11
THE TOHONO O'ODHAM RODEO

Sells, Arizona and El Bajio, Sonora, January 28-30

FROM THE OPENING PARADE TO THE LARGEST RODEO IN ARIZONA TO the Native American dancing competition, the Tohono O'odham Indian Nation Rodeo was always a huge success and a shot of adrenaline for the Sells, Arizona economy. Thousands of Native Americans and other tourists from around the United States and Mexico descended on that small town, devoured tequila, ate buffalo burgers, and bought various Native American tribes' crafts. The number of US Border Patrol agents was beefed up for the event, as the San Miguel non-gate/gate was constantly busy, day and night. Equally active were the essentially unwatched border areas near Sells, which allowed even more people on foot and small 4-wheel drive vehicles to cross into the US. Being a Border Patrol agent at this event was not fun, as they were stretched thin and underpaid. They received ever-changing guidance from Immigration and Customs Enforcement and the administration on just who to detain, who to release, and who to ignore altogether.

The town of El Bajio in Sonora also swelled during the festival. Carlos de Von Heim and Abdul bin Rastafa went unnoticed as they drove into town the night of January 28. Checking into a small hotel, they dressed as local Mexicans and partied that evening to shake the dust off their boots and the cobwebs from their heads after the long drive from Mexico City. Several other men from the Al Jihadi Levant (AJL) group arrived a few hours later, and all of them except Abdul found company that night in the arms of several local working women. Apparently, the Koran had a "three rivers" rule or something akin to it. That is, once you cross three rivers from home, you are released from all adult behavior and its consequences, at least until your wife or wives find out!

The next day, they painted their three pickups turquoise and orange as they prepared to use them in the Tohono O'odham Rodeo closing ceremonies on the night of January 30 in Sells. They were not alone. Thousands of people were preparing for the same thing. Carlos just watched and smiled since his efforts that evening focused on meeting with his "friends" who had recently been elected the police chief in Sells and a county board member in Pima County, Arizona. Around 9:00 p.m. on January 30 would be the best time for Carlos and his three "vehicles" to join the closing ceremony in Sells, they said. As they left, the police chief gave Carlos three Arizona license plates for his use after they entered the US. The board member reviewed the rezoning action with Carlos, which would change the zoning of an old, dilapidated house on the outskirts of Sells from residential to commercial, allowing for the future development of a "restaurant."

Abdul and his men spent most of the day on January 30 inspecting their backpacks. These were special backpacks with special payloads facilitated by a Canadian businessman, by way of Moscow, and finally by way of the Houthis in Yemen, courtesy of Iran. Initially developed by the Soviet Union during the Cold War, they were to be placed on significant obstacles and obstructions to their westward movement when they charged through the Fulda Gap in Germany. Soviet engineers finally made the case, and the Soviet generals finally listened to their argument. It did not make much sense to employ a strictly tactical nuclear weapon (backpack) on the battlefield, with possible strategic implications (and response) on the homeland. This was especially true when other weapons, such as fuel-air explosives, could reduce the obstructions almost as well. And since the Soviet engineers had to keep their eyes on the "backpack" before detonation, they began to realize the backpack's maximum effective range was farther than their ability to run, hide, or drive after detonation. However, for Abdul and his men, this was not a problem. *Allahu Akbar*, Abdul thought to himself. The time was getting closer for the Great Satan to experience the wrath of Allah up close and personal.

Carlos drove his Jeep Wrangler into the US late on January 30 through the San Miguel Gate. About an hour later, as a considerable commotion was occurring in the open area about a mile to the west of the gate, Abdul and his three pickups with well-hidden backpacks crossed through San Miguel Gate under the pretext of joining the closing ceremonies. The Border Patrol agent, all alone once the other agents went to quell the uproar, was doing his best to maintain order and control at the gate and quickly inspected the pickups. They were through. How easy it had been to fool the border agent and penetrate the hated America's belly.

Abdul and his three pickups drove with the mass of other brightly decorated vehicles in and around the closing ceremony that night. It was a wild and crazy time. After finding a dark and obscure place north of town, they changed their license plates and headed toward Phoenix. It was just under a hundred miles to Phoenix, and they made it there in a couple of hours by taking Route 86 to Tucson and then Interstate 10 to Phoenix. They had never seen anything like the Eisenhower Interstate System and were quite sure it was the work of the devil. Still, it would serve their purposes that day and in the coming months. Once in the Phoenix area, they found an old, dilapidated, extended-stay motel near Scottsdale and moved in. They would be there for a few months as they completed final preparations and then drove to their final destinations—one to the West, one to the East, and one to the Northeast. The choreography of this dance was precise.

CHAPTER 12
FRACKING'S DEATH KNELL AT THE UN

Key West, Florida, February 6

KEY WEST WAS BEAUTIFUL THIS TIME OF YEAR. HECK, IT WAS beautiful any time of the year, notwithstanding the occasional hurricane. The President gave Secretary of Defense Amanda Carson the lead for the administration's pursuit of a global climate change convention and treaty through the UN. She was determined to come through.

The science behind the global warming argument had never been unanimously agreed upon, and parts of it had always been a little suspect. When researchers from East Anglia in the UK and the UN's Intergovernmental Panel on Climate Change report admitted their results were faulty[1], one would have thought the issue would have faded a bit. It seemed the world's temperatures had not risen as much as had been stated. Yes, the last decade had produced some of the hottest years on record, and the drought in the western US was terrible. Still, it wasn't the hottest on record in North America, and temperature records had only been maintained since around 1880.[2] Additionally, the last decade had also produced some of the coldest weather recorded, a fact which the global warming advocates said proved global warming. Go figure! They had been warning of gloom and doom for more than twenty years and announced, as a fact, that the earth's sea levels would rise in fifty years. It would flood low-lying portions of Florida and island states in the Pacific. However, those fifty years kept sliding out into the future. Their concern for the Arctic and Antarctic ice caps was tantamount to religion. It yielded some of their best video clips, showing massive icebergs calving in the Arctic and Antarctic Oceans. Of course, in their minds, since the earth is warming, it must be caused by manmade CO_2 emissions and greenhouse gases from the western powers. Therefore, the western powers and nations becoming more industrialized must cut those emissions at any cost. The East Anglia emails had already faded from their memories, probably due to carbon emissions!

That is not to say rising temperatures and the potential for rising sea levels should not be studied, and preventive measures should be taken when there is a demonstrable, proven, and controllable cause and effect. There has been strong evidence of cyclical warming and cooling periods, including the mini-ice age in the Middle Ages and the ice age scare in the 1960 and 70s.[3] And one of the biggest questions remained: who caused the CO_2 emissions that melted all the ice, ending the ice ages before God put man on the earth? There were few industrialized nations back then! And so, the argument continued as Secretary of Defense Amanda Carson gripped the edges of the podium for her wrap-up speech.

"The future of your families and mine, the future of our existence, rests in our hands today. There can be no doubt that the earth is warming. And there can be no doubt that this warming is caused by human factors, chief among them the emission of greenhouse gases like carbon dioxide belching forth from our power plants, cars, and similar activities. And there can be no doubt that the sea levels are rising at an unprecedented rate. This issue, this global warming calamity, is a national security issue, indeed, an international security issue of the first order. That is why President Roland Justice has me, the American Secretary of Defense, in the lead for our country. It is the most important international issue, more important than terrorism, more important than the euro or dollar status, and more important than the several regional flareups over territory."

Carson surveyed the room and realized every eye was trained on her. She had them on the edge of their seats as she delivered her punch line.

"This threat, this global warming, is an existential threat. Therefore, I am pleased to announce that the President of the United States has agreed to stop all fracking operations within the United States by the year 2024. He has already directed the EPA to prepare the implementing instructions and regulations for this executive action. As you know, he stopped construction of the Keystone Pipeline in the United States when he took office, with almost complete public approval, and plans to eliminate all coal-fired power plants by the year 2030."

The room erupted with applause and shouts of acclamation as Carson continued, "Please, please, let me continue. We have spent several days here preparing the United Nations Global Climate Change Convention and Treaty, including specific actions that the signatories must take, and the timelines demanded. President Justice and Secretary of State Aranson, along with Secretary of the Interior Mills, have reviewed and approved these documents with the changes we mentioned yesterday concerning the management of the South China Sea, to which you have also agreed. The President has empowered me to sign on his behalf."

She reached into her pocket, brought out a large, ornate

Mont Blanc pen, and signed the treaty in large cursive writing. "There. Now even the MAGA (Make America Great Again) people can read my signature without their contacts in," ironically harkening back to John Hancock's signing of the Declaration of Independence in 1776. "This document is now part of the law of the land for the United States of America. Do not let your country be one of the last to sign, or not sign at all, as the repercussions could be telling."

———

THE CONGRESSIONAL DELEGATIONS from West Virginia, Kentucky, Pennsylvania, Wyoming, and Illinois were beside themselves as they listened to the news report. More than any others, their states were heavy into coal mining as part of their economies. They knew the President and the EPA opposed coal mining and coal-fired power plants due to their emissions, but this had gone too far. Their coal mining operations were abiding by the latest round of regulations and federal statutes, and the coal-fired plants in their states had all the required scrubbers. If left unchecked by Congress, this latest action by the President would severely damage their states' economies and any prospects for growth. The Supreme Court had recently issued an injunction against other far-reaching EPA rules on coal-fired plant emission standards. So why did the administration think it would get away with a UN treaty on emissions without Senate approval?

The delegations from Texas, North Dakota, and Ohio were equally incensed by the fracking ban, which came as quite a shock! Was not the boom in the US gas and oil industry directly attributable to fracking? Even when he had vetoed the Keystone Pipeline construction, the President had given no hint about banning fracking. And how could he ban fracking? What authority was he invoking to do this?

Both the Speaker of the House and the Senate Majority Leader appeared on the FTX and CTN networks that evening, decrying the President's action and the Secretary of Defense's signature on a treaty that had not been vetted by either the state governors or the Congress, let alone voted on by the Senate. "It was purely political theater," said the Speaker, ".... and we will have a hearing on this next week," said the senator. However, it was much ado about nothing, as they were becoming increasingly irrelevant in this administration. The President had discovered the condition that made executive orders and executive actions his most effective tool - the lack of term limits for senators and representatives and their concomitant unwillingness to take him on, short of impeachment, for fear of not being re-elected. Yes, they could file a lawsuit which could take years to play out. If they went the impeachment route, they could probably get a vote of impeachment in the House. But without a solid sixty-seven votes in the Senate to convict the President of "treason, bribery, or other high crimes and misdemeanors," it was a waste of time and a possible drag on their re-election chances. The resultant apathy and overwhelming concern for re-election and a polarized Supreme Court all but guaranteed a continuance of presidential overreaches from both parties.

Of equal weight was another condition that made executive actions so effective. Over the years, Congress took the easy way out when writing legislation, usually just listing the general policy guidelines and leaving essential details and controls up to the administration and department heads. In effect, this invited the administration to implement the legislation using executive orders and actions to excess. No wonder the EPA had almost carte blanche when deciding which industries to hammer and how hard! Congress had essentially abdicated.

The CEOs of several major petro giants could only shake their heads as the price of oil per barrel shot up 20 percent on the news of the UN treaty. It was already way too high due to the administration's anti-fossil fuels policies and Russia's stalled invasion of Ukraine. Yes, they would get a short-term shot in the arm, but if fracking stopped, the reliance on foreign oil would go back up, along with the instability in the regions from whence it came. And, lest we forget, fracking was also part of the natural gas boom in the US, which would also take a hit when fracking stopped. Constituents and Petro CEOs alike placed calls to key senators and congressmen, but most were not returned or answered with a "ringing of hands."

It was pathetic. Generals Yao and Borzovich could only smile and wonder how Carlos was doing. For Russia, the short-term would boost their oil-dependent economy, which bode well for their follow-on plans near and in Ukraine and elsewhere. General Yao relished the language in the agreement that reinforced the Security Council's treaty on the South China Sea and implied the PRC's primacy of exploration in the area for "consistency and efficient management of environmental issues in the South China Sea." It was truly amazing what one could do when most people did not thoroughly read what they were approving.

CHAPTER 13
KWAJALEIN GETS "WIND"

Kwajalein Island, Kwajalein Atoll, February 13

IT HAD BEEN A COUPLE OF MONTHS SINCE COLONEL GRAYSON FIRST heard rumors about the direction to support the PRC and Russian tests at US Army Garrison-Kwajalein Atoll and the Reagan Test Site. When the approved guidance finally arrived, it came in fits and starts, as the Chairman of the Joint Chiefs had contacted the Chief of Staff of the Army to give him the assignment. The Chief of Staff of the Army had, in turn, notified the Commander of Space and Missile Defense Command (who had already received a heads up from the Secretary of Defense), who advised Lieutenant Colonel Ron Bakerson, the Range Director of the Reagan Test Site. Bakerson spoke to Colonel Grayson about it. Seth had heard nothing official from the Installation Management Command chain of command but assumed it was part of what he heard at the Space and Missile Defense Command Conference about new users. Since it would be extremely costly to support the PRC and Russian tests, Seth wanted to ensure that the Installation Management Command would provide the added funding. His first few calls were to their Pacific Region Director in Oahu, who knew nothing of the new task and could not say anything about funding. Finally, Pacific Region contacted Installation Management Command headquarters in Washington, DC, and things got straightened out.

But they were here now, Saturday, February 13, a workday in Kwajalein. Both the PRC and Russian program managers had previously visited the Huntsville Offices of the Space and Missile Defense Command and met the Deputy Commanding General. All had gone well, although they discussed few details. After that, the two program managers and their translators arrived the night of February 12, landing at Kwajalein's Bucholz Airfield and rooming at the Kwaj Lodge. The following day, Seth and Ron invited them to breakfast at the Zamperini dining facility. They dined on made-to-order omelets and waffles, then moved on to the Reagan Test Site's Kwajalein Mission Control Center.[1] After a quick walk-through of the console room, they settled down into the user's bay for the rest of the briefings and discussion that day, or at least that was the plan.

As the senior American officer on Kwajalein, Colonel Grayson opened up the briefings by officially welcoming their guests and reminding them that their functions on Kwaj were restricted to:

1. Observing the program management techniques of the Reagan Test Site.
2. Observing the US Army Garrison-Kwajalein Atoll base operations support for such a facility.
3. Conducting low-level missile tests, which would be totally open to Reagan Test Site observers.

Neither Seth nor Ron had received much guidance as to what the low-level missile test parameters would be. So they had developed their own criteria and sent them to Huntsville for review. They were returned without comment. It required the tests to be short-range, less than 50 km, suborbital, and against stationary land targets. The feces hit the fan as soon as the translation ended.

The PRC program manager was insulted to be treated so poorly by such a low-ranking officer. The Russian program manager demanded to speak to Colonel Grayson and Lieutenant Colonel Bakerson's superiors immediately. The PRC and Russian program managers used the satellite phones they brought with them to contact their bosses. At the same time, Seth and Ron called their respective superiors at Installation Management Command and Space and Missile Defense Command. Seth then convened a video conference with Ron, the Pacific Region Director of Installation Management Command, and the Deputy Commander of the Space and Missile Defense Command to discuss the issue. Seth explained what limited guidance they had received, the criteria they had developed and sent forward to Huntsville, and their current situation.

The Deputy Commander of the Space and Missile Defense Command seemed to assess the situation correctly, but he also had recently received guidance from Washington, DC. "Colonel Grayson and Lieutenant Colonel Bakerson, we put you all in a tough spot with sketchy details. Hot off the presses. You must have really ticked off the Chinese and Russian program managers because the President called the Chairman and got involved personally with this. Your basic criteria are OK, but allow them to test up to 250 miles, suborbital, and against land or sea targets, no airborne targets. And make sure you all are on-site whenever they conduct their tests."

Lieutenant Colonel Bakerson chimed in, "Sir, I think we can make Aur Atoll work for that. It is to the southeast of Kwajalein

Atoll and we have used it successfully in the past to launch target missiles. So far, they have not requested a visit to our KREMS sensors. If they do, I would recommend just a VIP walk-through rather than any detailed capabilities briefing.

COL Grayson added, "Sir, we will put up trailers for both the PRC and Russian teams near the Kwajalein Mission Control Center for their workspace and a few to house them on the north end of Kwaj as long as their team members are here. Any idea of the number of people they will be bringing and for how long?"

"Gentlemen, this could last as long as a year from what I can gather. In terms of numbers of people, they have been capped at ten for PRC and ten for Russia. This is a fast-tracked initiative, and we are learning as we go, which is why we had not responded to your recommended criteria. I found out that the PRC could likely use someplace like Aur Atoll, and Russia could use Meck to launch from."

"Sir, we have an extremely heavy test schedule this year for the Meck launch facilities. I would recommend Wake Island if it were a US test, but since it is Russia we are talking about, how about they use the Roi launch facilities,[2] if, in fact, it would be a low-level test."

"Good point, Ron. OK, Russia must use the Roi launch facility, as long as they don't go snooping around the KREMS complex or its radars. Oh, by the way, both the PRC and Russia will have their own portable office facilities shipped into Echo Pier, so you do not need to drag any trailers down to the mission control center for them. Just make sure you have utility hook-ups in place. Include a landline over your mainland US network so they can call back to the Pentagon if they wish. Also, you might have some high-placed PRC and Russian generals visit at any time. Let us know when that happens, or if you get wind of it."

The Director of the Pacific Region, Installation Management Command, then chimed in, "Seth, I am sorry, but there is no additional funding for this effort for base operations. The President sees this as mil-to-mil cooperation that supports his overall international economic strategy. So, you and Ron need to eat this one. Let me know the impact on your overall budget by tomorrow."

"Sir, how can I let you know the impact tomorrow when we do not know the detailed requirements of the tests yet, and therefore do not know the base operations requirements to support them."

"Just do it, Colonel. Track your costs, and I will see if we can get some additional funding as the fiscal year progresses, but for now, it is yours for base operations support and Ron's for Reagan Test Site technical support."

Seth and Ron stared at each other as the video conference ended abruptly. They had a little more guidance but a lot more trepidation than before. What kind of mil-to-mil support was this, and what was the US Army getting out of it?

———

Kwajalein Island, Kwajalein Atoll, February 27

The Antonov AN 22 cargo aircraft landed a little after midnight. A massive four-prop plane, the AN 22 had been around for a long time and had a good record for hauling large loads into tight spots.[3] The Kwaj runway, Bucholz Airfield, was just a little over 6,600 feet long, so the AN 22 was a good pick. Both Russian and PRC crews deplaned, along with several pallets of computers, communications equipment, and several lengthy crates that were not marked. It was odd, but Seth had learned there was nothing normal about the new normal of testing with the PRC and Russia. His deputy, Lieutenant Colonel Eli Shan, had several minivans lined up to take the twenty men to their living quarters on the island's north end. The pallets of equipment were unloaded and temporarily stored in a warehouse near the airfield. The security contractor posted an unarmed guard on it, as did the PRC and Russian teams.

The ocean-going barge arrived at Echo Pier early in the morning. Despite little notice, Seth got his Goliath rolling crane to lift the modular structures off the barge. There were two of them, identical, except for the markings. One had the Mandarin markings for the Chinese, and the other had the Cyrillic markings for Russia. The flatbed trucks then rolled out of the pier area onto Lagoon Road and down to the Kwajalein Mission Control Center toward the island's southwest end, past the turtle pond, near the Japanese cemetery. It was tight, but the base operations contractor had done an excellent job finding a spot where both of the modulars could fit, and then he hooked up the water, power, and communication lines to them. By the end of the day, both modular structures were hot, occupied, and secured. By the end of the next day, the PRC and Russian crews had uploaded the pallets of equipment and long crates from the warehouse and then secured them inside their modular structures. Odd indeed.

———

Kwajalein Island, Kwajalein Atoll, March 7

Sunday in Paradise was how Seth described the day as he fixed coffee for himself and Sara. "Another Marshall Islands Chamber of Commerce Day," called Seth to Sara. "Deep blue skies, a gentle breeze, only 90 percent humidity, and eighty-nine degrees as the waves crash against the reef behind our quarters.

Do you remember when one of the American dependents, a young man around the age of twenty, tried to surf over the coral reef behind our house to impress Callie?"

"Yes, I remember that. As I recall, that was against garrison regulations, and you kicked him off the island," she said with a smirk. A short pause. "It doesn't get any better than this," cooed Sara as she finished getting ready for Sunday morning Protestant Chapel services. "How are our friends from China and Russia?" she asked with a hint of sarcasm. "You ought to invite them to church," she said, half-joking.

"Funny you should mention that," mused Seth. "Ron and I both asked the Russian program manager if any of his staff would be interested in the Protestant or Catholic service today. I thought one or two of them who speak a little English were about to accept when the PRC program manager just stopped all that discussion. He put the fear of Buddha into them. It seems evident that the PRC is running things regarding their tests and the Russians' tests. It is weird. In fact, ever since we had that meeting with the old Japanese soldier, and I sent up the information about untapped oil deposits in the South China Sea, things have been getting progressively weirder."

Seth and Sara enjoyed the Protestant Chapel service and then had brunch at the Zamperini dining facility. Ron and his wife and Eli and his wife joined them for brunch. Seth asked if he could say grace, which was his custom, and all agreed. "Father, thank you for the blessings you have given us. Great families, assignments in beautiful places like Kwajalein, and the opportunity to share our faith with others who travel through. Thanks for the meal this morning. Help us always do our duty to you first, then our families, and then for our country. Help us understand our role in your plan and give us the strength of character to question the status quo and buck the tide when necessary. Bless this food to our use and us to your service. I pray this in the name of your Son, Jesus, Amen."

Ron and Eli exchanged glances as Seth completed the prayer. They knew he and Sara were serious Christ-followers but were unaware of how deeply their faith ran and impacted their everyday lives.

"Wow, some prayer, sir," quipped Ron. Eli chimed in, "I thought church was over about thirty minutes ago." Both men grinned, but they were professional, and the respect among all three was mutual.

Ignoring their good-natured comments, Seth ate his ham and cheese omelet and shifted gears. "Have you been watching the news lately," asked Seth. "First, we find out about a long-lost study from an old Japanese soldier that suggests large and previously unknown deposits of oil and natural gas in the South China Sea. Then the UN resolution, basically handing over the South China Sea to the Chinese, was voted down by the Senate but essentially approved by executive action. Next, we hear that the PRC and Russia will participate in the next RIMPAC. Then the Secretary of Defense attends a global climate change conference, of all things! And, limits on fracking and CO_2 emissions are approved, and coal plants are banned without Senate advice and consent. Then the PRC and Russia are given almost carte blanche to conduct tests at Reagan Test Site. What is going on, and what is the common denominator? Are we big buds with those two countries now? And how about that open border with Mexico?"

Lieutenant Colonel Eli Shan echoed Colonel Grayson's concern. Sara surprised everyone with her following statement. "You know, as the head of the Yokwe Yuk Women's Club, I hear from ladies all over the lagoon. American ladies from Kwaj and Roi-Namur and the Marshallese women from Ebeye. They are scared. The last few nights, several of the PRC and Russian team members have been riding the LCM water taxis to Ebeye and cavorting with some of the less discreet women. However, there have been complaints of harassment and abuse. The ladies also told me that one of the Russian men who spoke a little English was bragging about how this would be a big year and something about Ukraine and Moldova. It will not be long before that comes through the Kwajalein Atoll local government channels."

"Well, that will stop immediately," declared Seth. "Eli, tell the security contractor to prevent PRC and Russian team members from crossing to Ebeye without my permission. Ron, pass that to the PRC and Russian program managers and ask them to see me tomorrow morning. I have to make a phone call back to DC right now."

A quick email confirmed Colonel Bishop was on duty that day. The phone call followed. "Will. Do you have a couple of minutes?" Colonel Bishop was assigned to the Joint Staff J3 Operations Directorate, specifically in the Pentagon's National Military Command Center. The center was the global hub of information and intelligence related to US military presence and concerns. The Services staffed it 24/7, 365, day in and day out. Seth and Will had known each other for years, ever since attending the Command and General Staff College and School of Advanced Military Studies. Yep, Will was a Jedi Knight too! Not bad for a Citadel grad!

"Will, I am trying to wrap my brain around several issues that seem to include or at least point to the Kwajalein garrison and Reagan Test Site. As you know, we are a highly classified facility, and we conduct some testing that even the President doesn't know about—at least, that is what we tell ourselves. But now, I am being forced to accommodate some missile and radar testing that the PRC and Russia want to conduct on Kwajalein itself. They have already set up their command center and plugged it into the Kwajalein Mission Control Center. Is that somehow related to the Secretary of Defense's global warming conference and the RIMPAC, both of which involve the PRC and Russia?"

"Hmm." Silence on the phone. "Call me back on your secure telephone unit. Here's my number."

Seth pulled the phone key out of his safe and dialed the number on the secure telephone unit. Will answered immediately. "You have hit a nerve, my friend. The Chairman and several service chiefs are concerned about the President's economic strategy, which cozies up to the PRC. The Joint Staff J3 Operations Section and J5 Plans Section had a beautiful scenario developed for RIMPAC involving the Philippines, the US Navy, and several other navies. Rumor is that the President scrapped that scenario near Scarborough Shoals in favor of combined US Navy-PRC naval presence maneuvers in the South China Sea. We wanted to exercise the Enhanced Defense Cooperation Agreement we signed with the Philippines in 2014, but political correctness prevents that."

"Have you heard about the letter from a World War II Japanese soldier I sent up through Installation Management Command Channels?" asked Seth.

"Not a peep. What is that all about?" retorted Will.

Seth explained his grandfather's letter in the attic and the chance meeting with Isao Akisao on Kwaj. But for Seth, there was no such thing as chance. He had been made aware of the letter for a purpose and was determined to follow that purpose.

"Hmm…" repeated Will, a man of few words. "I wonder if that has anything to do with something my wife Jill mentioned to me after the Senate voted against the proposed South China Sea Paradigm For Progress. She was in the UN Security Council when the discussion went down about that new resolution. It seems that China will play a prominent role in that area. I wonder if they were aware of the letter? And if so, who told them? I also wonder if that somehow plays into the decision on RIMPAC? I sure hope there aren't leaks in the Pentagon."

"Smells foul to me," said Seth, "but there is nothing yet that I could raise a red flag over with Installation Management Command or Space and Missile Defense Command. I will keep a close eye on the PRC and Russian activities on Kwaj if you can keep me informed of anything you feel comfortable with."

Will surprised Seth. "I know a guy over at the National Security Agency. I will ask him if he can keep me informed of any South China Sea and RIMPAC chatter. Since we are still planning the RIMPAC South China Sea Naval Presence Maneuvers, it makes sense that the Joint Staff J3 Operations Section should know. I will call you on the secure telephone if anything related to Kwaj comes up."

"Many thanks, and God bless you and Jill."

———

AMATA HAD WORKED for successive base operations contractors for more than twenty years and had risen to the ranks of a team supervisor. From the perspective of the Marshallese on Ebeye, that was impressive. He was almost a legend from the southern end of Ebeye to the northern end of Gugeegue (a tiny islet north of Ebeye) to the island of Ebadon in the northwest corner of the atoll. From Seth's perspective, Amata showed more gumption and determination than most Americans on Kwaj. He was honest, and he worked hard. His team provided maintenance service to the Kwajalein Mission Control Center buildings, and they did it well. By extension, Amata's team also cleaned up around the exterior of the PRC and Russian modulars. Lieutenant Colonel Ron Bakerson also thought highly of Amata.

A few days later, Amata approached Seth and Ron about his observations of the PRC and Russian facilities. They were messy and left trash everywhere, especially the Chinese. Amata also heard from some native women on Ebeye that the Russians had let something slip before they were stopped from traveling there. He handed Seth several crumpled pieces of paper that he found in the dumpster near the PRC modular. Seth had little knowledge of Mandarin, but he could plainly see sketches of several islands, Aur Atoll, and Roi-Namur among the written comments. He could also see several arcs drawn on the paper, centered on Aur Atoll, generally heading to the north and northeast. He could also see in large block letters the English acronym RIMPAC. Finally, there was a sketch of what appeared to be the coast of some landmass and some unknown island group, maybe another atoll in the Marshalls?

ONE OF THE lesser-known responsibilities of the Commander, US Army Garrison – Kwajalein Atoll, was his role as the Pacific Command, Commander's Representative to the Republic of the Marshall Islands. While wearing this hat, Seth Grayson placed a call to the Pacific Command J2 Intelligence Section. Ron Bakerson was also in the room with him when he called on the secure telephone. Seth talked to another of his friends in Pacific Command J2 Joint Intelligence Operations Center, about the chatter he picked up and the scraps of paper they found. His friend agreed to have the scraps of paper translated from Mandarin to English. Seth sent the papers over secure fax to the Joint Intelligence Operations Center at Camp HM Smith on Oahu and received a classified email response within hours. "Seth, not sure what you all have going on in Kwaj, but here is what we got off the papers. It seems there will be some significant PRC activity during RIMPAC in the South China Sea, which correlates fairly well with the planning J5 Plans Section has been doing. There is some vague reference to oil and gas reserves and Scarborough Shoals. Not sure where that came from. A few comments about Chinese and Russian initiatives before and during RIMPAC once the other things happen and the arcs. The arcs are a little disturbing. These appear to be consecutive range fan arcs, centered on Aur Atoll, to the north and northeast, like someone is marking the range fan of a weapon system. Oh, yeah, also a partial comment about the Al Jihadi Levant (AJL) and the US. I will discuss this with my boss tomorrow and let you know what he thinks. You may want to relay this to Space and Missile Defense Command and Installation Management Command."

"So which atoll is depicted in the sketch of islands?" asked Seth.

"Oh, I almost forgot," replied the J2 Intelligence Section rep. "That's the western coast of the island of Luzon, in the Philippines. It looks like it is about the same latitude as Scarborough Shoals."

Seth did not take long to contact the Installation Management Command Pacific Region Director and Ron to call the Deputy Commanding General of Space and Missile Defense Command in Redstone. While certainly not a smoking gun, the arcs were troubling, as were the comments about oil and gas in the South China Sea and the Russian initiatives. No one could make sense of the AJL comment. Soon, the Commanding Generals of Installation Management Command and Space and Missile Defense Command were informed and on the horn to each other. From five thousand miles away, the scraps of paper seemed less onerous and foreboding than they did to the Colonel and Lieutenant Colonel on site. However, since both had raised the "Japanese Soldier's letter" to the Chief of Staff of the Army, and now this revelation, there was sufficient concern that the two Commanding Generals requested a meeting with him in DC the following Wednesday, where they bared all.

———

Pentagon, March 9

That Wednesday afternoon in Washington, DC was exceptionally cold; more proof positive of climate change thought the Chairman of the Joint Chiefs of Staff. Admiral Halsey Burke was starting to consider retirement at this point. He was unhealthy and did not care for the President or the Secretary of Defense. His wife was also urging him to drop his papers soon. The Admiral and his wife were practicing Lutherans, or at least she was. Admiral Burke was what is politely called a carnal Christian. He relied more on himself and his own efforts than the guidance and comfort available from the Holy Spirit residing in the heart of every believer, whether Lutheran, Catholic, Southern Baptist, or even nondenominational. But the Admiral was not indeed a believer yet. The Chief of Staff of the Army was on his way to update him on a pressing issue in the Pacific, of which he knew nothing, at least that was what he thought.

The Chief of Staff of the Army relayed critical points from his meeting with the Commanding Generals of Installation Management Command and Space and Missile Defense Command and his concern for what that might mean to US Army Garrison-Kwajalein Atoll and Reagan Test Site. Admiral Burke's eyes opened wide, and his heart started beating rapidly. Just what was the President up to? First, the Joint Staff J3 Operations Section mentioned an NSA intercept regarding some chatter that AJL was seeking ways into the US, and now this? And most disturbing of all, who told the PRC about the large suspected oil and gas deposits near Scarborough Shoals?

———

Kwajalein Island, Kwajalein Atoll

Seth took Colonel Will Bishop's secure telephone call when he returned to the office that day. "Seth, look. Two things. First, my friend in the National Security Agency has picked up what you would expect as normal chatter when it comes to RIMPAC and Kwajalein. Secondarily, he also picked up some indeterminate comments about the AJL, a drug cartel, and access to the US in the same conversation. We are unsure what this means, but I had to let the J3 Operations Chief know what was happening. He has already talked to the Chairman of the Joint Chiefs. I had my hand slapped for asking the NSA for input on RIMPAC, but only a slight slap. Now we are officially tracking any chatter related to RIMPAC, Kwaj, and the AJL."

"Never thought I would hear those three names in the same sentence," smiled Seth.

CHAPTER 14

DISTRACTION IN LUANDA

Luanda, Angola, March 23

To say that the US government was surprised was the understatement of the year. Who would have thought that Luanda, Angola, would lead the news cycles for the next several days? Angola was a schizophrenic country if ever there was one. In the heart of Africa, with Portuguese as the national language. Its capital city Luanda boasts of being the most expensive place to live on the planet, just twenty or so years after a bloody civil war and only forty-seven years after obtaining independence from Portugal.[1] Now, Angola announces a joint venture with the PRC involving oil production and refining, pipelines across Africa to Kenya and South Africa, and another pipeline from Kenya down the Nile to Egypt.

The breadth of the agreement was staggering, but two other factors made it menacing. First, Angola planned to withdraw from the Organization of the Petroleum Exporting Countries (OPEC), which it had been a member of since 2006. Second, the PRC was guaranteeing Angola's uninterrupted access to its oil fields and pipelines with the stationing of a Peoples' Liberation

Army (Chinese) Division and Air Wing near Luanda. The PRC also envisioned a small naval presence there in the near future.

Neither Secretary of State Aranson nor Secretary of Defense Carson knew what to make of the PRC move. It did not seem to make sense. China already had a significant presence in Angola through its contractors and businessmen, as they had in several other African countries. The PRC had recently approached the governments of Kenya and South Africa about the initiative. Still, their ambassadors were surprised that Angola (and, by default, the PRC) had chosen to make the announcement so soon.

President Justice contacted the Chinese President, and they spoke for over an hour. The PRC President begged forgiveness for not forewarning President Justice about the initiative. He assured the President that this was just his country, China, continuing its business interests in western sub-Sahara Africa and bringing an infrastructure that could assist during any future Ebola outbreak. He further explained that OPEC was an outdated model for managing world oil prices and that Angola's departure from OPEC would bolster its economy and free up trading in Africa and with other world partners. The US President seemed to buy into the argument.

"Of course," said the Chinese President as the other shoe fell, "this initiative is costing us a great deal. So much so that I am afraid we will have to either recall some of the outstanding debt you have with us or we need to adjust the interest rate on your payments to allow us to generate the bonding we need. So sorry."

"Well, this is a bit of a surprise, but I presume this will in no way interfere with the proposed trade agreement we have been discussing," said President Justice.

"Not in the least," cooed the Chinese President. "I believe

our actions will make that trade agreement more likely and most acceptable by your businesses and industry."

President Justice hung up the phone, contented that his future trade agreement with the PRC was intact, not fully understanding the ramifications of what he had just heard.

CHAPTER 15
THE CARACAS ANNOUNCEMENT

Caracas, Venezuela, April 13

IT WAS A CRAZY, CRAZY SPRING. THE NEWS MEDIA (AND THE US government) was just getting over the "Angola Announcement," or the "Luanda Low-ball," as they had begun to call it, when lightning struck again. But this time, it was closer to home. The Russian foreign minister made a joint announcement in Caracas with the President of Venezuela and Raul Castro. Venezuela was leaving OPEC and would begin to increase its output with the assistance of Russian engineers and scientists. This included fracking technology that the Russians had invented and the Americans had stolen. It would have been bizarre if it was not so serious. The nation of Venezuela was near the boiling point due to hyperinflation; at the same time, governmental services had become a laughingstock. A Russian presence could slow the pending civil unrest while simultaneously giving them unprecedented access and influence in Latin America. In the same announcement, the foreign minister called for the US to withdraw from Guantanamo immediately and forever and renounce this, their last vestige of colonialism.

"To encourage our American friends to do the right thing and to ensure no harm comes to our friends in Latin America, the Russian people have authorized me to inform you that the Russian Navy will be homeporting two cruisers and an aircraft carrier at Puerto Caballo Naval Facilities in Venezuela. And we are concluding a refueling agreement with Havana for our strategic aerial assets should they ever be needed," announced the foreign minister.

Then, speaking to the US, he said, "The Guantanamo Bay lease you forced on the Cuban people in 1903 and renewed in 1934 with members of the oppressive regime in power then is null and void. Your actions in 1961, when the US cut all diplomatic ties to Cuba[1], and in 1962 when President Kennedy imposed a quarantine on that small island nation, abrogated the treaty. Russia renounces it, and so do the Cuban people. Adding insult to injury is the evil detainee facility at Guantanamo that has brought universal condemnation for your use of waterboarding and even more evil methods of forcing confessions from innocent people.

"Let the people of the Caribbean know that Russia is on their side and will help them whenever we can to rid themselves of imperialism that still exists today in the form of the United States of America. After our meeting here in Caracas, President Castro and I will be flying to Havana to sign our agreement.

We applaud the American government for allowing travel and trade between the US and Cuba. However, we are concerned that the recent overtures from Washington, DC to Havana about these more open relations are simply a disguise and a ruse, *maskirovka* (Russian for deception) at its best, to allow the CIA to take root on the island."

It was a large gauntlet thrown at the feet of the President for all the world to see. It was a direct denouncement of and challenge to the Monroe Doctrine and demanded a response. Or so one would think. That afternoon, at the daily conference with the President's Press Secretary, all the questions were related to the Russian foreign minister's announcement. The Press Secretary advised the press that President Justice and his national security staff were discussing the issue and developing a response to "our friends" in Russia.

Asked if they thought the latest Russian announcement was somehow connected with the PRC's move in Angola, the Press Secretary emphatically stated that it was not. And so it went for several days.

CHAPTER 16
THE GAUNTLET VS. THE HANKIE

White House PEOC, April 20

THE SECRETARY OF DEFENSE, SECRETARY OF STATE, SECRETARY OF Homeland Security, Vice President, National Security Advisor, Director of National Intelligence, Chairman of the Joint Chiefs, the President, his Chief of Staff, and his Press Secretary were all seated around the table in the Presidential Emergency Operations Center or PEOC.

Admiral Burke spoke first, "Mr. President. The Director of National Intelligence and I have been talking. In addition to the recent 'Luanda Low-ball' and Caracas Announcement, it has come to our attention that some unusual activity is being planned involving the PRC, Russia, and even a drug cartel and the AJL. It may also affect Kwajalein and the South China Sea. It is too soon to say precisely what is in the works or exactly who is driving the train, but here is what we know.

Per your direction, the PRC and Russia are both participants in the upcoming RIMPAC. The PRC and US Navy will conduct a naval presence exercise in the South China Sea as part of RIMPAC per your direction. The timing of which seems advantageous for some, as the new South China Sea Paradigm

For Progress is supposed to go into effect on July 4. Per your direction, the PRC and Russia are preparing for low-level missile and radar tests at the Reagan Test Site on Kwajalein. We have received intelligence that the South China Sea oil and gas deposits may be more lucrative and accessible than we previously thought. This intelligence also suggests Russia is planning some strange kind of activity before and during RIMPAC and that the AJL is seeking access into the US. We derived that last bit of information from some scraps of paper found on Kwajalein, of all places! It could be just disinformation to keep us on our toes or something else.

The NSA, CIA, DIA, and FBI are actively seeking additional information on all of this and trying to make some sense of it, but for now, they have not tied up loose ends, and we are not yet able to connect the dots. Suffice it to say that the Luanda and Caracas actions may be a part of this, or perhaps a planned distraction from something else, or they could be completely unrelated."

The President's face was turning red, but then Secretary of Defense Carson spoke next, "Mr. President, we cannot let the Russian announcement go unanswered. They have challenged our hegemony in the area and are acting on that challenge. Their actions are contrary to the long-standing Monroe Doctrine and the Roosevelt Corollary.[1] We need a strong statement from you denouncing their provocative actions."

"Of course, some of what the Russian foreign minister said is true," said the President to a stunned room. "We are guilty of war crimes at Guantanamo, and our presence there is tantamount to colonialism. I wish we had never leased that bit of land. I'm not too fond of the Russian presence in Venezuela, but they are independent nations with their own friends. Better the Russians do a little saber-rattling where we can see them than renew the fighting in Ukraine. Maybe elsewhere like Moldova or Finland."

"I concur!" shouted the Secretary of State. "We can use these two recent actions to our advantage. We are trying to consummate a new trade agreement with the PRC, and their actions should facilitate that when considered from their perspective. As for the Russians, they do not have the wealth or material wherewithal to conduct follow-on operations in Ukraine and Latin America simultaneously. So, if they spend some time and money at Puerto Caballo, they are reducing the threat to Ukraine."

"Sirs! That is just not true!" shouted Admiral Burke. "The Russians have the manpower, equipment, and intestinal fortitude to do both, especially if Caracas supplies the oil and gas. I am unsure what the PRC has up its sleeve, but the Russian Caracas statement must not go unchallenged."

"I agree with Admiral Burke," said the Vice President before the President could respond to the Chairman's challenge to the Secretary of State. "This is not the run-of-the-mill saber-rattling. This is in our backyard, and if it all goes forward as the foreign minister stated, it could be a real threat to us. We must do something visible that catches the Russians' and the world's attention, not to mention the American people. They are watching you, Mr. President."

The President smiled. "I have spoken at length with the PRC President, and he and I are in accord. First, let me say that this rumor of abundant and accessible oil and natural gas reserves in the eastern South China Sea is just that—a RUMOR!! Our own US Geological Survey (USGS) has laughed at it. Second, the 'Luanda Low-ball,' as some are loath to call it, will work to our advantage. We are working with the PRC on a new trade agreement that will favor our businesses in exchange for a short-term interest increase on the debt the PRC has with us. The PRC increased presence in Angola will benefit Africa economically. The Chinese President has also assured me that he does not know what the Russians are up to. Finally, he noticed that the Russians were becoming a nuisance on Kwajalein. So, here is what we are going to do. I will announce that due to their insult to the US and our allies in Latin America, the Russian government will no longer be able to participate in RIMPAC. Nor will they be able to use the Reagan Test Site on Kwajalein. And we demand their immediate withdrawal from there. I will also remind the Russians and Raul Castro that our GTMO lease is good until both nations agree to end it, or we pull out, which I am not prepared to do yet."

"Yet? Sir, your recommendations are a good start but pale compared to what the Russians may do in our own backyard," cried the Chairman, Admiral Burke.

"Ditto," chimed the Vice President as the President's face turned beet red. "It's like they threw down the gauntlet, and we threw back a hankie."

"And recent classified information we sent to you suggests significant gas and oil reserves…" started Admiral Burke before the President cut him off.

"Now, look," said the President with ice on his lips. "I know you military guys can never give up anything, but someday, we will leave GTMO. I am not so naïve that I believe whatever the Russians tell us, but if we can engage them here in a war of words, then perhaps we can take their focus off Ukraine, Moldova, and other eastern European nations. And don't forget what Putin said about Finland and Sweden joining NATO! I won't use the term 'yet when I talk to the press later today about Guantanamo, but I will tell them of my deliberate actions to counter Russian aggression. Amanda, please stay for a moment. The rest of you may leave."

As the door closed, President Justice whispered in Secretary of Defense Amanda Carson's ear, "Find a new chairman, fast."

———

White House, April 27

Finally! A week after the Russian foreign minister's announcement, word went out that President Justice would hold a press conference concerning both the Angola situation and the Russian pronouncement in Caracas. Reporters jostled for positions as the time approached. It was pretty obvious who the President was going to call on when it came time for questions according to the way certain reporters were seated. Other reporters were forced to stand, and some were not even admitted, even though they had the proper press credentials.

"Ladies and gentlemen, the President of the United States," announced the Press Secretary.

"Take your seats, please," stated President Justice emphatically. "Today's topic is foreign relations, specifically the 'Luanda Low-ball,' as some of you in the press have called it, and the Caracas Announcement of last week. First, Luanda. The President of China and I have spoken several times and at length concerning their plans in Angola and elsewhere in Africa. I have also talked with the leaders of South Africa, Kenya, and Egypt at length."

A bit of a stretch, thought Secretary Aranson. *I actually placed the calls with them to get their take on the situation.*

"Secretary of State Aranson and I have concluded that the Chinese Luanda Initiative is in the best interests of not only the PRC and Angola but also much of sub-Sahara Africa and, in a roundabout way, the United States. Economically, this will be a boon for much of Africa. It will reduce their dependence on international support, much of which comes from the UN, the European Union, and the USA. So, it will also work in our favor long-term. We will support this effort of the PRC with a slight increase in the interest we pay them on our debt. In exchange, they will agree to the trade agreement that Secretary Aranson has been working on, which will be a massive boon for our businesses and our trade deficit.

As for the Russian Caracas Announcement, this is serious business and will not stand uncontested. Therefore, I have decided that Russia will no longer participate in the RIMPAC exercise this summer. They will immediately cease all operations and testing at the Reagan Test Site on Kwajalein and remove all their equipment and personnel within the month. I will publicly call on President Putin to reconsider his actions in our backyard and invite him to the White House to discuss this."

"I will take your questions now."

A stunned silence fell over the reporters. Finally, a woman from MSNTC News asked the first question. "Sir, is there any truth to the rumor that you plan to meet with Raul Castro next week about the long-term viability of GTMO?"

THAT NIGHT on the FTX late news show, a junior congressman from the south and a senator from one of the western states argued about President Justice's actions related to the border, the PRC's new role in the South China Sea, and both the Luanda and Caracas Announcements. The Congressman raised the specter of impeachment, while the senator gave her support to the President working under difficult international conditions.

CHAPTER 17
AUR ATOLL SECRETS

Taiyuan, China, May 1

THE ROCKET LIFTED OFF THE LAUNCH PAD AT THE TAIYUAN SPACE Launch Facility southwest of Beijing.[1] It carried a communications satellite into a sun-synchronous, highly elliptical Molniya orbit[2] over the South China Sea. It seemed innocuous enough as communications satellites had frequently been put into orbit from that location, including US commercial communications satellites[3] when Canaveral went dormant for a few years. Several hours later, a second communications satellite launched into another highly elliptical Molniya orbit over the South China Sea. With both satellites in orbit, on opposite sides of the earth, they ensured communications coverage of the area. As one satellite was racing past planet earth at the perigee (lowest point) of its orbit, the other was dwelling over the South China Sea at its apogee (highest point). There was little time between the two of them when the PRC did not have excellent satellite communications in the area.

A few hours later, late at night, they launched another satellite into orbit, this time in an LEO,[4] or low earth orbit, with a westward regression ground track. But that ground track included occasional visits over Washington, DC; Huntsville, Alabama; Fort Shafter, Oahu; and Kwajalein.

Kwajalein Island, Kwajalein Atoll, May 3

Colonel Seth Grayson and Lieutenant Colonel Ron Bakerson met with the program managers from the PRC and Russia to bring them up to speed on the latest developments. They met in the small Reagan Test Site conference room just off the Kwajalein Mission Control Center. "Thanks for meeting us here so early this morning," Seth said. "I know you all have been following the news on our Armed Forces Radio and TV. I am sure you heard about the Luanda agreement between the PRC and Angola and, more recently, the Caracas Announcement made by the Russian foreign minister. Well, those kinds of actions can have repercussions even way out here in Kwajalein, as your governments must have already shared with you."

Speaking directly to the Russian program manager, Ron took over from there. "If you have not already begun, effective immediately, the Russian team must start dismantling their test infrastructure both here and on Roi. You will have until May 20 to complete that effort and remove yourselves from Kwajalein. Any test information you developed while using the Reagan Test Site facilities will be retained here. We have cut off all communications for the Russian team, except one landline to the US, through which you will be able to talk to the Russian Embassy. I know you all have satellite communications equipment, but let me assure you, those frequencies are either being monitored or jammed."

Seth and Ron waited for a harsh retort to begin pouring from the Russian program manager's mouth, but he said nothing. Seth thought he saw a slight smirk. "OK," said the Russian. Another smirk from the PRC program manager.

Ron continued, "As for the PRC tests, they are still on track, and we are happy to assist as we can. Oh, I almost forgot, the last time my inspector visited Aur Atoll to check on your progress, he was hassled when he arrived and was not allowed to exit our cargo ship for almost thirty minutes. What gives?"

"Please forgive me for that inconvenience," purred the PRC program manager in an unusual burst of politeness. "We are entering a sensitive phase of our testing, and any disturbance whatsoever could skew the results," he said in a blinding flash of obfuscation. "I must request at least twenty-four hours advance notice before any of your staff visits Aur Atoll again."

"Not going to happen," retorted Ron.

"No way," shouted Seth. "Our orders are that we will stay abreast of all your activities. Kwajalein is an American major range and testbed, not a Chinese outpost. We made this perfectly clear from the start and included it in the mil-to-mil agreement that the PRC and the US Army signed."

The PRC program manager smiled. "Gentlemen. You are correct about the agreement, but as you know, nothing in life or the military ever remains the same. Our respective leaders have had a lot of discussions about this point. Your military chain of command has accepted our need for the twenty-four-hour notice. If they have not informed you yet, I suggest you contact them. Good day."

———

A QUICK CALL by Ron to the Space and Missile Defense Command Deputy Commanding General in Huntsville confirmed what the PRC program manager told them. "Sir, this is nuts. How can we ensure the PRC is keeping their testing within the limits of the agreement if we have to give them notice before we inspect? They can cover up a lot of stuff on Aur within twenty-four hours."

"Ron, Ron, Ron. Calm down. Word is the President personally made this call in the interest of mutual and beneficial mil-to-mil cooperation and economic policy."

Seth called Colonel Will Bishop, at the Joint Staff J3 Operations Section, on the secure telephone unit. "Will, what is going on back there? Who is calling the shots on this PRC testing? I am thrilled we are booting the Russians off the island, but I've got to tell you, they seemed to expect it and made no fuss whatsoever. It is almost like this was the plan all along."

"Seth, this whole PRC and Russia issue is about to explode. Word has it that the Chairman is up to here with the administration on their actions involving the military. That includes adding the PRC to RIMPAC while not allowing the Filipinos in the South China Sea portion of the exercise and using highly classified facilities at Kwajalein. Not to mention the executive orders or actions, and now the executive agreements that the President has been issuing despite constitutional requirements not being met. And who has told whom about the old Japanese soldier's letter concerning the oil and gas near Scarborough Shoals is the question du jour. Everyone is on pins and needles."

"OK," said Seth. "Is the NSA still focused on the PRC and Kwaj? Did you hear more chatter about that or the cartel and the AJL?"

"Nothing recent. The AJL chatter has gone dark. The PRC chatter seems almost contrived at this point, like they are feeding us information."

"Roger," said Seth. "Just let me know if you hear anything of interest, especially about those range fan arcs at Aur. Meanwhile, Ron and I expressed our concerns up the

Installation Management Command and Space and Missile Defense Command channels. Just between you and me, I am keeping the Pacific Command J2 Intelligence and J3 Operations informed in my role as Pacific Command Rep to the Marshall Islands."

"Good idea. Talk to you later."

————

Aur Atoll, Marshall Islands, May 7

The work at Aur Atoll was at a fever pitch, and the PRC program manager spent all his time there. The Chinese had built the launch pad capable of launching small missiles at ground or sea targets. In an unusual twist, it appeared that the launch pad could swivel almost 360 degrees; it also had a rail launch capability in addition to the expected vertical launch. They had also built a launch control building, sleeping quarters, and what looked like several reinforced concrete bunkers, along with a long ammo bunker and fuel tank. Most surprising of all was the 250-kW generator they had somehow gotten to the island and been put in service.

Ron's review of their testing infrastructure included all of the above, except for the swivel capability of the launch pad. By the time he arrived after the twenty-four-hour warning, the PRC had effectively camouflaged that capability.

About the same time, at a nondescript location on the shore of the South China Sea, the PRC released a colossal "weather" balloon about as long as three busses. It was headed in the general direction of Guam and Kwajalein. But this was not your ordinary "weather" balloon. This one had solar panels, communications equipment, high speed cameras, and telemetry radars for tracking objects flying at high speed in the atmosphere. Traveling at 60,000 feet, this "weather" balloon could provide extremely clear pictures of the "weather" below, and anything else it might see, sense, or hear. A spy balloon, in every sense of the word.

CHAPTER 18
RIMPAC BEGINS

Pearl Harbor, Honolulu, June 25

THE BRASS HELD THE RIMPAC OPENING CEREMONIES AT THE USS Arizona Memorial in Pearl Harbor. The sheen from the fuel that continued to leak slowly from that revered battleship was a reminder to all of the need for vigilance. How easily we are lulled to sleep when all is going well, and how lasting the effects can be when we finally heed the wake-up call.

The American response to the Japanese surprise attack that Sunday morning in December 1941 brought to mind the quote by Edmund Burke: "The only thing necessary for the triumph of evil is for good men to do nothing." That is as true now as it was in the eighteenth century when the Irish statesman coined the phrase. But good men did not sit idly by and do nothing in 1941. They responded against tyranny and oppression on two fronts: against Nazi Germany in Europe and the Japanese Empire in the Pacific. Less than a hundred years later, in Colonel Grayson's opinion, history seemed to be coming full circle, but with slightly different players. In 1941, Japan sought oil and hegemony through the Greater East Asia Co-Prosperity Sphere in the Pacific. Germany sought to recover from World

War I and expand to their "rightful" boundaries, including all Germanic-speaking people. Now, it appeared to be China seeking oil in the South China Sea and hegemony in the Pacific. This involved the UN resolution called the South China Sea Paradigm For Progress. And Russia, seeking to recover from the Cold War and expand back to the Soviet boundaries with Russian-speaking people.

Seth could only frown as he recalled that Edmund Burke also said, "Those who don't know history are destined to repeat it."

Major exercises like RIMPAC can take months or even a year of planning and preparation. They tend to last a couple of months or more when you consider the advance parties that must be put in place, the support contracts the advance party negotiates, and the basing issues to be resolved. Finally, the conduct of the actual exercise includes the scenario to be fought and actions and reactions toward the RED team or Opposing Force (the notional enemy). In highly political exercises such as what RIMPAC had become, with the large number of nations involved, naming a RED enemy to oppose the good guys, could become problematic.

After much wringing of hands, wailing, and gnashing of teeth among the admirals, the Philippine Island of Mindanao became the enemy Nation of Mindanao for the exercise, run by the Islamic militant group Abu Sayyaf. The Philippines did not particularly like this scenario. But then, they realized they could use real-world intelligence assets the US Navy had to further their knowledge of that group and improve their tactics against it after the exercise was over. It was also a bit of a concession for the Filipinos since their activity related to Scarborough Shoals west of Luzon had been canned in favor of the PRC-US Navy combined naval presence exercise.

The RIMPAC scenario depicted a rapid growth of a brown

water navy consisting of small, shallow-draft ships for shoreline and interior or riverine operations by Mindanao, along with heavy naval support of cruisers, destroyers, and submarines from North Korea. Several ships from the US Navy's 3rd Fleet would be dispatched to play the North Korean ships and provide at least a radar signature for the exercise. Interestingly, Pyongyang's notional heavy naval support included their operations as far to the east as Wake Island, Kwajalein, and Aur Atolls, played by PRC ships. That was probably why the Pacific Command exercise planners included Colonel Grayson in some of the planning for RIMPAC. From Seth's perspective, the line between fictional scenarios and reality was getting a little blurred as he recalled the PRC's test site on Aur Atoll and the range fan arcs.

After the ceremony was over at the USS Arizona Memorial, several days of high-level briefings and photo ops followed. These days were used to ensure that the admirals from all the navies involved were brought up to speed in high-level briefings and memorialized with photo ops. The planners made final adjustments to the scenario and timing. The operations centers from Pacific Command and its subordinate commands, along with the exercise's Combined Operations Center, were dialed into the exercise and were good to go. The ships from the twenty-five nations' navies were provisioned, positioned, and leaning forward when the exercise started.

———

THE EXERCISE SAILED ALONG SMOOTHLY for a week or so, as the scenario drove the action exceptionally well. The Mindanao element of the exercise got exciting when some real-world Abu Sayyaf Islamic terrorist personnel showed up at one site but were quickly arrested by the Philippine Navy. They were Johnny-on-the-spot and prepared for such an eventuality.

Subic Bay Naval Facility played a prominent role in the exercise as a refueling and rearming site and as a command and communications node. The US Navy provided several landing and riverine crafts to supplement the Philippine Navy. Both parties learned a great deal. The scenario also used Clark Air Force Base as a resupply base and alternate headquarters for the exercise controllers.

————

Pacific Command HQ, July 4

July 4 was a date of great significance for both the United States and the Philippines. The exercise participants were upbeat and excited until they watched the news in the Combined Operations Center. Secretary of State Jim Aranson and the President of the PRC made a joint announcement about the implementation of the South China Sea Paradigm for Progress from the Paracels in the South China Sea. The Filipino participants at the Combined Operations Center were disgusted and cursed loudly in Tagalog, which most of the others, fortunately, could not understand. On the other hand, PRC participants were cheering just as loudly. This caused a momentary standoff in the operations center until the Australian Admiral on duty intervened. International incident averted!

————

Kwajalein Island, Kwajalein Atoll, July 12

Seth stayed abreast of the exercise from Kwajalein, mainly via Ron and the Kwajalein Mission Control Center. He also received classified email exercise play that he reviewed and answered. In the exercise scenario, Kwajalein would provide an alternate aircraft fueling and divert location and an alternate naval fueling site. US Army Garrison-Kwajalein Atoll had this real-world capability and serviced aircraft from friendly nations year-round. They also occasionally serviced US cruisers and destroyers when they were down that way. While not mentioned in the scenario per se, US Space Force tasked Kwajalein with near-earth surveillance, satellite tracking, and new foreign launch coverage, something the Reagan Test Site did day in and day out, anyway.[1]

On the morning of July 12 (July 11 in the US mainland), the two PRC Navy and several US Navy ships scheduled to take part in the naval presence portion of the exercise were slowly moving into position just west of Scarborough Shoals. Also, PRC and US Navy ships were near the Spratly Islands and the Paracels. There was a red sky that morning!

CHAPTER 19

AL JIHADI LEVANT STRIKES

Orlando, Minneapolis, and San Diego, July 12

Several months had passed since the Tohono O'odham rodeo—fond memories. Then Abdul and his cronies got down to business. It had taken months of preparation and coordination, done only face to face or by US Postal Service. There were no electronic signals to intercept. No phone calls to trace. No cell phones to ping or follow from tower to tower and no internet URLs to follow. Nothing. The six men had rented three adjacent rooms at the Scottsdale Extended Stay Motel, two per room. When they first arrived, they also purchased six "burner" phones and tested them by making innocuous "How are you?" phone calls in English. Then they turned them off and put them away for future use. As the leader of the six, Abdul bin Rastafa had set up the schedule and formalized the action plan.

After arriving and renting the rooms, they set up a meeting each Sunday morning in the middle room, ensuring that any sound that might pass through the walls would only leak into one of their adjacent rooms. At the weekly meetings, they discussed the functioning of the Soviet-style "backpacks" and their capabilities, the schedule, routes, corresponding distances and timings, and final destinations. They ended each session by unrolling their prayer rugs and facing the east to pray to Allah, the Salat, which was customarily required five times a day and was one of the Five Pillars of Islam. The other four, the Shahada or faith in Allah, the Zakat or giving alms/charity, the Sawm or fasting during Ramadan, and the Hajj or pilgrimage to Mecca,[1] were not required daily for their jihad. The Salat was the only time they allowed themselves to follow any of the five pillars of Islam as they prepared for their attacks.

To prevent suspicion, they remained clean-shaven, having shaved their beards before crossing into the US at the San Miguel Gate. They also occasionally went to the local McDonalds, but only in groups of two, and bought Big Macs, fries, and Coca-Cola. Most of the time, they cooked on hot plates and in microwaves in their room.

In the several weeks leading up to their departure, Abdul would call the motel's front desk and have them make lodging reservations in various cities en route to each team's final destination, always making sure a different person was at the front desk when he asked for that help. As model residents who paid early, they were gladly accommodated.

———

THEY DEPARTED their Scottsdale motel on July 5 and started on their way to their final destinations. One pickup headed east on Interstate I-10, the second generally headed northeast, taking I-17 to I-40 and then I-35 north, and the third, with Abdul driving, headed west on I-8. After four days of careful driving, never exceeding the speed limit, and always being courteous drivers, the three pickups arrived at their respective destinations from whence they would perform their jihad, enter heaven, and meet their seventy-two virgins[2] for the first time. It all seemed so simple and natural to them.

Each two-man team had three days to get situated, recon their route, and find alternate ways to their final destinations. They studied the formal entrances to each site for ingress and egress routes, the presence of security personnel, and the security and inspection procedures employed at each location before entry was allowed. Of course, actual entry into the facilities was not required nor desired, given the nature of their mission and the "tools" they had.

Late afternoon on July 12, the three pickup trucks drove to their final destinations and parked. One of the two men from the other two trucks placed a short phone call on their burner phone to Abdul, "We are here," in English. Abdul acknowledged both calls with a simple "You are cleared for your maintenance contract." At 8:30 p.m. EDT, they called Abdul back, "Cleaning supplies are in place." At 8:55 p.m. EDT, Abdul called the other two phones in conference mode and told them, "It is now 8:55, mark. *Ma'a salaam.*"

IT HAPPENED at 9:00 p.m. EDT, 8:00 p.m. CDT, and 6:00 p.m. PDT. Simultaneously, the men detonated the three "backpacks" just short of the security screening area for each location. It had not been necessary for the men to enter the facilities, as the estimated dirty nuclear explosions were more than sufficient to level them all, along with everyone in attendance. Approximately one-fifth the size of the atomic bomb that devastated Hiroshima in August of 1945,[2] three kilotons was more than sufficient for the tasks.

The two men in Orlando parked in the unbelievably large parking lot, rode the tram to the theme park's entrance gates, and loitered briefly before entering the restroom short of the security screening stands to await their 9:00 p.m. EDT swan song. It was timed for the start of the nightly parade when the maximum number of parents and children would be lining Main Street in anticipation of seeing their favorite cartoon characters.

The two men in Minneapolis had driven their pickup to the parking lot adjacent to The Mall of the Midwest and timed their approach to the mall entrance such that their "backpack" detonated at 8:00 p.m. CDT, as the nightly light and smoke show was winding down.

Abdul, and his partner in jihad, parked their pickup in a nearby parking lot and then walked toward Petinc Park as the Major League Baseball All-Star game was underway. Little did Abdul know, nor did he care, that the American League was leading the National League 4–2 late in the ninth inning. He knew, however, that more than fifty thousand screaming fans would soon die, justifiably in his opinion, as they were part of the Great Satan that constantly oppressed his people. At 6:00 p.m. PDT, his "backpack" also detonated.

The simultaneous explosions in three different states across the nation were felt by seismographs across the globe. The mushroom clouds that formed were soon 30,000 feet high and boiling with radioactive debris. Ugly was too gentle a word to describe the mayhem.

More than a hundred thousand people lost their lives that day as the combined effects of the nuclear devices took their toll. The blast effect was the most apparent and physically damaging, both the outward blast that could destroy skyscrapers and baseball fields alike, and the returning inward rush of air that filled the vacuum created by the explosion. Secondarily, but not by much, was the heat effect, with temperatures in the thousands of degrees incinerating everything in its path. Even those far enough away and somehow sheltered from the blast and heat but facing the noise lost their eyesight as the intense light burned their retinas. Finally, the most pervasive effect was the two-fold nuclear or radiation effect. The initial gamma rays could kill quickly out to a larger radius than the blast. Soon after that, the radioactive dust and fallout carried by the prevailing winds would irradiate everyone and everything not covered and protected. Radiation sickness from the fallout would manifest itself in some people within a few days and continue to kill others for weeks and months.

People were running and scattering everywhere, looking for their loved ones. Thousands of them were injured, screaming in pain. Tens of thousands more had died instantly or were soon to die.

What America used to end a war in 1945 and preclude a costly and time-consuming invasion of the Japanese homeland by war-weary allies, the AJL used to start one in America. The US was already war-weary from years in Iraq and Afghanistan, as evidenced by the administration's disastrous and embarrassing withdrawal from Kabul. Some say that incompetent withdrawal emboldened action by Russia and China and the AJL. And now, after years of "Mutual Assured Destruction" and other nuclear weapons strategies, and all the treaties that were in place to protect against nuclear weapons ever being used again, nuclear war was on the North American continent.

CHAPTER 20
DEPARTMENT OF HOMELAND
SECURITY AND SECONDARY IMPACTS

Washington, DC, July 12

THE DEPARTMENT OF HOMELAND SECURITY ON-CALL DUTY OFFICER called Secretary Jack Ruiz at his home around 9:15 EDT that evening. CTN and FTX newscasts were reporting all three blasts by 9:20 p.m. EDT. To say that the public was concerned by the morning of July 13 was an understatement, as mass hysteria prevailed in all three target areas, with seething anger and near hysteria everywhere else across the land.

———

Orlando, Minneapolis, and San Diego secondary impacts starting on July 13

As if the explosion and resulting nuclear bomb effects had not been enough, each location had secondary impacts unique to those regions. In Florida, the prevailing winds from the Atlantic pushed west and southwest until they collided with the breezes off the Gulf and spread the radioactive fallout across most of central Florida, contaminating orange fields, Plant City strawberry fields, and even the Ruskin tomato fields 40 miles away. Even if they survived the blast, the farmers in central Florida would immediately lose their livelihood for decades to come.

Worse than that was the fallout contamination that hit the Withlacoochee, Hillsborough, Alafia, Manatee, and Myakka River basins and their associated freshwater springs; from there, the Gulf of Mexico and its habitats. And if it could not get any worse, the Southwest Florida Water Management District began reporting soon after the blast about the damage to the Floridian Aquifer System running north-south in the middle of the state via the geologic substructure of the state. It serviced such large cities as Orlando, St. Petersburg, Tallahassee, and even Savannah, Georgia.[1] This source of pristine freshwater, one of the largest in the world, was rendered useless in just a few seconds as the shockwave from the blast fractured and destroyed the geologic formations beneath the surface. The fallout polluted the water in numerous locations. This was an environmental disaster of epic proportions affecting every man, woman, and child in Florida and points north.

In addition to the death and near-total destruction of the Orlando area, the short-term and long-term effects were crippling to the economy of the nation's third most populous state and most of the Southeast.

———

THE EXPLOSION in Minneapolis had a significant difference. It ignited another kind of fire, that of radical Islam in the homeland. In an area with many radicalized Imams, some of which were already sending fighters to AJL, the blast proved that the Great Satan was falling. In the Imams' minds, it was time for all good Muslims to start their own jihad in their neighborhood. As the people in the area scurried to find safety from these local Islamic terrorists, fear and horror reigned supreme in most areas near Minneapolis. Knife and ax-wielding young men roamed the streets, looking for any infidel they could find to convert or kill. While there were some instant conversions, there were even more instant killings than the police could handle. After calling in the Minnesota National Guard, which brought with it its own jihadist element to be weeded out, the state was finally able to enforce some sort of martial law in Minneapolis/St. Paul and surrounding areas.

The "Land of 10,000 Lakes" would never be the same as the fallout rendered the majority of them in the immediate area into nothing more than veritable hot spots for decades to come. As the fallout moved to the east in front of the prevailing west-to-east winds, hundreds of Wisconsin dairy farms were irradiated before the cloud began dropping its radioactive debris on Lake Michigan and Lake Superior.

Even parts of Canada were impacted by the fallout. The Canadian government rushed to assist their citizens and offered assistance to the US states of Minnesota, Wisconsin, and Michigan.

———

IN SAN DIEGO, the prevailing winds pushed the fallout to the east and south. A major effect of the blast so near the border and one that Abdul and Carlos Von De Heim anticipated and had prayed for, was the final and complete collapse of the international border between the US and Mexico in California. Petinc Stadium is about ten miles from the San Ysidro Gate. Neither the blast nor the heat effects of the explosion did much damage to that international border gate facility. The pandemonium that ensued, followed by the initial fallout effects, caused the Border Patrol to close the gate until they could find and don their protective suits. The need for protective suits did not seem to bother the estimated twenty-five thousand who crossed into the US from Tijuana on foot during the first few days after the blast when San Ysidro was "closed." This included families seeking asylum, young men looking for work, Cartel members selling drugs, and others with various motives. Large numbers started filling emergency rooms from California to Texas, and in the weeks after that, with radiation sickness due to the radioactive fallout. The Governor called in the California National Guard to regain control of the border, assisting the local Border Patrol agents as well as they could.

But they could not control nor contain the movement along the fault lines in the area. To the east of San Diego lay the Elsinore and then the San Jacinto fault lines. To the west of San Diego was the Newport-Inglewood fault line.[2] The shockwave from the blast immediately put these lesser fault lines into motion, not much, but enough that everyone felt tremors in Los Angeles. More ominously, gauges detected tremors farther to the east at the San Andreas fault line, the mother of all fault lines and the home of the soon-to-be "big one." Most residents felt—and all the seismic gauges registered—tremors along the San Andreas as far north as San Francisco. And then the tremors stopped. The people of California would have to wait for some time in the future for the long-expected "big" earthquake.

———

THE DEPARTMENT OF HOMELAND SECURITY was overwhelmed as this scenario was not one they anticipated nor practiced. Yes, they had conducted tabletop exercises where a radical detonated one small nuke in DC or NYC, but they had never exercised the effort on the ground; that would have been cost-prohibitive and consumed too much of their valuable budget. Yet, the personnel of the Department of Homeland Security led by FEMA performed as well as expected in coordination with the activated State Emergency Operations Centers. Florida, Georgia, Minnesota, Wisconsin, California, and Arizona State Emergency Operations Centers went hot ASAP. The Florida center, well-rehearsed from the hurricanes of 2004, 2005, 2006, etc., was on the line to the county Emergency Operations Centers of much of Florida within thirty minutes after the blast. They invoked mutual aid support agreements liberally and received the Governor's declaration of a state of emergency almost immediately. They requested, and FEMA quickly granted, a declaration of major federal disaster.

The other states also quickly responded with each governor's declaration of a state emergency, followed by receipt of FEMA's declaration of a major federal disaster soon after that. The President issued a full mobilization order for the National Guard in several states, starting with California and the Guard from neighboring states to reinforce the effort. In short order, the National Guard from California, Arizona, Nevada, Florida, Georgia, Alabama, Minnesota, Wisconsin, Iowa, and Nebraska had all been mobilized and placed in support of FEMA. FEMA wisely put these Guard units under the command and control of a coordination cell from United States Northern Command, which called the shots for the military units.

Selected US Army Reserve units were also activated, with specialty skills such as well drilling and firefighter detachments. The Joint Task Force-Civil Support out of Fort Eustis, Virginia, was the coordination cell for US Northern Command. Usually activated to coordinate Department of

Defense support during chemical, biological, radiological, nuclear, and high-yield explosive crises, the Joint Task Force-Civil Support coordinated all Department of Defense support in this case.[3] It immediately created three smaller task force coordinating cells which relocated to the State Emergency Operations Centers in Florida, California, and Minnesota. This all happened quickly, as their exercises in the past few years included activating and deploying the joint task force and its subordinate headquarters.

On the Road, July 14

President Justice had been rushed by the Secret Service to the underground Presidential Emergency Operations Center, or PEOC, in the White House within minutes of the blasts on July 12. In agony, he watched as news reports came in, and the governors of the affected states sent him updates and requests for assistance and prayers.

Against the wishes of his advisors and the Secret Service, he decided to visit all three states after the planned July 13 speech to the nation. With all the issues facing his administration from Russia in Ukraine, the RIMPAC exercise, and even the Caracas Announcement, he couldn't believe the unfortunate timing of these attacks nor the inhumane nature of them.

After addressing the nation on July 13, President Justice flew to California first, then Minnesota, and then Florida on July 14 to inspect the damage himself and talk to each governor. Even at 45,000 feet from Air Force One, he could see the extent of the damage. What had seemed unbelievable was now a reality. He pledged the nation's resources, time, and talents to restore law and order, rebuild the damaged cities and infrastructure, and bring the perpetrators to justice. It all sounded good, but making a speech and then making things happen on the ground are two different things. While the President was well-intentioned, as were FEMA and Joint Task Force-Civil Support, and all the state and county emergency operation centers, the task was monumental. And for a nation with $30+ trillion in debt (and growing), this would only compound that issue and bring the economy to the stalling point.

The President requested assistance with loans and debt forgiveness of some of the existing debt, at least publicly. Justice called on his new friends in Beijing. He also had his UN Ambassador address the General Assembly to issue a resolution to denounce the cowardly act and cut all funding to the perpetrators once that was determined. "Tilting at windmills" was a phrase some news outlets used to describe that action.

As the response and recovery played out, priority for limited resources eventually went first to California—the most populous state. Second, Minnesota received aid as the state whose damage and fallout after-effects could damage the Great Lakes system (and it also bordered Canada). And finally, Florida the third most populous state but also the one best prepared for disaster.

As one might imagine, when this priority went public, there was a fallout of the political kind, as some state officials in Florida began wondering why President Justice was still in office. Some firmly believed the priority had a political tinge to it. Who knew "Red State-Blue State" would be a factor in prioritizing FEMA assistance? "Are we not all American?" was the cry of millions.

A catastrophic event that should have brought the nation together was tearing it even further apart as it was being politicized by both major parties and the media.

CHAPTER 21

CHINA AND RUSSIA MAKE THEIR MOVES

Camp Smith, Oahu, Hawaii, July 14

THE CYBERATTACK CRIPPLED COMMUNICATIONS AT CAMP SMITH ON Oahu, including those headquarters and commands linked to the Pacific Command network for RIMPAC. It was the product of tech-savvy workers, an insidious and reproductive computer virus that attacked Internet-driven communications and databases. It also hit command and control center networks and even video-conferencing capabilities. Basically, if the system used any facet of the Internet, the virus disabled it. The only communications still available to Pacific Command were the landlines on Oahu and carrier pigeons. The PRC would point to Pyongyang when the crisis had passed. Still, large numbers in the US Military and the NSA continued to suspect Chinese involvement with the breach in security and communications that conveniently blinded the US Navy and Pacific Command for just enough time to allow the PRC Navy's bodacious move.

A pall descended over Pacific Command Headquarters. It was especially telling as they were still receiving and processing the details of the three attacks on the mainland when the screens went dark. The President expressed his desire for RIMPAC to continue in the face of the blasts, as a show to whoever did them that we would not be cowed.

President Justice had told the nation, "While we have received a cruel and cowardly blow, our banking centers, our significant population, and transportation centers, and most of our agricultural areas are still intact and supporting the rescue and recovery operations. FEMA and the National Guard from numerous states are responding quickly to aid those states affected. I have been in contact with the governors of all the affected states, and I can assure you they are on top of the situation. Their emergency responders are doing all they can, working around the clock. I personally visited all three areas. I am absolutely enraged by the atrocities that have been perpetrated. I am utterly amazed at the American people's spirit and ability to bounce back."

The President continued, "We are starting to hear a lot of chatter regarding who may have done these cowardly acts, and the Al Jihadi Levant, or AJL, continues to rise to the top. Let me be clear: they will pay and pay dearly. We are already on the road to recovery and will return even stronger. They cannot stop us. They have not deterred us but made us even more resolute in combating terrorism. For example, RIMPAC will continue as planned, as will our leading role in fighting global climate change. Our allies, such as the UK, Canada, and others, and new friends like China and Iran will work with us to rid the world of terrorists.

Whether they are from the Middle East, Europe, South America, or homegrown right-wing religious ideologues, we will seek you out and destroy you."

Admiral Halsey Burke did not know what to make of that speech, nor did Colonel Grayson.

'Continue RIMPAC —our new friends, the Chi Coms and the

Mullahs of Iran?' Not my friends mused the Chairman of the Joint Chiefs of Staff.

'Homegrown right-wing religious ideologues?' That sounds like me, thought Seth.

———

IT WAS a moonless night over the shallow South China Sea. With virtually no breeze, the sea was flat as the ships slipped through the silver expanse en route to their destination. Under the guise of moving into position for the naval presence exercise with the US Navy for RIMPAC and facilitated by the Pacific Command blackout, the PRC Navy moved its aircraft carrier, the *Liaoning,* two new cruisers, two more frigates,[1] and several support ships just east of the Scarborough Shoals. But in a bit of a surprise, this was one day early and involved more combatant ships than the two frigates the RIMPAC scenario specified.

Fort Meade, MD, July 15

It was a concise and simple phone call, and the NSA tech on duty, James South, did not know what to make of it initially. General Borzovich, Russian Strategic Defense Forces, called General Yao of the Chinese People's Liberation Army.

"How goes your testing in Kwajalein?" asked Borzovich.

"Well, we are on schedule and in place. How are your preparations?" queried Yao.

"Fine. Please confirm petrol from your new area will not be leaking west," growled Borzovich.

"Confirmed," stated Yao.

That was it. It lasted twenty seconds and seemed innocuous enough. Most in the administration and the military and intelligence departments of the government were aware of the PRC and the curtailed Russian tests at Kwajalein and therefore considered it linked to the situation on Kwaj.

Little did they know. The Russian piece of the cabal's agreement from the meeting near the US-Mexican border those many months ago was imminent.

———

Ukraine, July 16

After Putin's "special military operation" into Ukraine in 2022 had stalled, most leaders and pundits in the West, including NATO, the European Union (EU), and the USA, thought that Russia was years away from being able to reconstitute its forces such that they could strike again. At the end of 2022, Russian troops had consolidated control of the Donbas region in southeastern Ukraine, continued to hold and reinforce the Crimea Peninsula, maintained control of Transnistria in Moldova, and created a land corridor from the Donbas through the Mariupol region to the Crimea. They had significant forces in their newly acquired part of Ukraine, Crimea, and Transnistria. However, the heavy losses in 2022, combined with the economic havoc inside Russia due to the sanctions and banking isolation, appeared to have stopped further aggression for the time being. Putin was under indictment by the World Court for war crimes.

But sometimes, politicians only see what fits their narrative. The oil and gas pipelines from Russia to Western Europe were still off. However, the US (a little bit), Canada, and Saudi Arabia were boosting production enough to keep NATO and the EU functioning.

Ukraine was still not a part of NATO and continued to claim

sovereignty over the Donbas and Crimea. But possession being nine-tenths of the law, those areas looked Russian. Kyiv, Lviv, and Odesa were still Ukrainian and rebuilding slowly. The West was tired, almost broke, and looking for some economic recovery time, and only saw a Russian military that was licking its wounds. They failed to see or refused to see the reconstitution in place of the Russian mechanized and armored forces, the build-up of Belarus forces along the Ukrainian border, and a secret agreement between Russia and the rest of Moldova to allow the Russian air force to use their airfields and airspace. This was in addition to the Russian formations already in the Transnistria region near Odesa.

All quiet on the eastern front. At 0200 hours (2 a.m.), July 16, Russian and Belarus forces moved from multiple locations with the mission of taking or destroying Kyiv, the Ukrainian capital, and ending all political resistance. This mission included taking the port of Odesa on the Black Sea, creating a solid land bridge from Russia through the Donbas, then Crimea to Odesa to Moldova. Next, they would squeeze the central and western parts of Ukraine until it ceased to exist. From the Donbas area, more than forty thousand Russian mechanized forces streamed out of the woods and moved west to the Dneiper River toward Kyiv. From Crimea, more than thirty-five thousand Russians moved north up the Dnieper River toward Kyiv. From Belarus, twenty-five thousand soldiers in large mechanized and armored formations charged directly toward Kyiv. And from the west, in Transnistria along the Moldova/Ukraine Border,[2] ten thousand soldiers moved into the Odesa area and linked up with the forces from Crimea that were moving north.

There had been no preparatory artillery barrages nor air force bombing campaigns to prepare for or signal this phoenix-like event. Instead, it was a bolt from the blue and highly effective. It was a coup de main, which was over in forty-eight hours, as Putin's combined forces crushed an exhausted Ukraine. Russia now controlled the northern, eastern, and southern portions of Ukraine, the entire coastline on the Black Sea, including Odesa, the Dnieper River, and the capital of Kyiv. Their continued closure of the pipelines to Western Europe and the West's fatigue effectively initially deterred any significant response from NATO, the EU, and the US.

Adding insult to injury, Russian warplanes started making numerous incursions into Finland's airspace. They moved several thousand "exercise" troops to the Finnish border along with medium-range ballistic missile launcher systems. Belarus moved at least 10,000 soldiers to their border with Lithuania, the only thing blocking access to Kaliningrad, the Russian enclave on the Baltic Sea, an isolated residue of World War II.

The US administration appealed to President Putin, asking him to consider the malicious nature of his actions and demanding an immediate withdrawal.

After he stopped laughing, Putin considered his next phase. He would have already made his airborne insertion on Riga, Latvia, and then attacked west across the Russian-Latvian border with a tank division armed with the T-90 tanks to secure that warm water port on the Baltic. But the presence of several thousand American forces on the ground for an exercise since late June gave him pause. The reality that Latvia, Lithuania, and now Finland and Sweden are part of NATO further dictated his pause. Article Five of that august body (an attack against one was an attack against all) could be invoked to bring the wrath of God on his head if so inclined. As he stood at the podium, he stood tall and proud. He announced the Russian people's successful intervention in Ukraine. The Russian military had prevented the wholesale slaughter of Russian-speaking Ukrainians, killed the neo-Nazis, and provided humanitarian relief to the entire nation due to the famine and disease brought on by American sanctions. It was twisted logic at best, Machiavellian at its worst, and vintage Putin.

———

Fort Meade, MD, July 17

James South remembered the intercept of a few days before and then reminded his supervisor, who reminded her supervisor, who reminded the head of the NSA. An embarrassed NSA Director called the Director of National Intelligence. Late that night, there was a meeting of the National Security Council.

President Justice was insistent that there could not possibly be any linkage between Putin's renewed attacks and anything to do with the PRC or its actions in the South China Sea. The Chairman, Admiral Burke, silently recalled the old fairy tale of the *Emperor's New Clothes*. He and the Vice President exchanged glances.

CHAPTER 22
THE PHILIPPINES WEIGH IN

The White House, July 18

THE PRESIDENT OF THE PHILIPPINES CALLED PRESIDENT JUSTICE and requested immediate response and support from the United States per the provisions of the 1951 Mutual Defense Treaty. It had been four days since the PRC Navy had moved its naval presence forces into the far eastern South China Sea. The aircraft carrier was near Scarborough Shoals, as were two cruisers and two frigates. They had dispatched landing parties on Scarborough Shoals and forced the Philippine forces, ones they had recently reinserted, to depart. One frigate was boldly cruising between Scarborough Shoals and the coast of Luzon, getting as close as twelve miles from the beach.

The Philippine President was animated. "Mr. President, our worst fears have come to pass. The Chinese Navy is not protecting everyone's interest in the region; instead, they are expanding their own. They have effectively consolidated their control over Scarborough Shoals, which is historically considered part of the Philippines and lies only 124 miles west of Luzon.[1] In fact, they forced several of our Philippine Marines to leave, under threat of incarceration."

President Justice responded smoothly, "Oh, come now. I have been on the phone with the President of the PRC this morning, and he assures me their forces are just performing their RIMPAC naval presence task, including a NEO or noncombatant evacuation operations exercise. Your men will be allowed back in the area once the exercise is over. And your claim on Scarborough Shoals is a bit tenuous, as it is well outside the internationally recognized twelve-mile limit."

"I could say the same thing to you about the Hawaiian Islands, American Samoa, Guam, and the Northern Marianas, President Justice. They are much more than twelve miles away from California, yet you claim them. Scarborough Shoals, or Panatog Shoal[2] as we have called it for centuries, is part of the Republic of the Philippines, and I urge you to honor your nation's commitments under the 1951 Mutual Defense Treaty. To that end, I have directed my Chief of Staff to contact your Chairman of the Joint Chiefs, Admiral Burke, and the Pacific Command Commander about this. And I am sure you know that the Chinese are building new islands near the Spratly Islands in the South China Seas by dredging the shallow waters and depositing the sand on the coral reefs. Once built, they installed long-range artillery to control access to the shipping lanes in the area. Woody Island in the Paracels has become a Chinese fortress and now has surface-to-air missiles. Help us protect our land and our assets," pleaded the Philippine President.

"Mr. President," retorted President Justice. "The 2014 Enhanced Defense Cooperation Agreement we signed with you does not require us to respond to your beck and call. As for these new islands you mentioned, they are barely spits of land and will assist the PRC in supporting international trade and emergencies like search and rescue. The US Navy will watch the PRC Navy in our oversight role and report anything out of the ordinary or contrary to the UN South China Sea Paradigm For Progress Resolution."

"Oh, you mean that capitulation agreement that your Secretary of State crafted and your own Senate refused to approve? Please. Remove the scales from your eyes. Open them to the reality of what is happening around you. And the Enhanced Defense Cooperation Agreement is an extension of the 1951 defense treaty. It does not replace the requirements of mutual defense. I have also alerted our national press to my request and this phone call. That includes your CTN and FTX news correspondents and stringers in Manila. So again, please assist us in securing our vital national assets in the South China Sea."

President Justice felt his hand was being forced as he responded, "OK. Look, Mr. President. I will consult with my Secretary of Defense and the National Security Council about your request and get back to you." And then he hung up the phone.

———

THE PRESIDENT CALLED the meeting in the Oval Office, which indicated his sense of the meeting as being perfunctory rather than an actual strategic working session. His opening remarks set the tone.

"Ladies and gentlemen, the President of the Philippines called me a little while ago, trying to invoke the 1951 Mutual Defense Treaty provisions between our nations over his perceived threat by the PRC Navy against the Philippines, more specifically Scarborough Shoals. I have to tell you I am skeptical about his request. The PRC assures me they are merely performing two overlapping functions. That is the naval presence exercise as part of RIMPAC and the security provisions of the UN-approved South China Sea Paradigm For Progress resolution. Secretary Carson, any comments?"

Amanda Carson spoke as if rehearsed. "Yes, Sir, you are correct. I also spoke to the head of the Peoples Liberation Army and the PRC Navy, and they confirmed what you said."

Admiral Burke could no longer contain himself. "Secretary Carson, Mr. President. But did you talk to me? Or to the Director of National Intelligence?

"Our contact in the South China Sea, the US Navy, tells the Pacific Command Commander and me that the PRC Naval actions are inconsistent with the goals and objectives or even the scenario of RIMPAC. And from what I know of the South China Sea Paradigm For Progress, I would say the PRC has also gone a little overboard in that effort. I think we should seriously consider invoking the 1951 Mutual Defense Treaty with the Philippines and warn the Chinese Navy to back off."

Before the President could vent on the Admiral, the Vice President chimed in, "Mr. President, I think the Chairman has spoken wisely. The Philippines is one of our oldest, albeit contrary, allies in the western Pacific, and I am getting phone calls from other nations in the area who have similar concerns. The leaders of Australia, Japan, Malaysia, Viet Nam, and Taiwan all called me this morning."

"Why did they call you?" asked the President.

"Sir, they said they could not get through to you."

Having declined to take those calls, the President knew precisely why they had called his Vice President, and he was not happy.

Late that same night, the Vice President called the Chairman and asked for a strategic update the next day at the Pentagon. Admiral Burke said he would arrange it.

Also, that night, the President called Secretary of Defense Amanda Carson and inquired as to the status of her search for a new chairman. "Ongoing," she said. "But we need to be careful. Admiral Burke is well respected at the Pentagon, and we can't just "can" him because he voices his concerns from his perspective. That is what a Chairman of the Joint Chiefs of Staff should be doing. I am looking into his background for any skeletons we can find. But, considering we are still recovering from the terrorist attack last week, the Russians are showing no signs of withdrawing from Ukraine, and they are threatening Lithuania, Latvia, and even Finland, it is not a good time to replace a chairman."

"You have two weeks to bring me some recommendations for his replacement," fumed the President.

CHAPTER 23
AUR ATOLL RAISES QUESTIONS

Kwajalein Island, July 19

It was April 27 when the President proclaimed that due to their Caracas Announcement, Russia would not participate in RIMPAC and would no longer be able to use the facilities at Kwajalein Reagan Test Site. The Pacific Command planners had quickly struck them from the scenarios and escorted their naval planners from Camp Smith, Oahu. Almost three months later, there were few vestiges of the Russians anywhere on Kwajalein or in the Marshall Islands.

However, the same could not be said of the Chinese. Spurred on by the President's consistent support or, at least, acquiescence to their actions in the South China Sea, the PRC became even more active on Kwajalein and the Marshall Islands. To say they became emboldened was an understatement at best.

As more aircraft from the PRC began to seek permission to land and refuel, Colonel Grayson and Lieutenant Colonel Bakerson started noticing the ramp-up in May. A quick call to Space and Missile Defense Command and Installation Management Command produced permission to meet their needs. The same was true when several PRC Naval vessels made calls at Echo Pier, ostensibly to familiarize themselves with the area before the start of RIMPAC. These same ships also made clandestine stops at Aur Atoll, at which time they offloaded large crates.

"With all that has happened in the mainland, resources are appropriately being diverted to the recovery and intelligence efforts—as they should be. However, here in the central Pacific, I am a bit concerned with the number of large PRC aircraft using the Kwajalein runway, and now, parking on the taxiway," said Seth to Ron and Lieutenant Colonel Shan. "I know that both Space and Missile Defense Command and Installation Management Command have blessed it, but we are running low on jet fuel, and the barge does not arrive for another two weeks."

"And their ships are hogging the space at Echo Pier and in the lagoon itself," added Eli. "The base ops contractor complained to me yesterday that the pier is becoming unsafe."

"Does anyone know where the PRC ships are going when they leave Kwaj lagoon? One of my Marshallese sources said he thinks they are headed toward Aur Atoll," added Ron.

"That reminds me. We need to schedule another official visit to Aur Atoll to check on the PRC infrastructure and testing schedule. I would have expected that they would be ready for their initial test launch by now," stated Seth.

"We are in sync," responded Ron. "I sent that request to the PRC Program Manager yesterday. He said he would arrange it for the next week."

"That's unacceptable," said Seth.

"I didn't say I agreed with it, sir, but that was their answer. I told them I would talk to you. Oh, they also told me they plan to use Wake Island as a remote observation point for their tests."

"What? Call the base operations contractor there, the 8A Small Business set-aside contractor from Alaska. Tell him to inform us of any activity he sees from the PRC, anything, and I want to hear about it ASAP. I will send a classified email to Installation Management Command, and you need to send one to Space and Missile Defense Command about this new Wake issue."

———

THE NEXT DAY, Seth and Ron took one of their DASH 7 aircraft and overflew Aur Atoll. There was a small dirt strip on Tabal Island at Aur Atoll, but the DASH 7 could not safely land there. To their amazement, they saw a hub of activity at the test launch site and what appeared to be armed guards, a new wrinkle.

"OK, that is a little unsettling," said Ron to Seth. "Nothing in their test schedule calls for armed guards, and the RIMPAC scenario does not call for it either." Colonel Grayson spoke to the pilot of the fifty-passenger prop and told him to reroute to Wake Island. After some flight plan adjustments handled by the FAA air traffic controllers in the Kwaj tower, the pilot headed north. It was a cloudless and mild day, with little in the way of trade winds, so the pilot selected a low-altitude course. About a hundred miles north, they flew over a beached tanker of some sort that looked like it had run aground on that small reef fifty years ago.

However, they did notice what appeared to be several antennae protruding from what could have been the bridge.

A couple of hours later, as they approached the Wake Island runway, having made the 650-mile trip in a little over three hours, Lieutenant Colonel Bakerson asked Colonel Grayson what he thought about the entire situation and what he planned to do.

"I have been praying about the entire situation for months, Ron. And I need to tell you this is testing my faith; faith in myself, our higher headquarters, the military, and the President or whoever is calling the shots in DC. It is also testing my faith in God. Why would He allow three nuclear weapons to be detonated in the US with the devasting loss of life and property that followed? It seems like my prayers are going unanswered. I am getting nothing. So, all I can do is what I think is best. At the moment, that is to obey the lawful orders of those appointed over me and report what appears to be contrary to them. But..."

An extended period of silence followed, during which time both Seth and Ron gazed out the window and inwardly searched their souls.

"But?" echoed Ron.

"But what does 'support and defend the Constitution against all enemies foreign and domestic' legally mean from our oath of office? Why are we giving so much access to the PRC to highly classified facilities at Kwajalein and the Reagan Test Site? Why are they so deeply involved in RIMPAC, and apparently, now we have given them carte blanche in the South China Sea? I saw the news over the past few weeks when the President stated that there is no new 'discovery' of oil or gas in the area when we know differently and told Department of Defense. And it is apparently in Philippine waters. I also read about the controversy with the UN South China Sea Paradigm For Progress treaty that is now in effect, although the Senate voted against it. How can that happen? That is a constitutional mandate for the Senate to advise and consent to all treaties. How can the President conclude an international treaty by executive action or by executive agreement, as he is now calling it? I know the Senate can be slow about acting on treaties and that other presidents from both parties have done the same thing, but it is the Senate's duty, alone, to review, approve or disapprove treaties, to advise and consent. Especially this one that involves so many international partners and the UN. But in this case, the Senate did act and voted it down! And why are we not honoring our existing Mutual Defense Treaty with the Philippines? Of course, my favorite, how can the President override the laws of Congress regarding illegal immigration by a simple Executive Order or Action? How can he independently decide to outlaw fracking and coal-fired power plants? I have a friend, who is retired now, who worked at US Space Command on Peterson Air Force Base in Colorado Springs. He was there when a previous administration shared technology with the PRC, which eventually facilitated their leap into the ICBM club and moon and Mars shots. Now, this president is allowing access to highly classified facilities at Kwajalein. What sort of logic is that? From my perspective, some of these actions seem contrary to the Constitution, but no one is doing anything."

Another long period of silence.

"Don't get me wrong, Ron. I am not pointing the finger at any one person, but at a system that allows this to happen. Or better, at the failure of us to police the system to ensure these kinds of things either do not happen or are fully vetted and constitutionally approved. And where is the military's senior leadership when all this goes on?"

"Admiral Burke must be pulling his hair out," mused Ron.

"I truly hope so," responded Seth. "I really do. Until then, I will continue to pray for guidance, our elected leaders and Admiral Burke, and the strength to do what I think is right. But here is my bottom-line question. What happens when the provision in the Constitution that makes the President the

Commander in Chief of the military, conflict with other provisions of the Constitution, such as the Senate's advise and consent role related to mutual defense treaties? Or the provision that requires Congress to declare war and no one else? And what constitutes a war? We never declared war in Korea, but more than thirty thousand Americans lost their lives. We had the Gulf of Tonkin Resolution that gave the politicians some top cover for Viet Nam, but we lost another fifty thousand troops. Grenada and Panama were not preceded by any declaration of war. I understand that in our fast-paced, computerized, and social media world, sometimes there is the need to act quickly before Congress can respond, which was the rationale behind the 1973 War Powers Act. Still, some presidents don't even follow that. So, since we have taken an oath to support and defend the Constitution against all enemies, foreign and domestic, is there a hierarchy of provisions in the Constitution that guides senior military officers on what to do when provisions are in apparent conflict? I don't think so."

Seth and Ron landed on Wake Island, the site of one of the fiercest battles in the Pacific, but it got lost in the fog of history. In December of 1941, starting the day after Pearl Harbor and lasting until December 23, Wake Island was the cause du jour, a shiny spot in an otherwise dark period of American history. A small contingent of US Marines and civilian contractors held out against overwhelming odds from the Japanese Navy intent on taking the atoll. After inflicting tremendous casualties on the first Japanese landing party and damaging several Japanese Navy ships from the air, the American forces finally surrendered. The US naval task force from Hawaii, which was supposed to provide relief, was delayed and eventually halted in order to protect the remaining American naval assets, which were in short supply after December 7.[1]

COL Grayson spoke to the Space and Missile Defense Command tech rep assigned to Wake Island and the head of the base operations contractor. He warned them to be alert at all times. Seth acknowledged that the PRC may be allowed to use Wake for remote observation of the tests at Aur Atoll and that they had to report to him or Lieutenant Colonel Bakerson daily on all PRC activity. He also told them that the PRC was a little aggressive in demanding access to facilities and assets and that the garrison at Kwajalein and the Reagan Test Site were still in charge. He cautioned them not to let the PRC do anything he had not approved. Then he and Ron flew back to Kwajalein.

Aboard the Kwajalein Safety Ship, July 21

Bright and early, Seth and Ron boarded the range safety ship and headed to Aur Atoll. They did not tell the PRC of their intended destination, but as they headed east from Kwajalein, the PRC project manager quickly deduced it and called his team on the ground at Aur to prepare the area for inspection. He also called General Yao, who called the Chinese President, who called President Justice, who called the Secretary of Defense, who called the Commanders of Space and Missile Defense Command and Installation Management Command directly, and then the Chairman of the Joint Chiefs of Staff. They were all reminded that the PRC was our ally, and they were not to interfere with their legitimate testing.

Washington, DC

Admiral Burke was beside himself. What could be so crucial that the Secretary of Defense would bypass him and the Secretary of the Army. Why would she call the Commanding Generals of Space and Missile Defense and Installation Management Commands directly with guidance on coordinating on the ground with the PRC at their missile test on Kwajalein. What kind of hold and influence did the PRC wield on the President? It was a crazy thought that had entered his mind often times over the last few months and that he could not shake. He, too, had taken the oath of office when commissioned as an ensign in the US Navy from Annapolis "to support and defend the Constitution of the United States against all enemies, foreign and domestic." Forty-eight years later, did it matter? Were they just words on paper? After everything he had seen during that time, after all he had seen presidents from both parties do, and the frequent strange Supreme Court decisions........and after all the times the Congress had done nothing when faced with tough choices, what difference did it make?

Was the Constitution still a viable document for running a country? Was it ever? Or had it been polluted beyond cleansing over the years by judicial activism, corrupt lobbyists, executive orders and actions, executive agreements, and signing statements? Now there was a good one, signing statements! Over the years, presidents from both parties had taken to issuing signing statements alongside the legislation they approved, indicating their level of approval or disapproval with selected provisions of the law they just signed into effect. And in some cases, implying their intended nonenforcement. Lately, though completely unconstitutional, the signing statements were actually being included in the federal records.

President Reagan even had some entered into the judicial record when some laws were challenged in the Supreme Court.[2] What good is a document, i.e., the Constitution, when it is not followed? He wondered what a domestic enemy of the Constitution looked like and what could be done to thwart them.

Admiral Burke was not a praying man. A died-in-the-wool Lutheran, he called himself Christian because the Lutheran Church was a Christian denomination. But his knowledge of the Scriptures was minimal, and more importantly, his knowledge of, belief in, and reliance upon Jesus Christ was nonexistent.

Admiral Burke, like many in the military, was a self-reliant man. He was intelligent, hard-working, and a good man. But the last few months had tested his belief and confidence in himself and the system of government he was sworn to uphold. Maybe not the system as it was initially designed and intended, but the system as it had evolved in more than two hundred years. Can the Commander in Chief simply ignore the Constitution without repercussions?

His meeting with the Vice President on July 19 regarding the strategic update was enlightening. He always liked the Vice President and saw him as one who sought the best for the United States, even though they disagreed politically on several issues regarding means and methods for solving the nation's ills. Though not stated, from what he could ascertain, the VP had some concerns over how close the President had become to the Chinese President, his overriding concern for the proposed trade agreement with the Chinese, and how he imposed the Paradigm for Progress on the nation. It was also apparent, though not stated, that the VP neither liked nor trusted the Secretary of State.

The VP had closed their strategic update with several quotes from the Scriptures. As to the United States of America, he said the following: "If my people, who are called by my name, will humble themselves and pray and seek my face and turn from their wicked ways, then will I hear from heaven and will forgive their sin and will heal their land," (II Chronicles 7:14). After the Admiral had hinted at his concerns and his feeling of aloneness, the Vice President offered him the following verses: "For it is by grace you have been saved, through faith…and that not of yourselves, it is the gift of God…not by works lest any man boast," (Ephesians 2:8–9) and "Here I am, I stand at the door and knock. If anyone hears my voice and opens the door, I will come in and eat with him, and he with me" (Revelation 3:20). Finally, the VP asked Admiral Burke to look up a verse from the Book of Esther, chapter 4, verse 14.

As Admiral Burke searched for that verse in his dusty Bible in his home office that night, he felt an overpowering sense that he was not alone in the room. His heart began beating rapidly, and his chest filled with excitement as he experienced the presence of God's Holy Spirit surrounding him. The Admiral began to weep from the pressures of his job, from what appeared to be unconstitutional actions of his government, and from his own condition of being isolated, doomed, and lost. Admiral Halsey Burke, a graduate of the United States Naval Academy and Chairman of the Joint Chiefs of Staff, knelt down on the floor of his home office and prayed for forgiveness. Forgiveness for all that he had done or failed to do that fell short of God's plan, for all those times he had ignored God, for the times he had used his name in vain, for not being the best husband he could have been, and for not taking a stand when he should have. Halsey Burke asked Jesus Christ, the Son of God, to forgive him, wash him clean, give him the strength to do what was right, and let his yes be yes, and his no be no.

Aur Atoll

Seth and Ron, aboard the range safety ship, landed at Aur Atoll a few hours later. It was apparent they were expected. When the PRC Site Manager met them on the dock—the dock they had improved since being there—he immediately took them to the nearest temporary building for a briefing on the status of the PRC missile tests. Seth listened for a while and then requested a tour of all the facilities and infrastructure. They showed them the launch pad and one control building and then were directed back to the dock. Seth stopped and demanded to see the entire launch pad structure inside and out and inside every building on the island. A guard physically stopped him as he walked back to the launch pad. As he tried to push past him, another guard arrived, and this one was armed. The PRC Site Manager quickly jumped between Seth and the guard and said something in Mandarin to the guard. Then he addressed Seth.

"Please, sir, I know you are just doing your job, but so are we. There are proprietary factors at work here, and we cannot yet show you everything you want to see. In due time, you will see it all, and you will be amazed. But for now, I must ask you to leave."

Grayson continued to argue for a bit longer as Bakerson continued to secretly tape the entire event on his smartphone, which no one noticed at his side, in the palm of his hand. Then, ninety minutes after they had arrived, Seth and Ron boarded the range safety ship and headed back to Kwajalein.

CHAPTER 24

GROWING CHINESE ON KWAJALEIN

Kwajalein Island, July 22

When COL Grayson and LTC Bakerson returned to Kwajalein the following morning on the safety ship, they noticed what appeared to be an increased number of PRC personnel on Kwajalein. The approved PRC numbers had started out as ten when they first arrived and then went to twenty once they set up on Aur. But now, there appeared to be another fifty or so on Kwajalein.

Seth spoke to Lieutenant Colonel Eli Shan and the base operations contractor, who confirmed that fifty PRC soldiers had just arrived via a Peoples' Liberation Army cargo plane. They had called in an inflight emergency and been granted permission to land by the FAA air traffic controller in the Kwaj tower. Eli told Seth they were put up in the Kwaj Lodge while repairs were made to their cargo plane. Eli also mentioned that a PRC captain led the fifty soldiers.

With Ron and Eli in the room, Seth called the Space and Missile Defense Command Commanding General about the latest developments: their trip to Aur, the PRC's refusal to show them everything at the test site, and the suspicious arrival of fifty Chinese soldiers.

"Sir, I just wanted to make sure you are aware of what is really happening on the ground in Kwaj. It may be different from the perception of your staff in Huntsville and DC. We just discovered that the PRC plans to use Wake Island as a remote observation site for their Aur Atoll test launches. Also, they recently declared an inflight emergency and landed a cargo plane on Kwaj. Now, while they are ostensibly awaiting repair parts, a company of fifty armed soldiers led by a Chinese captain is on the island. They have used our airfield for other flights before, but I am not sure why that cargo plane would be anywhere near Kwaj. They claim to be part of RIMPAC, but my reading of the scenario does not include them. And worst of all, Ron and I were refused access to some structures that the PRC erected on Aur Atoll and only partial access to the launch pad. I can tell you that the launch pad appears to have the capability for vertical launches and 360-degree launching with a swivel launch pad for horizontal launches off the rail, which could explain what those range fans were all about. I am not positive about the swivel capability, as the PRC has hindered me from seeing some things, but it appears so."

"Colonel Grayson, the Secretary of Defense, just called me directly with guidance from the President to not interfere with the PRC testing. The final negotiations between the Secretary of State and the PRC regarding the new trade agreement are underway, and they are very sensitive. I had heard about their ideas to use Wake as an observation site and am a little confused by that request, but I understand the President's concerns. So, tell the base operations contractor on Wake and my Space and Missile Defense tech rep there to keep you informed, but we will allow it. I have already contacted the

Commanding General of Installation Management Command about this."

"Sir, sir, let me send you a short video that Ron and I took while on Aur and some footage we took here on Kwaj when the PRC program manager was not looking. There are Chinese military personnel, ships, and planes everywhere. I cannot vouch for what they plan to do under the auspices of their so-called limited test on Aur Atoll and now Wake Island. Nor can I vouch for what they plan to do on Kwaj, given the number of assets they have here. They have armed guards on Aur and soldiers with machine guns on Kwaj. I told the PRC program manager to have the weapons stored in my arms room, and he said he would but has done nothing."

"Seth, you are overreacting. Just do your job. I will contact General Yao about the armed guards and soldiers and get that resolved, but go ahead and send me the video you took. I will talk to Installation Management Command again after reviewing it," replied the Commanding General of Space and Missile Defense Command. And then the line went dead.

———

SETH WENT HOME to Quarters 241 for lunch and met Sara there. He explained the entire situation to her and asked what she thought.

"Ladies on Kwajalein and some Marshallese women from Ebeye working on Kwaj are seeing the same thing, Seth. They are worried, especially when an armed Chinese soldier stares at them and smirks. I think you should be prepared for whatever may come. Use some of that School of Advance Military Studies contingency planning you learned and develop some what-if scenarios and possible responses. You know, I think you call them branches and sequels."

"I knew there was a good reason I married you," sighed Seth.

"Easy, big boy. It's only lunchtime, and besides, I will be here tonight," she smiled. With tears welling in her eyes, she added, "Having seen what happened in the US, we are all a little jumpy and scared. I am worried about my Aunt Sally, who lives near Jacksonville. I have not heard from her since before the July 12 attacks, and she is not answering her phone. Let's pray about all of this." Then she said, "Father, we ask that You be with the President and Governors in the US. Give them the wisdom and resources they need to deal with the chaos in the States. Please be with the families who have suffered so much. It is awful. Here on Kwaj, you know Seth's heart and his concerns about the Chinese presence on Kwajalein and their planned testing. I ask that you give Seth wisdom and the insight to handle this difficult situation as you would want him to. Give him the courage to act when and where he should and the confidence to restrain himself when he should. Please protect him at all times, in Jesus's name, I pray, Amen."

"I love you," said Seth as he headed back to the office. That afternoon, Seth knelt in his office and prayed for guidance and strength. He pulled out the small King James Bible he had received as a plebe at West Point and read a passage from Esther 4 and then II Chronicles 7. "God, I am not sure what to do, but I know you guide my steps. So, for now, I will update my superiors on everything I am seeing and hearing, whether they want to hear it or not, but I will keep them updated. I will prepare for possible contingencies and develop plans to respond to the most likely ones. Please give me wisdom in dealing with my bosses."

This last prayer request resulted from his unique position. His immediate boss, and rater, was the Senior Executive Service (SES) Director of the Pacific Region Office of Installation

Management Command in Oahu. But he also worked for Space and Missile Defense Command, supporting their mission by supporting the Reagan Test Site. Yet, as the Pacific Command Commander's Rep to the Marshall Islands, he also worked for the Commander of Pacific Command. In a roundabout way, he also had to keep the US Ambassador to the Marshall Islands satisfied. All in a day's work!

———

Kwajalein Island, July 23, (July 22 in CONUS)

"Will, can you talk?" asked COL Seth Grayson of COL Will Bishop.

"Call me back on your secure telephone unit," said Will.

Several minutes later, Seth had Will on the secure phone line and told him what was happening on Kwajalein and Wake Island.

Will responded, "Not good. The official party line here in the five-sided building is that the ChiComs are our new best friends, and we need to stop hounding them. However, I can tell you that several general officers in J3 Operations Section, including my boss, are more than concerned about the PRC Navy's actions in the South China Sea and our Mutual Defense Treaty with the Philippines. They are equally worried by the Russian operations in Ukraine and their continued aggression in and near the former Soviet Republics and the Baltic states. Most of all, the NSA continues to pick up chatter regarding the Al Jihadi Levant and possible links to the PRC and Russia. Nothing concrete, but references to a meeting in Mexico several months ago and, even more ominously, a possible link between the AJL and Iran. Sunnis and Shias working together. Now that is truly scary! And not only has Russia been providing Iran assistance with their 'peaceful' nuclear program, but I have also heard some scuttlebutt that the source of the enriched uranium used in the terrorist attacks on July 12 may have come from a Canadian source. It was probably vetted by one of our previous secretaries of state via a Russian uranium business and then to Iran. It is getting really sour around here."

"Will," replied Seth. "This is bad and getting worse. Here is what I plan to do. I will keep you in the loop on everything happening on Kwaj, Aur Atoll, and Wake Island regarding the PRC if you can keep your boss informed. I will call the Pacific Command J3 Operations Section and update them regarding the PRC's actions and RIMPAC play. Then I will call the Pacific Command J5 Plans Section in my role as the Pacific Commander's Rep. I have already called the Commanding General of Space and Missile Defense Command and updated him. He is calling the Commanding General of Installation Management Command. And I almost forgot. Ron Bakerson has been taking video clips of activities on Kwaj and Aur Atoll, highlighting some of our concerns, especially the armed Chinese guards and soldiers. He took it surreptitiously, so the quality is not too good, but I think you will find it enlightening. I hope it also finds its way up to you via the Space and Missile Defense channels, but I wanted you to have it, just in case it doesn't."

"OK," answered Will cautiously. "I will hold onto it for now."

"And another thing I almost forgot," added Seth. "The US Ambassador to the Marshall Islands has requested a meeting with Ron and me in Majuro on Tuesday, which is your Monday. Not sure what it is about, but I will let you know. It could just be about the drought we are having due to the El Niño. They are in dire straits on Majuro. We are doing better in Kwajalein Atoll due to the mobile ROWPUs (reverse osmosis water purification units) we brought in to supplement our lens wells and desalination plant. The drawdown on our lens wells has been tremendous to the point of some saltwater intrusion into them. But with some recent tweaks to our desalination plant, we've been able to scale back on the lens well pumping and seem to be turning the corner."

About an hour later, Seth and Ron called the Pacific Command J3 Operations Section and updated them on the status of the RIMPAC play and asked if the scenario required the PRC to have armed guards or the use of Wake Island. The answer was no, but guidance from the Secretary of Defense directly to the Commander of Pacific Command indicated that they were to remain flexible in working with the PRC during RIMPAC. Seth also called the Pacific Command J5 Plans Section and gave him the same update he had given Colonel Bishop at the Joint Staff J3 Operations Section. Not yet fully recovered from the cyberattack of several days prior, the Pacific Command J5 Plans Section was all ears regarding the activities of the PRC. Pacific Command had established a working group with their J6 Communications Section, the Joint Staff J6, US Cyber Command (located at Fort Meade, Maryland), and reps from the Department of Homeland Security, FBI, CIA, and NSA. This group was developing information that tied the attack to Pyongyang but also found indicators of support from Beijing. They kept both the Commander of Pacific Command and the Chairman of the Joint Chiefs apprised of their efforts.

CHAPTER 25

AMBASSADOR'S MEETING IN MAJURO
AND THE 65TH ARRIVE ON KWAJ

Majuro Atoll, July 26

MAJURO IS THE CAPITAL OF THE REPUBLIC OF THE MARSHALL Islands. A long semicircle, the atoll is home to about thirty thousand Marshallese, which is nearly half of the total population in the Marshall Islands. Unfortunately, for the people who live and work there, the gaps between most of the islands surrounding the atoll had been closed by causeways over the years to improve travel between the islands that made up the semicircle. The causeways, while facilitating travel, had the adverse effect of significantly dampening the flushing action of the tides as they rushed in and out in the gaps between the islands. The tides fed the coral reefs inside the lagoon with much-needed cleansing action. As a result, the coral system inside the lagoon was moribund, and the water quality was abysmal. The law of unintended consequences in effect!

As COL Grayson overflew the Majuro lagoon in the Air Marshall Islands puddle jumper that the Marshallese President sent them and landed at the Amata Kabua/Marshall Islands International Airport,[1] he could see the effects of the causeway.

The contrast between the lagoon's murky green/gray water and the crystal-clear blue water on the ocean side was starkly evident.

When they landed, Seth and Ron were escorted into the VIP lounge of the airport, where, much to their surprise, Ambassador Jane Taylor met them. Also meeting them was the Deputy Assistant Secretary of State (DASS) for Eastern Asia and the Pacific, Marsha Eckerd, and the Marshallese President Markus Kabua. He was a relative of the airport's namesake and previous President and Iroij of the Marshalls.

"Good morning, Mr. President, Madam Ambassador," said Seth. "So good to see you again. I believe you both know Lieutenant Colonel Ron Bakerson, the Director of the Reagan Test Site. To what do we owe the pleasure of meeting you all in the VIP lounge?"

"Seth, I want you and Ron to meet Deputy Assistant Secretary of State Marsha Eckerd.

She and I have discussed several issues related to the Marshall Islands and recent Chinese initiatives in the western Pacific. Then, President Kabua called me a couple of days ago with his concerns over increased Chinese presence on Majuro."

"COL Grayson, we are seeing Chinese military and businessmen all over Majuro. The businessmen have purchased some small businesses, and the military personnel seem to be inspecting the atoll, with a particular interest in our airport and piers," blurted out the Marshallese President. "We are concerned. And my cousin called from Gugeegue last week and said he had seen great numbers of Chinese on Kwaj. Do you know what is going on?"

The Ambassador added, "Marsha and I called the Secretary of State last week about the unexpected and increased PRC presence but were pretty much blown off as if we were some petty worrywarts. He told me not to contact him about the

Chinese again," She continued more loudly, "We are getting a little paranoid, I admit, but it is not paranoia if someone is really following or watching you."

"Is that why we are meeting in the VIP lounge?" asked Seth.

"Absolutely," answered DASS Eckerd. "The Ambassador and I have observed PRC personnel following us and watching her quarters. We went on a shopping and handicraft hunting trip this morning until we lost our tails and then headed here by prearrangement with President Kabua."

"And why we sent you the small twin-prop Air Marshall Islands plane to get you here instead of your DASH 7, which the Chinese could easily track," added President Kabua. "And why I slipped in here under the premise of inspecting the airport facilities in advance of the upcoming Central Pacific tennis tournament."

"So, tell us, COL Grayson and LTC Bakerson, what the heck is going on in Glocca Mora?" asked Ambassador Taylor. "And be specific. I am trying to represent the United States to the Marshallese government but am unclear on the approved PRC's role. If we need to get into classified or sensitive information, President Kabua understands he may have to leave."

Seth and Ron spent the next hour explaining their guidance regarding the PRC's role in RIMPAC, the direction to allow the PRC to use Kwajalein and the Reagan Test Site for limited missile and sensor testing, and the role that Aur Atoll was playing in that testing. They also discussed the PRC's planned use of Wake Island as a remote sensing site, which disturbed President Kabua quite a bit, as the Marshallese contend that Wake Island is one of theirs and not a US possession.

The discussion that followed showed how some PRC presence could then be expected on Majuro, albeit it seemed a little large, given the supposedly limited nature of the testing on Kwajalein. After that, President Kabua departed to attend a joint, but closed, session of the Council of Iroij (upper chamber of the legislation) and the Nitejela (lower chamber) regarding the Chinese.

"Seth, this is unnerving," fretted the Ambassador.

"You can say that again," said Seth. "I did not mention it with the President here, but the Chinese have armed guards on Aur Atoll, and a company of armed soldiers recently deplaned at Bucholz Field on Kwaj under the pretense of aircraft maintenance problems. I have called this into my bosses, and we even sent some videos that Ron took. So far, no response. And if that isn't strange enough, the launch pad they have built on Aur Atoll seems to be much more capable than just launching small test missiles. In fact, it has a prescribed set of range fans that point to the east and north for up to 750 miles. It has vertical and horizontal launch capability, and perhaps it can swivel a full 360 degrees. The PRC has built more than a test facility."

"OK, OK, OK then," said the Ambassador. "I am allowed to call the Vice President directly on urgent matters when the Secretary of State is unavailable or, in this case, won't talk to me. I will contact him tonight via secure phone and ensure that there is some sort of visibility regarding the PRC's actions out here, at the highest levels of our government," stated the Ambassador. "Marsha, I want you in the room with me when I call."

"And Ron and I will contact Space and Missile Defense and Installation Management Commands about our information exchange with you all today, and the Pacific Command J5 Plans Section, since I am the Pacific Command's rep to the Marshall Islands. We will have to inform them about your plans to call the VP to give them time to prepare. So please wait until tomorrow to make your call, if I may be so bold as to ask, Madam Ambassador."

"OK, Seth, we will play it your way, but tomorrow at noon our time, when I know the Vice President will be at his quarters in DC tomorrow night, I will make the call. Please update your bosses before then."

As the meeting broke up, Seth called his office to arrange the calls to the Pacific Command J5 Plans Section, and the Commanding Generals of Space and Missile Defense, and Installation Management Commands upon their return to Kwajalein.

Late that night, after his and Ron's calls to the general officers, Seth picked up his secure telephone unit and called Will Bishop at Joint Staff J3 Operations Section.

———

Kwajalein Island, July 27

COL Grayson was at his office near the terminal on Kwajalein when the C17s started arriving. They were bringing the personnel and some of the lighter equipment for the 65th Brigade Engineer Battalion (Combat Effects) from Oahu. The heavy vehicles and equipment from their TOE (Table of Organization and Equipment) and the even heavier construction equipment they leased would arrive by barge the next day at Echo Pier (assuming the PRC ships would make room). As the engineer battalion that supported the 2nd Stryker Brigade Combat Team of the 25th Infantry Division[2], they were battle-tested and competent.

It wasn't the complete battalion, but with more than three hundred personnel, including the battalion headquarters and most of the three operational engineer companies, Seth felt a little less isolated. He and the battalion commander met to discuss the projects for the various civic action teams (CAT)[3] the battalion would deploy in and around Kwajalein for the next ninety days. Typically, construction units such as the 84th Engineer Battalion (Combat Heavy) were tasked for these CATs. But this time, the 65th was about to foray into the civic action arena. And as a last-minute change to their manifest, they were told to bring their individual weapons and basic load of ammo, as they would be building a Known Distance range and would need them to "proof it" once completed. These weapons included 9mm pistols, M16A4 assault rifles, some with M203 grenade launchers, a few M4A1 carbines, and even several M249 squad automatic weapons.[4]

These civic action teams had been deploying to various parts of the western Pacific for years and had made quite a name for themselves, building schools, roads, clinics, and even piers. Now, the soldiers of the 65th were about to spend three months in the relative comfort of Kwajalein Atoll. They would be improving the dirt airstrip on the southernmost island in Aur Atoll, and building a new water catchment system, school and medical clinic on Ebadon, in addition to the Known Distance range on either Kwaj or Roi-Namur. Seth was not quite sure yet, since he just added that mission as a cover for the 65th bringing their weapons. In a bit of irony, Seth recalled that US Army engineer units from Hawaii were no stranger to the Marshall Islands. The 84th Engineer Battalion from Oahu visited Eniwetok Atoll in the '70s to put a concrete cap on the nuclear crater there from the 1954 Bravo Blast.[5] In the late '90s, they constructed several small facilities for the Marshallese in Kwajalein Atoll.

As the wheels started turning in Seth's mind, he could see the potential for much greater use of the 65th Engineers relative to the PRC's significant increase in personnel on Kwajalein. But first, he needed approval from US Army Pacific and the Commander of the 25th Infantry Division at Schofield Barracks on Oahu, to whom the 65th were assigned. And since he had no direct authority with either of those commands, COL Grayson contacted the Pacific Command J5 Plans Section and presented his idea for the use of the 65th Engineers. In COL Grayson's mind, possession was nine-tenths of the law—he aimed to ensure he had possession of the land rather than being squeezed out of the garrison's leased land within Kwajalein Atoll.

CHAPTER 26
THE VICE PRESIDENT AWAKES IN DC

Washington, DC, July 28

AFTER HIS SECOND STRATEGIC UPDATE ON PENTAGON ISSUES WITH the Chairman of the Joint Chiefs of Staff, the Vice President was more than troubled by what he heard. After the room had cleared, he suggested that he and Admiral Burke have an informal chat in the Chairman's office. "Admiral, is your office clean?"

"Absolutely, Mr. Vice President. It is swept weekly, the last time being this morning. There are no listening devices in here"

"So, tell me again about your concerns with the recent PRC initiatives," demanded the VP.

"Certainly, sir. There are several from a military perspective. First, I question the almost unrestricted and growing use of the Reagan Test Site and associated support structure on Kwajalein. That is a highly classified facility, and the PRC is an untested friend at best. Second, and closely related to that, are the armed guards on Aur Atoll and a company of armed Chinese soldiers who just showed up at the Kwajalein airfield. We have complained to the PRC, as that is not permissible, but to no avail. Also related to Kwaj is the handwritten note we found and the chatter the NSA has collected that suggests some link between the Al Jihadi Levant, or AJL, and the PRC. This one is still tenuous, but we are exploring it further, especially after the attacks of July 12. The third is the idea of the President inviting both the PRC and Russia to participate in RIMPAC. Yes, China has exercised with us before, but not to this extent. Fourth, and closely related to that, is the recent UN Action, the South China Sea Paradigm For Progress, which the President approved by executive agreement instead of the Senate advise and consent route. Of course, the Senate did consider it and soundly rejected it. And fifth, and further exacerbating our Paradigm for Progress concerns, the President is seemingly refusing to adhere to the Senate-approved 1951 Mutual Defense Treaty we have with the Philippines regarding support for their effort to defend the Scarborough Shoals.

Let me tell you, sir, the reports I get from the Chief of Naval Operations and the Commander of Pacific Command all tell me of an extremely aggressive PRC Navy. It is far exceeding both the scenario of RIMPAC and their role under the Paradigm for Progress. If that isn't bad enough, they are continuing to build new islands in the South China Sea near the Spratly Islands under some of the flimsiest excuses I've heard in a long time. And, installing long-range artillery and anti-ship missiles on them. They already have surface-to-air missiles on Woody Island. And then, there is the Russian Caracas Announcement. It is a direct affront to us, and that comes at a time when Putin restarted his operations in Ukraine and is poised to expand further if it were not for the airborne units we had in Latvia. And yet, the Commander in Chief does not seem worried. I could go on and forgive me if I have overstepped my bounds."

"No," said the VP. "I hear you loud and clear."

"Sir, when taken piece by piece, none of these items seem that egregious, except for the July 12 Islamic terrorist attacks or the renewed Russian attack on Ukraine. Most of the things going on could be mere policies that I happen to disagree with. But when you look at the whole set of them, you have to ask yourself, what the heck is going on at 1600 Pennsylvania Avenue? Who is whispering in the President's ear? And what is the connection among all of it? The President and the Chinese?

"Oh, and I need to add some details to the thing that seemed to kick all this into motion—the letter by a Japanese soldier who fought on Kwajalein during World War II and was captured by our forces. He was also a geologic engineer and had worked on some rigs in the South China Sea before the war. His findings show significant, and I mean vast, oil and gas reserves there, especially near the Scarborough Shoals. Given today's technology, those deposits could turn a third-world country such as the Philippines into a thriving and democratic economic force. In the wrong hands, it could influence world oil markets. That tidbit of information came from US Army Garrison-Kwajalein Atoll through Installation Management Command, Space and Missile Defense Command, and Department of the Army to the Secretary of Defense and the President. It was classified SECRET when it left Kwaj. I reclassified it as TOP SECRET. So why is this being bantered about in the public media yet passed off as worthless by the President? And who shared it with the Chinese?"

"Did you read the scripture from the book of Esther that I mentioned, Admiral?"

"Yes, sir, I did. Chapter 4, verse 14. 'Who knows whether thou are come to the kingdom for such a time as this?'"

"Yeah, so have I, over and over again," whispered the Vice President, "'… for such a time as this.' And for what it's worth, Ambassador Jane Taylor called me from Majuro yesterday with similar concerns."

When he reached his quarters at the Naval Observatory in

DC, the VP told his senior military aide to set up a meeting the next day in his office with the Speaker of the House and the Senate Majority Leader regarding some proposed legislation to amend the Clean Water Act.

The idea of impeachment had been perking in the House for several months. A tense relationship between Congress and the administration already existed after the President imposed his views on immigration using executive action.

The more recent events in Ukraine and Moldova and the "Luanda Low-ball" and Caracas Announcement only added fuel to the fire. However, it was still just a smolder among some junior representatives and a few junior senators.

The event that genuinely stoked that fire was the President's decision to move ahead with the South China Sea Paradigm For Progress via an executive action that directed the Secretary of State to continue negotiations. The administration worded it carefully, not to say the Paradigm for Progress was approved, but it authorized the Secretary of State to continue working on it. Then it was announced as if it were in effect by the Secretary of Defense. And now, it had recently been formalized as an executive agreement. Yes, presidents from both parties have concluded executive agreements with foreign nations, and the Supreme Court has tended to uphold their agreements. However, it was presented initially as an executive action related to a potential treaty, and the Senate voted it down 70–30. After the Senate vote, the step from executive action to the executive agreement infuriated many of the senators. Both sides of the aisle took it as a direct affront to them and their constitutional role in treaties. When the news of the large oil and gas deposits leaked out, that was more fuel to the fire (no pun intended). That was followed by the Secretary of Defense's announcement about the UN climate change agreement. When the President refused to honor the 1951 Mutual Defense Treaty with the Philippines, a treaty the Senate did advise and consent to and approved, that sent hold-outs over the top. Not to mention the porous border with Mexico that the AJL used to bring in the three nuclear devices for the July 12 attacks. It was more than most members of Congress could stand.

And when the President canceled the title 42 policy that prevented some illegal immigrants from crossing the southern border due to Covid concerns, then sued to stop the "Stay in Mexico policy," caravans of Central American illegal immigrants grew exponentially. Congress had had more than enough!

So, as he continued to sense the growing angst among the senators and congressmen, the VP met with the Speaker and Senate Majority Leader.

———

Washington, DC, July 29

"Gentlemen, I have been listening to you and some of your fellow legislators on some of the news talk shows. I believe that we may have a bit of a constitutional conundrum on our hands. The President does enjoy certain freedoms as the Commander in Chief of our Armed Forces, and he can use his executive authority to implement the laws that Congress passes. But, there are some, not only on Capitol Hill but also in the Pentagon, who think he may have exceeded constitutional limits.

"The purpose of this meeting—and, no, we are not being taped—is to get your initial reaction. I can swear to you that those reactions will remain with me and me alone."

The Senate Majority Leader spoke first, "Sir, this meeting is quite unusual, but let me say first that impeachment…"

"Whoa," yelled the VP. "I said nothing about impeachment."

"No, you did not, sir, but if you want our opinion on what we think about the President's constitutional overreaches, then it must be considered. In fact, if he simply goes around us via executive actions, executive orders, and now executive agreements and the courts do nothing to correct the matter, then impeachment is the only tool we have left."

"Go on," said the VP.

"So, impeachment of a sitting President by the House and the subsequent vote in the Senate has only been tried four times in the entire history of our country, and all failed. President Andrew Johnson was impeached in 1868 after he attempted to remove Secretary of War Stanton without Senate approval required by the Tenure of Office Act. He narrowly escaped conviction even though that particular law's constitutionality was suspect.[1] Bill Clinton was impeached in 1998 for perjury, for lying to Congress about his affair with the young lady on his staff. The Senate quickly acquitted him in early 1999.[2] And you know, the House impeached, and the Senate acquitted Trump twice. Once for the phone call between President Trump and Ukrainian President Zelensky regarding the withholding of funds, and once for his alleged role in the January 6, 2021 capitol riot. So, impeachment proceedings are not something one jumps into lightly, although certain senators from the coal-producing states and others from states involved in fracking might argue that point with me."

The Speaker was a little more forthcoming. "Sir, more than just a few representatives would jump on the impeachment bandwagon ASAP. And some from both sides of the aisle. I am not sure, however, that I have the simple majority needed."

"Well," mused the VP after much discussion. "I am neither for nor against impeachment. What I am for is preserving the integrity of the US Constitution. Let's see what develops in your respective houses over the next few days. And I must insist, that this conversation never occurred."

The talk of impeachment began to heat up on News Talk Radio first, as the inevitable leaks from the corridors of Congress occurred. Then the talking heads on several cable TV news shows, fanned the fires. What in the world did the President think when he got so close to China, and how could he allow Russia to take over so much of Ukraine again? And now Moldova? And for some, how could he change how immigrants are handled by an executive action contrary to the existing legislation? The coup de grâce was the combined effect of allowing the AJL to attack three US cities with small nuclear devices while allowing Russia to flex its muscles in the Caribbean. Not honoring our treaty with the Philippines and threatening to stop all fracking and coal plants were beyond the pale.

Was the President actually doing all he could "…to preserve, protect, and defend the Constitution of the United States?"[3] people were asking. Does President Justice not remember his oath of office?

And where is the senior leadership of the military on all of this, asked some of the pundits. Their oaths of office require them to "support and defend the Constitution of the United States against all enemies, foreign and domestic." How can they look at themselves in the mirror as the President does what he is doing, primarily those actions directly related to the military in his role as Commander in Chief that seem to run crosswise with other constitutional provisions? At what point should a senior General Officer or Admiral simply tell the Commander in Chief, "No, and retire or— resign if necessary—rather than carry out unethical or unconstitutional orders"?

The first poll on the issue came out on August 1 by FTX News. It found that 53 percent of the population supported an impeachment process or at least a discussion of impeachment by the House. But with a margin of error of +/- 10%, that poll was a little suspect.

Then the ATC/Washington Chronicle poll on August 2 reflected 58 percent in favor of an impeachment process or at the least the discussion of it, with only a +/- 5% margin of error.

But the real shocker was the MSNTC poll on August 7. MSNTC news was known to favor most of what the President was trying to do globally, yet its pollsters found that 48 percent of likely voters polled would support an impeachment process.

CHAPTER 27

IMPEACHED!

Washington, DC, August 8

AFTER HE MET WITH THE VICE PRESIDENT IN LATE JULY, THE Speaker of the House began to informally canvas his party members. Then he talked to a few from the other party in a most casual and off-the-record way. The Speaker found that a majority of the congressmen and congresswomen favored or at least would consider an impeachment process if the President did not change his ways rapidly. The Senate Majority Leader got similar results when he informally polled his party's members.

In a meeting facilitated by the VP, the Speaker and the Senate Majority Leader met with the President in the Oval Office on August 8. They brought the Senate and House Minority Leaders, who attended grudgingly. The Speaker presented their concerns and broached the subject of impeachment that was gathering momentum in their chambers. Both the Speaker and the Senate Majority Leader pleaded with the President to make some announcement and concession regarding his immigration executive action and the South China Sea Paradigm For Progress executive action/agreement immediately. He also needed to soften his recent edicts on coal-fired plants and fracking. Something that would show the members of Congress that he understood their concerns and intended to work with them on these issues added the House Minority Leader.

It did not take long for the President to react and react strongly. He insisted he was well within his constitutional authority and vehemently proclaimed, "How dare you insinuate that I am not doing all I can for the American people after the horrendous terrorist attacks of July 12?"

"Sir," inserted the VP. "Some of the latest polling actually shows that a large percentage of the American people are laying the blame for those terrorist attacks at the doorstep of 1600 Pennsylvania Avenue, as your positions on border security are perceived as soft. I think you would be wise to address the public on your recent initiatives and explain your rationale and processes, but also clarify that you intend to work with Congress on the myriad of issues facing us now. The latest polling also shows a groundswell in favor of impeachment. Now, we all know that polls can be misleading, and we should not govern just to get better poll numbers, but the consistency in these polls is worth noting."

"I will hear no more of this. The people elected me to govern, and govern I shall. This impeachment talk is opposition rhetoric, nothing more. Now, get out, all of you."

While he had never trusted the Speaker of the House nor the Senate Majority Leader, the President had trusted his VP in the past as an honest broker. He was like a voice in the wilderness that he could rely on to present the other side, a devil's advocate if you will. But now, not so much.

———

IT TOOK a few days for the Speaker and the Majority Leader to get their acts together, but they did. The Speaker and his legal staff drew up the charges pursuant to Article I, Sections 2 and 3, and Article II, Section 4 of the Constitution. The charges needed to be specific, as impeachment by the House and the subsequent trial by the Senate were essentially political theater superimposed on extremely serious charges. The theatrical aspects could overwhelm the script and the facts if the charges were unclear and unsubstantiated. They had to lay out the specific charges and relate them to either "Treason, bribery, or other high crimes and misdemeanors." While treason and bribery are very specific and well-defined in legal journals and seemingly not in play given the current scenario, the terms "high crimes and misdemeanors" in the context of impeachment, while ill-defined, were much in play in this case.

Neither the Andrew Johnson trial, the Bill Clinton impeachment trial, nor either of Donald Trump's trials had ended with a conviction. For those reasons, the House legal staff decided to develop charges related to the President's specific constitutional duties, the defined limits on his powers, and how they related to the enumerated powers of Congress. To that end, they developed the following charges:

Charge 1. That the President exceeded his constitutional authority by changing the way illegal immigrants are assessed, processed, and returned—or not, via an executive action contrary to the nation's legally approved laws. This led directly to multiple nuclear attacks directed against the United States of America on 12 July of this year.

Charge 2. That the President exceeded his constitutional authority by approving a treaty with the UN and specifically the People's Republic of China regarding the South China Sea Paradigm For Progress (SCSPFP) by means of executive action, later redefined as an executive agreement. And that he directed the Secretary of State to continue working on the "refinement and implementation of the SCSPFP," even after the US Senate had rejected the proposed treaty, 30–70 in their constitutional role to advise and consent on proposed treaties.

Charge 3. That the President failed to carry out his constitutional duties when he refused to adhere to the provisions of the Senate-approved 1951 Mutual Defense Treaty with the Philippines, in that he knowingly allowed the People's Republic of China Navy to conduct operations that endangered the Scarborough Shoals, a reef and coral shoal known to belong to the Philippines, and failed to come to the aid of the Philippines when so requested by the President of the Philippines, as agreed to in that Mutual Defense Treaty.

Charge 4. That the President knowingly provided classified information regarding natural resources in the South China Sea to the People's Republic of China and then deliberately allowed false information regarding those resources to be publicized. This false information was then used, in part, to facilitate the United Nation's approval of the South China Sea Paradigm For Progress.

Charge 5. That the President knowingly put classified facilities and information at risk at the Reagan Test Site in the Kwajalein Atoll by allowing unprecedented access to facilities and infrastructure and by allowing a build-up of armed People's Republic of China personnel and equipment on the installation beyond what they required for their testing.

The House legal staff considered other charges, such as allowing or not preventing the renewed Russian attack on Ukraine and the discussion of giving back Guantanamo. But those could be portrayed as policies or, in some cases, policy failures. Or, in the case of Guantanamo, a trial-balloon policy.

There was also a growing suspicion that the PRC was somehow connected to Pyongyang's cyberattack, but Department of Defense could not yet prove that, nor was there any evidence the President had any knowledge of it.

Most felt the first two charges were the clearest and with the most proof behind them. The third charge was also clear and easily proved but could be considered a policy change given the thaw between the Philippines and the US since 1951 and their requested departure of our forces from Subic Bay and Clark AFB in the 1990s. Charges 4 and 5 were the weakest but by no means wrong. The President's lawyers could argue a simple professional difference of opinion regarding the potential oil and gas reserves in the South China Sea since none had been extracted yet, and the US Geologic Survey did not see the potential. And Charge 5 could be read as simply a shift in focus to facilitate economic gains, which to some degree was what the President wanted to do.

Some wanted charges related to the UN environmental treaty the Secretary of Defense had signed. But it was working its way up the court system courtesy of a lawsuit filed by several states, so the House decided not to include it as an issue.

The House Judicial Committee reviewed the charges, then approved them, and recommended that the Speaker refer them to the House as a whole for consideration.

———

House of Representatives, August 15

The House members, media, and observers packed the House floor and the visitor's chamber above it. The tension in the hall was beyond electric when the Speaker mounted the dais. Every news outlet in North America and worldwide was on hand as the Speaker rapped his gavel, bringing the special session of the House to order.

As the Speaker started the roll call vote, it soon became apparent that the vote would run mainly along party lines, but not entirely. The representatives from the coal-producing and oil-fracking states all voted for impeachment. And most of the representatives from two of the states hit hardest by the July 12 terrorist attacks also voted for impeachment; California did not. When all was said and done, the vote was 249–186 for impeachment. It wasn't overwhelming, but it was more than the simple majority needed to complete the impeachment and send it to the Senate. Now, all the House had to do was select the Representatives who would act as the prosecutors for the case in the Senate Chambers.

At the press conference after the vote, the first question to the Speaker came from the Al Jazeera Washington bureau chief. "Mr. Speaker, can you please tell me why the House decided to take up this action, to tilt at this windmill so late in the second term of President Justice's presidency? I mean, the elections will be on November 8. And then, the new President will take office in January. President Justice will be gone, and perhaps your party will win. This effort does not seem to pass the common-sense test."

"Well, Ahmed, I am glad you asked that question and especially glad you asked it as a foreigner and visitor in our country. The United States of America was founded on the Declaration of Independence and launched into exceptionalism under our Constitution. It is not perfect, but it is the best governing document the world has ever seen. It is careful to separate powers so that no one part of the government—executive, legislative or judicial—can reign supreme or rule as a de facto sovereign. Sovereignty in the US rests with the people. Our government is supposed to be of the people, by the people, for the people, to quote Abraham Lincoln. If a president or any other government official acts outside the Constitution, allowing that to go unchecked is unacceptable and weakens the Constitution. Yes, the President's term ends in January, but bad things can happen between August and January, some of which could become difficult if not impossible to reverse. This is especially true of what is happening in Ukraine, Moldova, Finland, the Caribbean, the South China Sea, and on our southern border. And, since we are going to change presidents one way or another between November and January, why not change presidents now, at least temporarily, to preserve the viability of the Constitution? Our government will not collapse if the Senate votes for conviction. We have a VP who would become the new interim President and a process for installing a new VP. The world did not end when President Nixon resigned in lieu of facing an impeachment process, nor will it end after the Senate takes action.

"Given where we are now, this is a great time for the impeachment process because the election is so near. It would only be a few months after the Vice President takes over as interim President before the new President is elected and then installed. Next question."

"Sir, it is rumored that the Vice President is behind all this, and he has his sights set on the White House. Any comments?" from the MSNTC reporter.

"Well, you need to ask the Vice President about that. As far as I know, he cannot possibly run for election in November because his party's convention is next week, and he has not filed the necessary paperwork with the Federal Election Commission. Last I heard, he planned to retire from public office after President Justice's term ends. But ask him."

"Mr. Speaker, what happens if the Senate fails to convict?" from FTX News.

"Then President Justice remains the President of the United States until January. If that happens, Congress will work with him to uphold the Constitution and govern the country."

———

The White House, August 16

As expected, the President sent his Press Secretary to the podium the following day to denounce the House vote as a partisan and divisive act, taken at a time of national mourning, which would amount to nothing. He also said that the IRS had opened investigations into the Speaker's tax returns for the last seven years after noticing several anomalies and that the FBI was actively investigating the Chairman of the House Judicial Committee for child abuse.

The political theater had just seen its opening act. The impeachment trial was set to begin on August 22. The President's Chief of Staff requested a delay, but the Senate Majority Leader was not in the mood, nor was the Speaker. Both the Speaker and the Judicial Committee Chairman vehemently denounced the charges as political blackmail.

The President called a meeting of his National Security Council and told them that this would all soon pass. To the Secretary of Defense, he told her to continue with RIMPAC, keep a close eye on the PRC Navy near the Scarborough Shoals, but do not engage them under any circumstances. He also told her that the PRC was not to be interfered with during their missile tests on Kwajalein. The economic/trade agreement with the PRC was hanging in the balance, and any small thing might upset them. To the Secretary of State, he told him to complete the economic/trade agreement with the PRC, warts and all, as a weak deal was better than not having one.

"Look, people," said President Justice. "This will all blow over. I have done nothing wrong, and neither have any of you all. This is partisan politics at its worst. The House vote was not that convincing, and the Senate will never go along with this. No way they can muster sixty-seven votes."

The President grabbed his Press Secretary and Chief of Staff as the meeting concluded. He told them to start making the case hard—that the opposition party was being partisan, the impeachment vote in the House was an ugly stain on Congress, that the Senate was more reasonable, and that he was protecting American interests around the globe.

Neither the VP nor the Chairman of the Joint Chiefs of Staff was invited to the National Security Council meeting, so the Secretary of Defense relayed to Chairman Burke the President's guidance on the PRC Navy, Scarborough Shoals, and Kwajalein.

Late that night, Admiral Burke placed a call to the VP.

CHAPTER 28
THE KUDZU STRATEGY

Video Conference from the Pentagon, August 17

THE COMMANDING GENERAL, SPACE AND MISSILE DEFENSE Command convened the classified video conference attended by the Commanding General, Installation Management Command, the Pacific Command J5 Plans Section, Joint Staff J3 Operations Section, COL Seth Grayson, and LTC Ron Bakerson.

"Seth," said the Commanding General of Space and Missile Defense. "We have reviewed the video you sent us and discussed it with the Joint Staff J3 Operations and the Pacific Command J5 Plans. Funny, but they did not seem too surprised. Someday, I will ask you about that. We have also heard the results of Pacific Command's J6's cyberattack assessment and an NSA laydown of the chatter about the AJL and the PRC. The Commander of Pacific Command and I spoke at length about what he sees in the South China Sea, specifically the islands the Chinese continue to build and arm near the Paracels, the Spratlys, and their apparent complete takeover of Scarborough Shoals. It seems there may be a bigger picture being painted by our friends, the ChiComs."

"Sir, I can explain about the video."

"Not now, COL Grayson. We need an honest description of what you and Ron are seeing on the ground in Kwajalein, Aur, Wake, and Majuro. Your meeting with the Ambassador and President Kabua the other day raised eyebrows but got some key people talking. The Chairman is aware of this video conference, so what you say will carry much import, as I will be meeting with the Army Chief of Staff and the Chairman tomorrow. Therefore, make sure you do not exaggerate, but neither should you leave out any detail."

"OK, sir. Since last we talked, the number of armed Chinese on Kwajalein is now around seventy-five. A second PRC aircraft had maintenance problems and had to land at our airfield with twenty-five more armed Chinese soldiers to add to the original fifty. A captain leads them. He is charming to talk to but will not follow my instructions to disarm his men and lock up their weapons while they are here. They have also positioned one armed soldier in the tower with the two FAA air traffic controllers. I had my security contractor put one of his men in the tower, armed, so we are at a Mexican standoff. As a reminder, I have been putting all this in my daily situation reports to Installation Management Command, and Ron has put them in his reports to you, sir."

A long silence ensued as the Commanding Generals of Space and Missile Defense and Installation Management Commands conferred, with the video conference muted. "Yes, you have. Unfortunately, we did not give them enough consideration due to other pressing needs in DC and around the globe, such as Ukraine, Moldova, the 'Luanda Low-ball,' the Caracas Announcement, and, of course, the July 12 attacks, until the Chairman recently talked to me. Now continue."

A much-appreciated admission, thought Seth. *Integrity has a way of showing up, or not, in difficult situations.*

"Roger," said Seth. "At Aur, there are ten armed guards and

about twenty more personnel intent on completing their preparations for their vertically launched missile test. And possibly for manning the railed missile launcher that is part of the apparent swivel launch pad assembly. In addition to being able to launch their test missiles toward Kwajalein's impact sites, something that is not so unusual, we believe they could also aim to the east and north. I am unsure if the missile launcher supports surface-to-air missiles, is for anti-ship missiles, or both. On Wake, the Space and Missile Defense tech tells me a platoon of twenty-five armed Chinese soldiers arrived yesterday, led by a lieutenant. And Ambassador Taylor tells me about fifty PRC business types and approximately fifty armed Chinese soldiers are in Majuro, led by another captain.

"Oh, and significantly, a Chinese major arrived on the same plane with the additional twenty-five soldiers that landed at Kwajalein. Ron and I met him and explained that he and his soldiers had to leave, and until then, they had to surrender their weapons to the security contractor. He just smiled and said they would be going the next day, but that has not happened. We have the same discussion each day. We tried to disarm one of their squads the other day, but it escalated quickly, and we came to another stalemate. The PRC has more armed personnel on Kwaj than I do—seventy-five to twenty security contractor personnel.

"Yesterday, a squad of five Chinese soldiers hopped on one of my catamarans and rode to Roi-Namur. Ron and I weren't sure what they were up to but grew suspicious, had enough time to alert the security contractor, and flew eight of his men to Roi on one of the Hueys. They landed before the catamaran got there and stationed themselves at the KREMS complex, just in case. Good thing, too. The Chinese soldiers showed up at the KREMS but backed down when faced with eight armed contractor personnel and rode the next cat back to Kwaj.

"The Bucholz Airfield and Echo Pier on Kwajalein are crowded with two PRC cargo aircraft and two cargo ships. No heavy military equipment has arrived yet, but one of the cargo ships is loaded with military connex shipping vans, and the cargo airplanes have yet to be offloaded. There is also a PRC Navy frigate in the lagoon, pretending to be part of RIMPAC, and another near Aur Atoll, doing the same.

"It feels like a slow but steady hostile takeover or maybe a "kudzu" offensive strategy. You know kudzu, that noxious weed in the southeastern US along major roads and interstates, quietly growing everywhere, taking over trees, shrubs, and everything. Or better, do you recall the story of the frog and the pot of boiling water? If you throw a frog into a pot of boiling water, it will jump out quickly. However, if you put the frog in the pot of water at room temperature and slowly turn up the heat, the frog will stay in the pot until it is boiled to death. The PRC are slowly taking over Kwaj, Aur, Wake, and Majuro. They are usually quite polite and pleasant but steadfast when we try to impose our rules and restrictions. With the implied rules of engagement we live under, like do not interfere with their testing, it appears that I am the frog, but I have noticed the heat.

"From the way they arrayed their units, it looks like Kwajalein is their primary location, as the largest armed contingent is here and led by a major, but with a significant presence in Majuro and smaller contingents on Aur and Wake."

Seth continued, "As to your assessment that there may be a larger picture being painted, I do not have the same perspective as you all do. But I cannot help but consider the possibility of some linkage between the July 12 attacks, what the PRC is doing in the South China Sea and the Marshalls, and probably what Russia is doing in Ukraine and Moldova. While Putin pushes west using one technique, could China be extending its influence to the east using another?"

"Thanks, Seth. Besides your security contractor's twenty staff members, what other assets do you have out there?" asked the Commanding General of Installation Management Command.

"Sir, I have twenty military personnel assigned to US Army Garrison—Kwajalein Atoll. I have directed that each military member takes one of the security contractor's spare weapons home each night with ammo, mainly M16 and 9mm. That has happened. We also have most of the 65th Brigade Engineer Battalion from Hawaii here for Civic Action Team, or CAT missions. They have three hundred personnel with small arms. I planned to start them on their CAT missions in and around Kwaj and Aur atolls and perhaps out-kudzu the PRC by sheer numbers. We let Pacific Command J3 Operations know about the potential use of the 65th, and they are coordinating with the 25th Division, but no word back yet. However, the CAT teams of the 65th are in position at their project sites and armed."

CHAPTER 29
RECOVERY AND DENIAL

Orlando, Minneapolis, and San Diego, August 17

IT HAD BEEN MORE THAN A MONTH SINCE THE JULY 12 ISLAMIC terrorist attacks. The trail of Abdul and his friends had been traced back to Scottsdale, AZ, but was cold before that.

The effort had changed from search-and-rescue to recovery operations in San Diego, Orlando, and Minneapolis. The cleanup of radioactive materials was in process. FEMA set up regional headquarters in each of the emergency operation centers for Florida, California, and Minnesota, as did Joint Task Force-Civil Support from Northern Command. The regional Joint Task Force cells were extremely effective in coordinating military support to the state governments—always in coordination with FEMA. Government agencies in all three of the attacked states and adjacent states worked feverishly to identify the extent of the environmental impacts and develop mitigation plans. Using the National Incident Management System promoted by FEMA, the regional FEMA office led each region, but the state and county emergency operation centers did most of the heavy lifting. Each county designated an incident commander and received the necessary staff to run things primarily from local governments. Five sections reported to the incident commander. These were operations, plans, logistics, admin/finance, and intel/investigations.[1] This enabled coordinated efforts across most of the nation.

The significant reduction of fresh water in Florida due to the radioactive fallout and the gross alteration of the Florida aquifer was having dire impacts. Fresh water was in critically short supply and the agricultural industry was at a standstill, which included production, packaging and shipping.....everything in the food distribution system.

In coordination with FEMA, the state Emergency Management Office brought in more than two hundred small reverse osmosis water purification units, or ROWPU, from across the nation. They produced fresh water with the ROWPUs and also imposed draconian restrictions on water consumption. The US Army Corps of Engineers Jacksonville District Office issued emergency design-build contracts for new desalinization plants near the Gulf Coast and the Atlantic. Still, these would take at least nine months to bring online, if then. Sadly, much of metropolitan Orlando was evacuated, and the theme park areas just west of town had been essentially obliterated.

In Minneapolis and the surrounding area, including the Great Lakes, radioactive monitoring identified the extent and expected spread of the contamination and radiation, as hospitals were full of new cases of radiation poisoning. The mall area was still too hot to start the cleanup. The blast had severely damaged the US Army Corps of Engineers St. Paul District offices. Hence, the Mississippi River Division (St. Paul's higher headquarters) ordered the Rock Island District to send a mobile team to the twin cities area. They began emergency contracting for clean-up and construction of emergency shelters.

In San Diego, the Petinc Field area was still too hot for cleanup. Geologists and scientists from across the nation convened in Los Angeles to study and discuss the impact and potential for aftershocks based on the movements observed (and felt) to date at the fault lines in the area. While there had been some reaction in the San Andreas Fault region, most experts believed that the "big one" was not imminent. The Corps of Engineers Los Angeles District had the lead for emergency debris removal contracts and other contracts as required in the Southern California area.

An unexpected result of the attack was occurring at San Ysidro Gate. Even though the area was hot with radioactive fallout, tens of thousands of illegal immigrants from Mexico and other Central American countries were streaming into the San Diego area every day. They moved north and east toward specific towns in California and Arizona. All of them had the most current list of sanctuary cities in the states[2] and were heading towards them. San Francisco was the most popular destination as its reputation for protecting and servicing illegal immigrants was well known south of the border. Los Angeles, Oakland, and San Jose were other popular California destinations. Phoenix, Tucson, and Mesa were popular destinations in Arizona. The federal government's failure to prevent illegal sanctuary cities in most of the states was a proximate cause of some of the ever-growing unlawful immigration crises. As the San Ysidro Gate area was officially closed due to the fallout, the Border Patrol pulled all but a few of their agents in chemical/radiological suits off the site. It was basically an open border.

Unfortunately, thousands of those crossing the border were exposed to lethal doses of radioactive fallout. These individuals showed signs of radiation sickness within a few days or weeks. This added to the already over-crowded emergency rooms in

California, Arizona, and other states, caused by the nuclear explosion effects radiating from Petinc Stadium.

Another group that followed the same path was Abdul's follow-on buddies. This was a preplanned assault on the US, and these guys had no illusions as to how long they had to live. No one was sure, but conservative estimates put the number as high as a hundred or more AJL terrorists that had slipped into the Southwestern US. Since they probably knew their lifespan could be counted in weeks, once they passed through the contaminated areas, the expectation was they would begin to hit their assigned targets and targets of opportunity as soon as humanly possible.

That expectation was quickly fulfilled. Car bombs seemed to be the preferred modus operandi (MO) of the terrorists, which indicated they had AJL cell members already in the US. They had secured and prepositioned the cars and loaded them with explosives shortly before the July 12 attacks. Otherwise, the chaos north of the border would have prevented or possibly hindered the acquisition of the cars and explosives. The preferred target for the car bombs included power substations, fire stations, police stations, and the building in the San Diego area where the California emergency operation center had set up, along with the Joint Task Force-Civil Support regional office.

A different group of AJL terrorists attempted to attack the naval base at San Diego, but the Navy's Shore Patrol members thwarted that at the gate, giving their lives in defense of the base. The car bomber sent to Miramar US Marine Corps Air Station was also foiled. The word had gotten out, and the Marines were fully prepared.

Those terrorists not chosen for car bombing duties were armed to the teeth with small arms and machetes and given specific government buildings and banks in the area to enter and kill all they could find. They were very successful initially —the surprise approach was their best friend. Others were directed to soft targets such as malls, churches, synagogues, and movie theaters east of San Diego. The mayhem started in late July and continued through August, covering an area from San Diego, California, to Yuma, Arizona. The National Guard units assigned to recovery operations were quickly re-tasked to work with local police departments to stop this flood of smaller radical Islamic terrorist attacks. Smaller, but no less terrorist and evil in nature.

President Justice contacted the Mexican President and made sure he was aware of the radioactive fallout along the California-Mexican border and subsequent poisoning of those who tried to cross there. President Justice requested the assistance of the Mexican government in containing the flow but to no avail.

Farther to the east in Arizona, there was another kind of problem at the border. The Arizona National Guard was on high alert, and some units were sent to support recovery operations in California. The Secretary of Homeland Security convinced the governor to let the US Border Patrol units maintain control over the border in Arizona without additional Guard personnel. In Sells, Arizona, the newly elected county commissioner of Pima County and freshly elected Sells police chief hailed this decision as a victory for the voice of reason. But in reality, this resulted in dozens of more places along the border that were inadequately secured, causing thousands more illegal crossings

In Texas and New Mexico, the governors did not ask the Department of Homeland Security for additional help. They called up their National Guard units (those not already activated for federal service due to the three terrorist attacks). They sent them to the border to reinforce and ensure that the

Border Patrol effectively stopped the flow of illegal immigrants into the US. When asked about Posse Comitatus limitations which restrict what the military can do, both governors responded that their Guard units would support the Border Patrol and not take over policing the border. However, one does what one needs to do.

———

IT HAD NOT TAKEN LONG for Carlos de Von Heim to move in and take over. First, he opened a new franchise restaurant in Sells. Then he expanded his control of Sells by use of the new police chief and the new county commissioner through selective blackmailing of the other commissioners and threats of physical violence against them and their families if they seemed reluctant. One unexplained death had already occurred, and one commissioner's teenage daughter was kidnapped. Carlos also brought in more "mules" from Mexico and more muscle to maintain control of his organization and his "customers." In short order, more than twenty members of his organization were in the Sells area, doing pretty much what they wanted to do. Carlos sent mobile teams to Phoenix, Santa Fe, and Austin to establish additional "restaurants." He knew this situation would not last long. Sooner or later, some do-gooder would report him, or some news organization would do a broadcast on the "trouble in Sells." But until then, his cartel would reap enormous profits and continue to grow and find other areas where he could expand. Life was good! He simply could not believe his good fortune that the US Government was unwilling or unable to address the fentanyl he was bringing across the border, even though it was a leading cause of death among the young in the US. At his current outrageous profit margin, he would be able to make $100 million before another president could be elected who would secure the border.

———

Sells, Arizona, August 19

Both CTN and FTX reporters had been alerted to strange activity in Sells, Arizona, by anonymous phone calls. When the reporters from those two stations left the heavily damaged San Diego Public Information Office in a hurry, the BTC reporter noticed and followed. As all three correspondents knew each other well and had worked other disasters together, the three quickly shared what they knew and started a three-car convoy to Sells. After driving the four hundred miles to Sells in their HAZMAT (hazardous materials) suits in just under six hours, the three reporters and their cameramen sought a meeting with the mayor. Since they were unable to contact the mayor, they tried the Public Works Director, who met with them on the condition that they take no pictures, alter his voice, and tell no one about him.

The interview was sensational and hit all the airwaves simultaneously on all three networks that evening. Within two hours the governor was interviewed, and he declared he would look into the matter immediately. The Arizona attorney general echoed the same comments.

However, when the President was queried about the situation, he became animated.

———

Washington, DC, August 20

"I am just about fed up with some news organizations that go out of their way to make this administration look bad," said the President. "Look, our border with Mexico is as secure as it has ever been, and we are adding agents to the Border Patrol to ensure they can handle the crisis in San Diego. I am aware that a two-bit drug dealer has crossed into Arizona, but let me tell you, we have known about it for weeks. We are watching him to see what he does and to ensure we do not violate his constitutional rights before we bring charges."

"Sir," said the BTC reporter timidly. "Are you aware that the report is from three very different news organizations with very different political perspectives, and that the operation that has been set up in Sells, is not two-bit? It is large and growing fast and involves some elected American officials. And how does the Constitution afford an illegal immigrant and drug dealer constitutional rights?"

"Rumor and hearsay," responded President Justice. "Except for perhaps in San Diego, our border is secure and controlled thanks to the executive action that we implemented a year ago. I welcome our brothers and sisters from south of the border who want to improve themselves and our nation. Next question."

"Sir," yelled the reporter from CTN. "Any truth to the rumor that the drug cartel action in Arizona is related to the three terrorist attacks, as some in the NSA believe?"

"Poppycock. This news conference is over."

CHAPTER 30
THE PRESIDENT BLINKS

Various places around the world, August 21

PEOPLE EVERYWHERE WATCHED THE EVENING NEWS ON AUGUST 19 and the President's news conference on August 20 that covered the Sells, Arizona situation. That group included the Chinese president, the Russian president, and the leader of the AJL. In what appeared to be a synchronized effort, the Chinese sent several more submarines and their remaining frigates into the South China Sea with the bulk of their naval assets near the Scarborough Shoals and the Spratly Islands. Their island-building operations continued unabated near the Spratlys and the Paracels.

Then suddenly, a dredge flanked by two frigates and led by one submarine stopped just east of the Scarborough Shoals and began dredging operations to build a new island between the shoals and Luzon. Chairman Admiral Burke ordered his US Naval forces to stay in close proximity and report through Pacific Command to him every four hours or more frequently if needed. He also contacted his Philippine counterpart and updated him. He sent word through the Secretary of Defense to the President, of his actions, with nothing in return.

On Kwajalein and neighboring atolls, the PRC forces threw away any pretense of a simple missile test and barred Colonel Grayson and Lieutenant Colonel Bakerson, and any of their staff from visiting Aur Atoll or Wake Island. For his part, Colonel Grayson cut off all support to the PRC and ordered his security contractor to prevent any PRC from using the garrison aviation or naval assets. The security contractor was also able to surprise and overwhelm the armed Chinese soldier in the tower at Bucholz Field and escorted him from the airport. Simultaneously, Seth had the base operations contractor position two of his DASH 7 fixed wings birds and three of his Huey helicopters along the runway and taxiway to prevent any further arrivals of PRC aircraft and provisions. He also positioned his largest ship, the *KMRSS* safety ship, at the South Pass into the lagoon near Carlos Island to physically block any other large PRC Naval vessels from entering it. He positioned a large cargo ship at Tabik Chan Pass near Ebadon and another large cargo ship at Mellu Pass near Roi-Namur.

—————

At about the same time, Vladimir Putin went on state TV in Moscow. He announced that the Ukrainians in the Donbas region and the Moldovan people had just decided to re-enter the Russian Federation. This was as his armored and mechanized forces proceeded to take the remaining portions of Ukraine and overwhelmed Moldova, stopping only at their western borders. Simultaneously, he moved another armored division to his border with Latvia, flew several more sorties into Finland's airspace, and then called the Secretary-General of NATO.

"You have one day to contact the Supreme Allied Commander of Europe, and then the President of the United

States," said Putin. "Have them remove their airborne forces from Latvia, which are there for a supposed training exercise. Unless, of course, the European Union and NATO can continue to exist without gas and oil that used to come through our pipelines to you. You can also forget about beefing up your imports from the Organization of Petroleum Exporting Countries (OPEC) and Venezuela, or even the Chinese. Once the Americans have departed, we will move in to protect our brothers in Latvia from the Americans and their NATO lapdogs. If you do not do this, and we are listening to you, or if the Americans refuse to move out, then I will be forced to move my forces in and rescue Riga. Any bloodshed will be your responsibility. Let's see if article 5 of the NATO charter, 'an attack against one is an attack against all,' is the glue and trigger it is made out to be."

———

IN THE MOST unusual aspect of this highly orchestrated ballet, a large AJL formation armed with abandoned US Abrams M1A3 tanks, Bradley Fighting Vehicles, and several drones went around Ramadi and rolled into the western portion of Baghdad. To say that terror reigned supreme in Baghdad was an understatement of the highest order. In addition to the aforementioned heavy equipment, the AJL also brought with them about twenty-five abandoned Humvees packed with C4 plastic explosives. They used them as improvised explosive devices at every roadblock and other chokepoints to blow their way into the Green Zone. Quickly, they captured the US ambassador and the president of Iraq, set up their TV cameras, and sent a live feed to U-tube. Within minutes, the leader of AJL himself carried out the beheadings on live TV and threatened more such killings if the Americans did not immediately remove their forces from all countries of the Middle East and the "stans."

Furthermore, they had to renounce their support of Israel, cancel the Abraham accords, reject their Christian faith, and allow Sharia law in areas with large Muslim populations in the US, such as Minneapolis, Detroit, and Atlanta. He also publicly stated what the NSA had already guessed, that the AJL attacks on July 12 were planned in conjunction with ISIS and that the hundreds of fighters carrying out more attacks in the US were under the direction of a joint AJL-ISIS-Taliban committee. "There will be more heads rolling, literally, unless I hear from the President within the hour." Then the feed went dark. Quietly, the Shia fighters in Iraq who had been opposing AJL received orders from Tehran to cease fire and infiltrate back to eastern Iraq and then into Iran.

While the impromptu press conference was being conducted, a select team of AJL fighters with clandestine Iranian backing invaded the House of Saud and captured the king. They tortured and killed the king slowly in excruciating pain as his family watched, including the next in line to the throne. The king was drawn and quartered, a process used in centuries gone by, including some European kingdoms in the Middle Ages. It is a process still "alive and well" in some parts of the Middle East. Not wanting to end up like his predecessor, the king-select went on state TV to announce that the king had died of a sudden and massive heart attack and that he and his new regime considered the AJL fighters as friends of Mohammed and worthy of their support and praise. The Saudi-led aggression on Yemen stopped immediately, and they reoriented their ground and air forces toward Jordan and Israel. The Russian military in Syria rejected all pretenses about fighting AJL and viciously attacked the rebel forces on the ground, shoring up the Assad government. A tenuous cease-fire among the Russian forces, the Assad forces, and the AJL went into effect in Syria, tacitly ceding portions of eastern and northern Syria to the AJL.

It was stunning in its tenacity and ferociousness. In a matter of days, a rejuvenated AJL caliphate sprung into being, as only Jordan, Egypt, Morocco, Lebanon, and what was left of Assad's Syria had refused to join their Islamic brothers from the Middle East and Northern Africa. But the handwriting was on the wall. To some, there appeared to be a two-headed hydra in that part of the world, growling and snarling at each other, but working together when necessary—a Sunni-dominant caliphate led by AJL and a nuclear-armed Shiite Iran supported by Lebanon and a fractured Syria.

Late that night, President Justice spoke to the head of NATO, then the Supreme Allied Commander of Europe, and then he talked to the AJL leader. The press conference was scheduled for early the following day.

The Rose Garden, August 22

The President started slowly. "As most of you know, there have been a number of occurrences around the world over the last few weeks and months, and indeed, the last few days and even hours. Concerning the Russian aggression, I have been in contact with our NATO allies, and we are in accordance over what to do. In order for oil and gas to flow back into Western Europe and prevent bloodshed on a massive scale, we agree if the Ukrainian Donbas and Moldovan people want to re-enter the Russian Federation, then we should not stand in the way. There will be a special referendum held next month in Ukraine's Donbas region and Moldova to put that notion to the vote. Until then, Russian forces will remain in both countries to keep the peace. If the referendum reveals that the Ukrainians or Moldovans want to stay independent, then so be it, and President Putin has agreed to withdraw. As for Latvia, our military training exercise with them is now complete, and we are returning those forces to Fort Liberty (formerly known as Fort Bragg) starting three days from now. The Latvian president has indicated his preference for a new trading relationship with Russia, which will take advantage of and use the new port facilities in Riga.

"In the Middle East, it now appears that AJL has taken over much of Iraq, including Baghdad, and that most of the citizens in that country are sympathetic to their cause. While I condemn their methods and the beheadings of government officials, including our own ambassador, we must all yield to their tenacity and pure motives for the creation of a caliphate in the Middle East. Of course, I cannot and will not demand that all Americans renounce Christianity and convert to Islam, nor do I renounce Israel, although their past actions in large part are somewhat responsible for AJL's rise to power. Therefore, we are withdrawing all support for the Abraham Accords.

"I acknowledge AJL as the de facto government of Iraq. We have agreed to take into consideration their request for selective Sharia law implementation in the US for our Muslim brothers where they have a significant presence. In response, the AJL leadership assured me that the jihadist attacks here in America would cease immediately.

"Finally, I am aware of the PRC's actions in the South China Sea, and I am a little concerned about the apparent exceedance of their authorities under the South China Sea Paradigm for Progress and the scenarios of RIMPAC. Therefore, I am calling back our forces from RIMPAC in the South China Sea to make it clear to the PRC that we will not tolerate such action. They must play by the rules if they want to participate in any future RIMPAC exercise. I am not taking any questions."

The room full of reporters sat in stunned silence. The President of the United States had just blinked, and blinked, and blinked. Western Europe, long too dependent on Russian and OPEC oil and gas, was now paying the price for it, as were the Ukrainians, Moldovans, and Latvians. The South China Sea was just handed over to the PRC without so much as an acknowledgment of the mutual defense treaty with the Philippines. And the President had just apparently indicated his approval of Sharia law in American cities with large Muslim populations.

Unstated, but not going away, was the strange linkage among the AJL, ISIS, the Taliban, and Iran—Sunni and Shia terrorist organizations fighting each other on the ground at the tactical level. But working with each other at the operational and strategic levels for larger goals such as the caliphate or humiliating the United States and obliterating Israel? It was perhaps the scariest result of the administration's foreign policy or lack thereof.

Admiral Burke was livid. His Commander in Chief was timid at best, he thought, as he turned off the newscast of the President's press conference. And while perhaps not a "domestic" enemy of the constitution, President Justice was certainly no friend to it, Burke mused to himself.

The Chairman called the Commander of Pacific Command on his secure line. "To clarify what you heard during the press conference today, you will not immediately pull your RIMPAC naval forces from the South China Sea. We must adequately prepare to safely extricate our forces from such a large international exercise as RIMPAC in the midst of such international turmoil. Put your ships between the PRC Navy and Scarborough Shoals as best you can without drawing fire.

Contact the Pacific Fleet and tell him to assemble two CVBGs (carrier group task forces), and start steaming west—one will take up position between Guam and Kwajalein and the other will steam toward the South China Sea. Contact US Army Pacific and put the 25th Infantry Division and all attached and supporting US Army Hawaii assets on high alert. Also, notify US Army Alaska to put the reactivated 11th Airborne Division on alert.[1] Give Commander, Marine Forces Pacific a heads-up also. Put him on notice that I may need First Marine Expeditionary Force at Kaneohe to have a Marine Air-Ground Task Force ready to go within forty-eight hours. Put the Marine forces at Camp Blaz on Guam on alert also.

"And just so you know, I am also telling the Commander of Special Operations Command and Special Operations Command–Pacific to prepare several Operational Detachments Alpha (ODA) for airdrop as required.[3] Cancel all leaves and stop all ETS (estimated time of service) and retirement actions. If these prep actions somehow leak or when they leak and you are asked by the press, tell them that this is related to the Commander in Chief's directive to us regarding RIMPAC, and are in preparation for safely extracting ourselves from the South China Sea and the RIMPAC exercise area."

"OK, boss, but I gotta tell you, this sounds a bit disingenuous. We are supposed to be pulling out of the RIMPAC exercise area in the South China Sea immediately."

"Right," said Admiral Burke. "And we will, and these actions will facilitate that. These are very tense times and a miscalculation on our part or the Chinese could have grossly negative consequences. We don't want the PRC to misread or take advantage of our extraction. You and I have had several long discussions over recent policy directives as they relate to China, the Mutual Defense Treaty with the Philippines, and what some consider presidential overreaches by the current

President. This includes his use of executive action to excess. Well, now he is undergoing the impeachment process, and I believe he is not thinking correctly or not understanding what we are seeing and telling him. I know he is not getting the correct picture from the Secretary of Defense and the Secretary of State. I believe that if he were in his right mind, he would order something similar to what I am telling you. How palatable is that? I am not saying that he should be considered part of the 'against all enemies, foreign and domestic' clause of our oath of office, but something is terribly wrong in DC. He is, in effect, capitulating to the enemy before we have engaged them, but based on incomplete information from some of his other senior advisors. His current guidance to us could have long-term negative consequences. The Vice President, Chief of Naval Operations, and Chief of Staff of the Army are aware of what I am telling you and are in agreement. I am waiting for the Marine Corps Commandant and Chief of Staff of the Air Force to call me back."

"Uhhh," said the head of Pacific Command. "OK, I am on board. Can you please send me a classified email to this effect, one that gives me a clear mission statement? I will respond with my assent."

"Consider it done," yelled Admiral Burke. "Your CYA email will be there within thirty minutes, but get your forces moving now. The Joint Staff J3 Operations Section is drafting the alert order as we speak. Make hard contact with the J3 in the National Military Command Center ASAP. I have to talk to the Supreme Allied Commander Europe about a totally different matter. Out."

CHAPTER 31
THE SENATE TRIAL

Washington, DC, August 22

THE IMPEACHMENT TRIAL STARTED AT TEN THAT MORNING. THE President refused to attend but sent a low-level staffer from the Attorney General's office and his Chief of Staff to monitor the events. Reporters and cameras from across the globe were in the chambers, as tension was sky-high even before the gavel came down.

The Chief Justice of the Supreme Court sat as Judge, ninety-nine senators sat as the jury, and five congressmen from the states of New York, California, Florida, Texas, and Iowa served as the prosecutors—all as prescribed by the US Constitution. One senator was confined to his bed at Bethesda Naval Hospital, undergoing some intensive cancer treatment. He watched the proceedings via closed circuit TV hook-up and had a direct phone line to the Senate floor to ask questions and vote when it came time.

The senior congressman first made a motion that the senator in the hospital be considered "not present" since he was not physically in the Senate Chambers. After much hullabaloo from the Attorney General's staffer, the Chief Justice said he would take the motion under advisement. The senior congressman then presented the five charges and made the general case for impeachment to the Senate. Then the President's Chief of Staff, who was also a lawyer, made a simple statement that the charges against the President were unfounded and politically driven, that no matter what the outcome, the President intended to serve his entire elected term of office, and he sat down.

For the next three days, the congressional prosecutors presented their evidence and arguments for each of the five charges, with challenges occasionally raised by the staffer from the Attorney General's office.

Witnesses for the prosecution included the Chairman of the Joint Chiefs, Admiral Halsey Burke, the Commander of Pacific Command, the Commanding Generals of Space and Missile Defense Command and Installation Management Command, the Director of the NSA, Colonel Seth Grayson, Lieutenant Colonel Ron Bakerson, Colonel Will Bishop, and Jill Bishop. Occasionally, the testimony was of such a classified nature that the Chief Justice convened a smaller working group, with all parties concerned represented, in the Senate Armed Services Committee's secure conference room. Afterward, he summarized what had transpired for the whole Senate in an unclassified way.

The Attorney General staffer tried to have the Secretary of Defense and the Secretary of State testify on behalf of the President, but both declined per direction from President Justice. The administration sent a note to the Chief Justice informing him that the Secretary of State was in Beijing to sign the long-awaited trade agreement with China, for which the UN's South China Sea Paradigm For Progress played an integral role. The note also stated that the Secretary of Defense was in Amsterdam for a meeting with the European Union related to climate change. The Congressional Prosecutors had subpoenaed both the Secretary of Defense and the Secretary of State as hostile witnesses, but neither appeared, given their "pressing" needs overseas. Nor did the Secretary of Homeland Security, Interior, or the Press Secretary, all of whom were subpoenaed. The President's Chief of Staff was also subpoenaed, and he appeared long enough to assert executive privilege and then leave the room.

Each evening, the Press Secretary would hold the daily news briefing and refuse to comment on the proceedings or even acknowledge their existence. He did comment on the recovery operations, and the fact that Russia had turned the oil back on for Western Europe, the fighting had stopped in Ukraine, and the terrorist attacks in the US were slowing down.

When reminded that the terrorist attacks were supposed to stop immediately, the Press Secretary responded that it would probably take a little while for that order to filter down to all the operatives in the field. He did not say that the main reason the attacks were slowing was that the jihadists' numbers were decreasing as they blew themselves up or died of radiation poisoning.

When asked about increased US Naval activity in and around the South China Sea, the alert status of the 25th Infantry Division, and rumors about Marine Forces Pacific preparing to stand up a Marine Air Ground Task Force, the Press Secretary balked. Eventually, he said that all those actions were related to the ENDEX of RIMPAC and the withdrawal from the South China Sea, as the Secretary of Defense had told him. When pressed for an explanation of the two carrier battle groups heading toward the South China Sea, he seemed caught off guard and abruptly ended the press conference.

———

August 25

The congressman from Florida took the floor on the morning of the fourth day of the impeachment hearing. As he asked for quiet, three protestors who were apparent fans of the President ran down the aisle carrying a US flag, a UN flag, and a Honduran flag. They shouted in Spanish and English, "*Fronteras abiertas, ahora! Fronteras abiertas, ahora!* Open borders now! Open borders now!"

It took about thirty minutes for the capital police to clear the three from the room, along with the other fifteen protestors just waiting for the flag bearers to make their run before joining the fracas. But finally, cooler heads prevailed, and the proceedings continued.

The Florida congressman started again. "Your Honor. Ladies and gentlemen of the Senate. We have spent the last three days laying out the case for a guilty verdict of President Roland Justice for the five charges stated. We presented the evidence and witnesses for each charge. We then offered the opportunity for the administration to cross-examine, present their own evidence and witnesses, and counter each charge. As you have seen, the administration not only chose not to cross-exam our witnesses, but they did not present their own evidence or witnesses. In fact, they were pretty much absent from the proceedings except for one staffer from the Attorney General's office and the occasional 'drive-by' of the President's Chief of Staff.

"We, the Congressional Prosecution Team, have answered your questions to the best of our abilities. We have presented the case for each charge to the best of our abilities and have actively sought input from the President and his advisors but to no avail. The prosecution rests. At this point, we defer to the Senate Majority Leader."

"Now, just a minute," shouted the Chief Justice, loudly pounding his gavel on the podium behind which he sat. "Per the constitution, I preside over these proceedings, not a handful of wet-behind-the-ears congressmen. All of you, sit down."

"As we all know, there is not a lot of precedence for impeachment trials involving the President of the United States. And when we consider the four cases that were tried, I think we can agree that the Andrew Johnson, Bill Clinton, and the first Trump impeachment were politically motivated and overreaches of the parties in power. The current proceedings have the same aroma and…"

Before he could say another word, the Senate Majority Leader was on his feet. "Your honor. You are discrediting yourself and the US Senate. Did you not see the evidence? Did you not hear the witnesses, some of whom are senior administration members?"

"Sit down, senator."

"No, I will not sit down, your honor. We are in the Senate Chambers, of which I am the majority leader. Your duties here are to preside over the proceedings and ensure we follow the law, and provide due process for the President, which we have done. You are not here to impose your personal preferences for or against the administration."

"But I am here to preside over the proceedings, as you have just confirmed, senator, and presiding I am. So, sit down, senator, before I have you forcibly removed. I will make a ruling if you are so kind as to sit down and shut up. Bailiff, please seat the good senator," and the Chief Justice wrapped his gavel loudly, over and over, until he had the attention of all ninety-nine senators, the congressional prosecution team, and the world via the live feeds from all major news networks.

"Now, I want the Senate Majority Leader, the head of the Congressional Prosecution Team, and the Attorney General's staffer to meet me in my chambers at my Supreme Court office in fifteen minutes. This hearing is adjourned until I return, which will be in about two hours."

Stunned was too mild a word. Nothing was said for about two minutes as the Chief Justice left the room. The Senate Majority Leader conferred with the head of the Congressional Prosecution Team. "Why don't we just move ahead without him?" asked the Senator. "The evidence has been presented, and the witnesses have been examined."

"But he is the Chief Justice of our Supreme Court, and by the Constitution, he does preside over the proceedings. We have to follow his lead," said the Congressman.

"But what kind of ruling can he make at this stage?" asked the Senator.

"He's a judge, and for the moment, your Senate floor is his courtroom. He can do pretty much what he deems legal and constitutional," whispered the Congressman. "And we have no recourse but to do whatever he says or decides."

Two hours later, the Senate Majority Leader, the congressman, and the Attorney General's staffer took their seats on the floor of the Senate. None of them were smiling. All the other members of the Senate were already seated, with the one senator watching from Bethesda while his senior aide was on the Senate floor. Every camera focused on the door from which the Chief Justice would enter.

It seemed like an eternity until the Judge entered, but it was only three or four minutes. The Chief Justice strode in, and all rose to their feet. The silence was deafening. While there was no sound in the room, no one could hear anyone else. It was like white noise ruled the Senate chamber airwaves for a few seconds.

Wham! resounded the gavel as it hit the podium so hard that the head separated from the shaft of the gavel and flew toward the Senate Majority Leader.

"Before anything else happens in this courtroom, in these hallowed halls where great men such as Adlai Stevenson, Howard Baker, and Ted Kennedy used to legislate, I will now issue my rulings.

"As to the charges, I rule that charges 1, 3, 4, and 5 are without merit, and the House prosecutors presented insufficient evidence to warrant any action. These proceedings may continue based only on Charge 2. To wit, the President exceeded his constitutional authority by approving a treaty with the UN and specifically the PRC regarding the South China Sea Paradigm for Progress employing an executive agreement. That agreement directed the Secretary of State to continue working on the refinement and implementation of the South China Sea Paradigm for Progress, even after the US Senate had rejected the proposed treaty, 30—70. This one was tough because there is much precedence for Presidents approving international agreements via the executive agreement route instead of using the Senate's advise and consent process. But in this case, the Senate did act, and the vote was 70—30 not to approve the proposed South China Sea Paradigm for Progress. So, for the President to proceed is rightly called into question.

"As to the process going forward from here, I rule that the US Senate must decide whether the good Senator who is in the hospital at Bethesda but who has taken part in all the deliberations via closed circuit TV and phone line is considered as being part of the 'members present' or not, before any vote can occur on Charge 2. I further rule that the Senate must make a formal and public decision on this matter. The net result will be whether one hundred or ninety-nine senators will constitute the 'members present' of the Senate for the verdict. More simply, will sixty-seven or sixty-six senators be required for a guilty verdict—if it goes that way."

Senators, Congressmen, American citizens, and news pundits were aghast. Yes, charge 2 was serious and should be included in the trial, but even more so was charge 1, which included the terrorist attack on 12 July. How could that not be included? It took a long time before the Senators calmed down.

The Senate being what it is, formal and process-driven if nothing else, adjourned for the rest of the day while the Senate Majority Leader met with the Senate Minority Leader, both Whips, and the President Pro Tem. The Vice President recused himself from the meeting and anything to do with the procedural vote that could decide the President's fate.

When all was said and done, they decided to have four hours of discussion on the issue the next day as a Committee of the Whole and then take a vote for cloture at noon, which required sixty votes to stop the discussion. Then, they would vote whether the senator at Bethesda was part of the constitutionally dictated "members present" or not by a simple majority. The Senate Majority Leader held an impromptu news conference to relay their plan. He took no questions.

———

August 26

By a vote of sixty to forty (the senator in the hospital was allowed to weigh in on the process), with much of the world watching, the Senate voted for cloture of the issue at noon. Then by a vote of fifty-one to forty-nine that strictly followed party lines, the Senate voted that the senator in the hospital would not be considered as part of the "members present" for the verdict on the impeachment charge. While there was obviously some waffling on issues related to the process, it appeared that the Senate would not have the necessary sixty-six votes required for a guilty verdict if party lines (and loyalty) held true.

LATE THAT NIGHT, the President was taking no chances, so he met with his Chief of Staff and prepared a short executive action, adjourning the Senate for the next week, effectively immediately. He then sent it via secure email to the Senate Majority Leader and the Chief Justice. Then he sent an email to Admiral Burke, relieving him from duty as the Chairman of the Joint Chiefs of Staff and appointing no one in his place, which meant the Vice-Chairman would act in his place, temporarily. The Chairman's position is in the direct chain of command for the nation's combat forces, from the President to the Secretary of Defense and then the Chairman. It was essential to have someone still designated for that role.

August 27

The Senate Chambers were packed again as the Chief Justice brought his gavel down on the podium on the dais. The mood was not quite as somber as the previous few days, as most expected the vote to be no better than sixty to thirty-nine for a guilty verdict. This would not meet the constitutionally required two-thirds of members present, which in this case, were sixty-six of the ninety-nine members present. The President's Chief of Staff represented President Justice and his administration. He was smiling and waving to a few senators he knew, especially ones he knew would be part of the essential thirty-four or maybe thirty-five or more!

Hardcore supporters of the President. Party loyalty above all else, he mused quietly. *So, what if they ignored the adjournment executive action from the President; it was on flakey legal ground anyway.*

A roll call vote has its pros and cons. On the one hand, it lets a senator's constituency see what their senator thinks about an issue in public. For the popular or non-contentious issues, it would look good in the newspapers—instant gratification. On the other hand, for complex issues, as the vote proceeded and if the vote was very close, there could be tremendous pressure on some of the last to vote. This was especially true if they were uncertain of their position or did not want the public or the President to know how they voted as they voted. Not that it wouldn't become public information later on, but the pressure of the moment could be overwhelming.

As the last senator stood to make known her position, the vote incredibly stood at 65–33. It was apparent to all that the actions of the President over the last few months had angered more than just the opposition party! But now, all eyes were on her. She was a junior senator from the high plains west, one known to curry favor with the administration and his party—a former US Army officer and West Point graduate, with two tours in Iraq and one in Afghanistan. The President's Chief of Staff had called her the night before to make sure she would toe the party line, that is, that the entire impeachment process was politically motivated and a mockery of justice. She questioned the timing of his phone call but agreed that there was some degree of political hanky panky involved in the process. And then she told him that she would do what was best for the nation at this point in time. The President's Chief of Staff immediately took that as support of President Justice.

What the Chief of Staff knew and what the President was banking on was that she was also a constitutional lawyer, scholar, and patriot. Her country and the party needed her to be strong! As she rose and made her remarks, she electrified the room.

"My fellow senators and all the Americans watching these proceedings," she said. "Let me start by saying that I am a big fan of the President and most of the policies he has implemented. He has supported women's rights and a process for bringing at least eleven million undocumented immigrants out of the shadows. He opposes the Supreme Court's recent decision on Roe v Wade. He supports our LGBTQ brothers and sisters. He was at my election headquarters last year, and we toasted my win. I named my son Roland after him. He is my hero for all that he has done to put this country on the right track."

She paused for what seemed like an eternity. Cameras clicked and whirred. The Senate Majority Leader was visibly shaken and leaned over to say something to the Pro Tem when she continued. "And I am an even bigger fan of the Constitution and its inherent checks and balances. The Senate is the body charged with the advise and consent role in several areas by that Constitution and is also charged with hearing any impeachment charges brought to us by the House. If we fail to act in accordance with the Constitution to preserve its integrity when it is under siege, even in the face of a charismatic and popular president, then what are we? Who are we? And how long can a self-governing people remain free when the 'members present' refuse to follow their own processes and procedures?"

A smile appeared across the face of the President's Chief of Staff. *The Senate's vote to disallow the good senator's vote from his Bethesda hospital suite did not sit well with her,* he thought.

This will come back to bite the Senate Majority Leader in the rear, he thought.

But as she continued, the Chief of Staff's countenance dropped, unsure of the rabbit trail she was on.

"I am reminded of Brevet Major William Jenkins Worth's Battalion Order, issued on December 22, 1820, at West Point. It says: 'But an officer on duty knows no one—to be partial is to dishonor both himself and the object of his ill-advised favor. What will be thought of him who exacts of his friends that which disgraces him? Look at him who winks at and overlooks offenses in one, which he causes to be punished in another, and contrast him with the inflexible soldier who does his duty faithfully, notwithstanding it occasionally wars with his private feelings. The conduct of one will be venerated and emulated, the other detested as a satire upon soldiership and honor.'" She paused and smiled. "Right is right, and wrong is wrong, whether as an individual or an organization, no matter how far up the flag pole they have risen.

"Has there been an offense in this case against the constitution? And if so, should we wink at it or correct it, and who committed it—the President or the Congress?"

Every eye was trained on her. Every media microphone boom inched closer to her. No one in the room was breathing, let alone making any noise. The only sound was that of a clock ticking under the balcony that seemed to slow down and echo loudly: it is time. It is time. It is time.

"I vote guilty on Charge 2."

The Senate floor exploded into a cacophony of noises and cheers and expletives. The press area instantly vacated as reporters dashed to talk to their contacts in the Senate. Some talking heads immediately sent live feeds of themselves talking about the momentous decision, while some read prepared statements about the illegality of the decision taken by the

Senate. Others cried, and some were even speechless for a little while.

Guilty, 66–33 stood the final tally, two-thirds of the votes, two-thirds of the "members present" all day long.

The Chief Justice had a shocked look on his face and quickly escaped from the Senate Chambers and made his way back to the Supreme Court building. He ripped up the President's e-mail and then deleted it from this computer. At least, he hoped it was gone.

The vote was heard around the world. It was more than electrifying. It was shocking. It was compelling. It was ridiculous. It was illegal. It was unconstitutional. It was the greatest thing since sliced bread. It was Armageddon. It was about time. It all depended on where you stood on the Constitution for some Americans. For others, it all turned on which party you identify with. And for far too many—who cares? What vote? Will this have any impact on my welfare check? Can I still use any restroom I want to, male or female, based on how I feel that morning?

But in the larger picture, this was a first. No president had ever been found guilty of high crimes and misdemeanors before. What was the next step? How could the government processes possibly continue uninterrupted? How and when would the transition take place? Most assumed the Vice President would automatically become the President, and they were almost correct, but only after he was legally sworn in. But who would be the new VP? When Nixon stepped down, he had already replaced Vice President Spiro Agnew with Gerald Ford, who became the first and only unelected president in our nation's history.

The current legal line of succession for the presidency is the Vice President, followed by the Speaker of the House, followed by the President Pro Tem of the Senate. It almost makes sense that the Vice President, once he moved up to the position of President, might nod to the Speaker to take his position as VP. But the 25th Amendment provides a process to select a new Vice President. It was used for the first time when Gerald Ford nominated Nelson Rockefeller as the new VP after Ford became President when Nixon resigned.

———

No one knew what would happen next, as the Vice President called a meeting that night at his quarters with the Chairman of the Joint Chiefs, the Speaker of the House, the Senate Majority Leader, and the Attorney General. The Secretary of Defense had been invited as part of the national command authority (NCA), but she declined the meeting. The Secretary of State was not invited, nor were any other department heads. The Chief Justice feigned illness and sent his clerk instead.

"Mr. Vice President, or I guess I should say, Mr. President, I want you to know that President Justice sent me an email late last night ordering me to adjourn the Senate for a week to forestall the vote, I guess. I ignored it, as he does not have that authority. But you should know that," said the Senate Majority Leader.

"OK, thanks, Bob. What we want to do at this meeting is lay out the next steps now that the Senate has found the President guilty of Charge 2. The only recourse now is his removal from office, which I expect he will acknowledge sometime tomorrow. But what happens next? We are in uncharted waters."

"Sir," said Admiral Burke, "So, that you know, the President relieved me of my duties as the Chairman last night. Here is the email."

The Attorney General spoke next. "Gentlemen, as you know, I am a long-time supporter of President Justice, and I am very saddened by the events of the last few days and by the vote the Senate made. However, his last-minute executive action to adjourn the Senate was done without my knowledge and was patently absurd. He is becoming desperate. The Chief Justice's rulings on the charges, while perhaps politically motivated, or perhaps he was misreading the vibes in the Senate, are legal and will stick. I am surprised he let Charge 2 stand. Still, he did, probably because talk radio made such a fuss about his executive action and the executive agreement to override the Senate's 70–30 vote on the South China Sea Paradigm for Progress. It was quite an overreach. He also let the Senate decide on what constitutes 'members present' as it falls under the rubric of the Senate deciding how to run the Senate. Perhaps, he thought the Senate would never reach the required cloture count of sixty or that the final vote on Charge 2 would be 60–39, or at worst, 65–34 instead of 66–33."

"What I am saying is that the decision has been made. I'm not too fond of it, but it was legally sound. So, some next steps from my perspective are as follows:

1. Find a federal judge to swear the Vice President in as President.
2. Nominate a new Vice President. I suggest you leave the Speaker and the President Pro Tem out of that discussion, as it might look self-serving if either one of them is even in the mix for consideration.
3. I assume you will want to keep Admiral Burke on as the Chairman, so issue a voco order to reinstate him as soon as possible, with no service break.
4. Talk to the current department heads about staying on, at least the ones you can work with. Then develop some good candidates to replace the ones you just cannot live with for the next four to five

months. The seconds in command, the 2-ICs, AKA the Deputy Secretaries, will have to step up while this is happening. Or you may choose to let the deputies just run out the clock until after the elections and the January swearing-in ceremony of the newly elected president, whoever that may be. As for me, I am resigning after this meeting.

5. Appoint a press secretary and hold a press conference ASAP.
6. Work with the Pentagon on some sort of strategies for what is going on in Europe, China, and the Middle East."

And to the Vice President—the new President—the Attorney General added, "I know you have already stated that you have no intention of running for president this year, but I highly recommend you state that again, emphatically, in public. And then make sure you do not change your mind. If you do, I will do everything in my power to roll back the recent events based on ulterior motives. Nothing would stick, of course, but I would make things miserable for you."

The new President shook his head and replied, "I will gladly make that announcement on several occasions in the near future. I have no Political Action Committee or election committee set up, nor was I registered or on the ballot for any primary. My only purpose for the next few months is to shepherd the country to the next election and then hand it off to whomever the people elect. I will also do my best to make the transition from President Justice and his team to our interim team as smooth, painless, and professional as possible. You have my word and my handshake on that." The Attorney General refused the handshake.

CHAPTER 32
POTUS REACTS STRONGLY

Washington, DC, August 28

PRESIDENT ROLAND JUSTICE WAS IN NO MOOD FOR A RECALCITRANT and blustery Senate that was obviously bent on finding him guilty of high crimes and misdemeanors. Just who did they think they were? He, Roland, was the elected President of the United States, the POTUS, the most powerful man on the face of the earth, leading the most powerful nation in the history of mankind.

As he took the podium in the Rose Garden that morning for the hastily called press conference, most reporters and onlookers expected to hear his formal resignation, acceptance of the Senate's guilty verdict, or some sort of remorse on his part. Were they ever in for a surprise!

Not the usual group of credentialed White House Press Corps awaited his comments. Only NTC, MSNTC, CTN, and Al-Jazeera, along with the *New York City Crier* and *Washington Chronicle*, had been invited, with strict instructions to tell no one else about the press conference on pain of expulsion from the White House Press Corps and pulling credentials.

"My fellow Americans and distinguished members of the

Press Corps. Yesterday, the US Senate voted on the issue of Charge 2 of the impeachment charges that the House preferred a few days ago. That kangaroo court completed their 'hanging' by finding me guilty of Charge 2. However, that entire process was flawed and illegal for many reasons.

"First, the charges were politically motivated, and my administration did not participate in the proceedings. We all have plenty of things to keep us busy these days without the political rhetoric of my opponents. Russia, AJL, the South China Sea, and of course, the recovery from the recent terrorist attacks should be our focus and will be our focus as we advance.

"Second, I adjourned the Senate twenty-four hours prior to their vote by written executive action, so their vote is null and void. Both the Chief Justice and the Senate Majority Leader received that executive 'adjournment' notice from me the day before, and apparently, both chose to ignore it.

"Third, the vote was actually 66—34, which does not meet the required two-thirds vote per the Constitution. The Senate Majority Leader did not allow the senator confined to his bed in Bethesda to vote even though he actively participated in the proceedings via closed-circuit TV and phone. I spoke to him yesterday, and he confirmed that he would have voted not guilty. He was the thirty-fourth dissenting vote!

"Therefore, by executive order, I pronounce the Senate's vote null and void and adjure them to get back to work.

"I am firmly in control of my administration and have taken the following steps to ensure the American people that their president is on the job and looking out for them. These steps include:

1. Order the Secret Service to maintain their standard protection of me vigorously.

2. Request the resignation of the Chairman of the Joint Chiefs of Staff, Admiral Halsey Burke, for failing to follow my orders to him regarding RIMPAC and withdrawing our forces from the South China Sea.
3. Request the Vice President to submit his resignation within two days for his deception regarding this entire fiasco.
4. Request the Chief Justice submit his resignation within two days for his failure to follow my executive action regarding the adjournment.
5. Suggest the Senate Majority Leader's governor remove him from office and appoint a new Senator.
6. Order the Secretary of Defense to recall our forces from RIMPAC, including those sent by Admiral Burke, which exceeds what is necessary for extraction from the exercise.
7. Call on the European Union to become more proactive in its defense of Europe and learn how to manage its relationship with Russia better.
8. Approval of the long-awaited trade agreement with China by executive agreement, which has the South China Sea Paradigm for Progress as an integral part of its terms of reference.

"Finally, let me applaud the hardworking Americans who are putting their lives on the line daily during our recovery operations. They should be the headlines today, above the fold, not the Senate's misguided and illegal vote.

"Let's get back to work."

———

Chairman's Office, Pentagon, August 28

Unbeknownst to the White House Press Corps reporters in the Rose Garden that day—except for the CTN crew, which was invited to both press conferences—the Vice President and the Chairman were holding a joint news conference at nearly the same time. Their meeting was in the Chairman's office at the Pentagon with CTS, ATC, CTN, FTX, the BTC, and the *Wall Street Sentinel*. The Vice President, the new President, also had persuaded the Attorney General to remain on the payroll for the press conference in case questions of legality arose. Of course, having the Attorney General at that press conference instead of being with President Justice would significantly suggest legitimacy merely by his presence.

"Ladies and gentlemen of the press, and to all Americans who are watching, listening, online, and those who will read about this tomorrow. Thank you for your patience over these last few weeks and your understanding as we begin implementing the decision of the US Senate, finding the President guilty of Charge 2 of the five charges proffered by the House.

"We are in unchartered waters, on new and unstable grounds. No President has ever been impeached and then also found guilty before. However, we know from the resignation of President Nixon in 1974 that we can survive this constitutional crisis and come out stronger than ever.

"I was just made aware that President Justice has completed his news conference and seems determined not to move. However, I appeal to his sense of fairness and legality, which will enable him to understand that he must step down and he needs to release the reins. He must abide by the decision of the Senate, which followed the constitutional process. Two-thirds of those senators present voted guilty. Senators from both parties and the two independent senators voted guilty. This was not a party line or politically motivated vote. The Chief Justice he appointed allowed Charge 2 to stand and the Senate to decide the issue of 'members present.'

"I am working with the Department of Defense and Chairman Burke to refine or develop strategies and operational plans to address our national security interests. These include Europe as it relates to Russia, the Far East as it relates to China and the South China Sea and Taiwan, the Middle East as it relates to AJL and the revived caliphate, and here at home as it relates to our porous borders and inconsistent policies on immigration. The last one has resulted in foreign and homegrown fighters carrying out radical Islamic terrorist attacks against the United States.

"On the home front, thirty-one governors have already contacted me about the transition from President Justice's administration to the interim administration I will put in place until the November elections and the January swearing-in ceremony. The Secretary of Homeland Defense and the Director of FEMA are on board, as are the Secretary of the Treasury and the Secretary of Health and Human Services. Unfortunately, the Attorney General who is here with us today as an act of legal affirmation of the impeachment process is resigning tomorrow. I am accepting the resignations of all other department heads and will employ the Deputy Secretaries as my department heads until January. Please bear with us as we sort out who is staying and who is moving on in each department and agency.

"I am now actively considering several names for appointment as the new Vice President, as I was sworn in as the President late last night by the Chief Judge of the Eastern District of Virginia.

"As for the South China Sea and our relationship with the PRC, I am hereby revoking the United States' approval of the

South China Sea Paradigm for Progress and the trade agreement that President Justice says he approved, even though the Senate did not approve it. As those were executive agreements, and he is no longer the chief executive, they are no longer in effect. I am also reviewing the recently 'approved' UN Treaty on Global Climate Change to see what is in the treaty that may be of use and what is not.

"Included in the review process is the immediate rejection of the 20 percent additional reduction of CO_2 emissions, the ban on fracking, and the closing of all coal-fired power production facilities. That is not to say there are no issues embedded within those areas that need further review and resolution, but the meat cleaver used on them was inappropriate.

"Additionally, while some in the press and at the Pentagon are aware, most Americans are probably unaware of the aggressive actions the PRC has been taking in the South China Sea. This includes creating and militarizing new islands near the Spratly Islands, arming Woody Island in the Paracels, blocking commercial traffic across the South China Sea, and even expelling Philippine forces from their own Scarborough Shoals. Eastward of that, in the middle of the Pacific, their illegal occupation and use of portions of the US Army's Reagan Test Site on Kwajalein for what appears to be future offensive actions will not be allowed to stand.

"To counter this aggression, Chairman Burke and his staff have been working with our allies to form a coalition that will force China to reconsider its moves. So far, the following nations are in agreement with us and will provide forces, overflight rights, basing support, and financial support. These nations are the UK, Australia, New Zealand, the Philippines, South Korea, Japan, Malaysia, and the Republic of the Marshall Islands.

"We already have some forces in the area from the RIMPAC

exercise, and the Chairman and Pacific Command are marshaling other assets to move there or to be prepared to move. Two carrier battle groups are already steaming west—one towards the South China Sea and the other towards the Central Pacific. The 25th Infantry Division in Hawaii and the 11th Airborne Division in Alaska are on high alert, and the Marine Forces Pacific is assembling two Marine Air-Ground Task Forces, just in case.

"The mission of this coalition and American forces is to prevent the PRC from controlling all of the South China Sea. To demilitarize the new islands the PRC built and to specifically return control of the Scarborough Shoals to the Philippines per our 1951 Mutual Defense Treaty. Furthermore, US forces also have the following mission: to remove the PRC military from the Marshall Islands, specifically from Kwajalein Atoll, the Reagan Test Site facilities, and the capital of Majuro, and to remove them from Wake Island. At the same time, putting the 11th Airborne Division on alert provides us with Arctic capabilities that should deter Russia from getting too cute in that arena.

"Per the 1973 War Powers Resolution, I submitted our initial plans and concept of operations to the House and the Senate. I will keep them apprised of our plans to return the South China Sea to its pre-Paradigm for Progress status and remove the PRC from the Marshall Islands. I will return to Congress for additional authorization if the planned actions take longer than sixty days.

"Until President Justice vacates the White House, I will use my quarters to operate from and will use my VP Secret Service detail. My new Press Secretary is here, and she will begin daily press conferences with you all starting tomorrow morning at nine.

"As a final note, please know that I am not now, nor have I

ever been, nor will I be a presidential candidate in November or any time after that. Once the elections are held in November, I will transition the president's responsibilities to whomever the American people elect by January and retire from public service."

Kwajalein Island

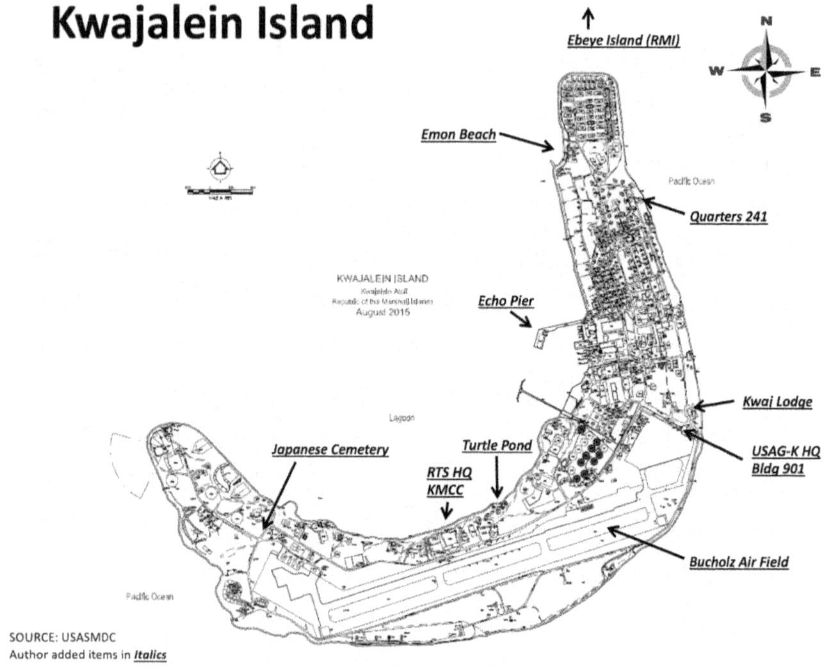

SOURCE: USASMDC
Author added items in *Italics*

Map of Kwajalein Atoll

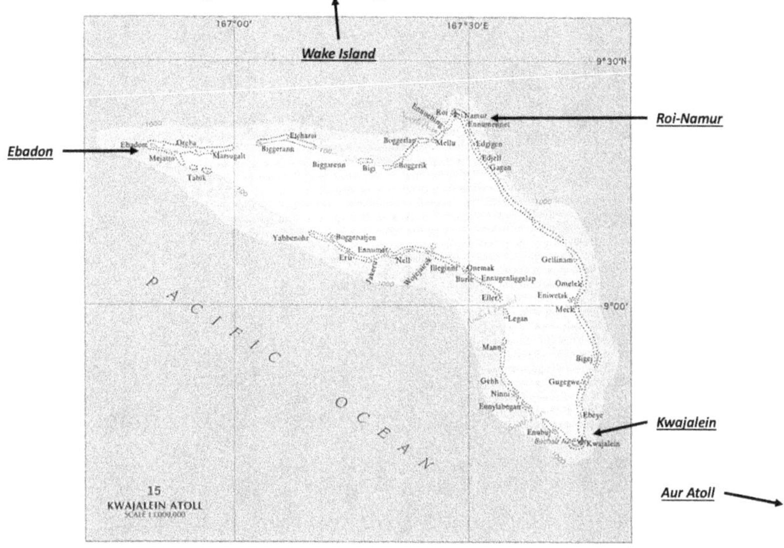

SOURCE: US Dept of Interior, Public Domain
Author added items in **_Italics_**

UNCLASSIFIED

CHAPTER 33

ACTION FROM KWAJALEIN TO WAKE
ISLAND

Kwajalein Island, August 29 (August 28, DC time)

COLONEL SETH GRAYSON HAD SPENT THAT MONDAY MORNING
meeting with Lieutenant Colonel Ron Bakerson, Lieutenant
Colonel Eli Shan, the Kwajalein garrison staff, the Reagan Test
Site staff, the security contractor, and the commander of the
65th Brigade Engineer Battalion, Lieutenant Colonel Smith.
They had already heard the verdict and knew about the
political standoff back in DC.

There were pleased to hear about the two US Navy carrier
battle groups, one of which might come into play at Kwaj as it
would take up position between Kwaj and Guam, where the
Navy had a small base, the Air Force had Anderson Air Force
Base, and the Marines had Camp Blaz.

They were also pleased to hear about the 25th Division
being put on alert, especially as they were the divisional
headquarters for the 65th Engineer Battalion back on Oahu.

"All right, so let's go over the situation, mission, and concept
of operations again," said Seth. "Nothing has changed in the
PRC situation for the last twenty-four hours. They still have
twenty-five soldiers and a lieutenant on Wake, fifty soldiers,

and a captain on Majuro with another fifty businessmen, or so they appear. There are ten armed guards and twenty techs on Aur Atoll, seventy-five soldiers with a major and a captain on Kwaj, with twenty or so scientists and techs in their headquarters modular van near the Kwajalein Mission Control Center."

"Don't forget their naval assets in the area," said Eli. "Now they have three frigates. One in the lagoon here, one just off Aur Atoll, and one just arrived yesterday west of Wake."

"And they still have an unloaded cargo ship at Echo Pier and an unloaded Antonov 22 at the airfield," said Ron. "No telling what might belch forth from those things."

"So, here is our mission statement from Pacific Command," said Seth. "We are to escort the Chinese from Kwajalein, Aur, and Wake and assist in the removal from Majuro, as requested. We are to conduct this removal as peacefully as possible, but in no uncertain terms are we to engage the PRC with live ammo unless fired upon first. If the PRC resist, we are to stop immediately to ensure the safety of all the civilian contractor personnel and their families."

"This sounds like a 'mission impossible' for us," sighed Ron.

"Are we supposed to argue them off the islands or use fire hoses?" asked Eli facetiously, with a large grin.

"I am glad you asked," retorted Seth. "We have some help coming our way. The 25th Division is gearing up the 1/27th Infantry Battalion, their alert battalion, and they will be flying in here within thirty-six hours. We need to ensure the runway is cleared by then. We don't want the Chinese frigate loose inside the lagoon where they could threaten us or take aggressive action, so we need to disable it. To help clear the way for the 1/27th, a battalion of the 1st Special Operations Group is going to airdrop several Operational Detachments Alpha, or ODAs, into the area tonight. Two will come in via low-level 500´AGL static line drop, and three will arrive via HALO (high altitude low opening), that is from 25,000.' One ODA will arrive on Aur Atoll via the 500´ low-level static line drop and will link up with the 65th Civic Action Team (CAT) team at the small overgrown dirt strip on the southern island of the atoll. The sound of the PRC's power generators on the main island should mask the sound of their arrival via the MC130. The CAT team has been improving it and building a new lens well for the locals, so hopefully, this will not tip anyone off. The second one will drop in on Wake Island at the end of the runway via the 500´ low-level static line drop and contact the Space and Missile Defense tech there. And a third ODA will HALO onto Roi-Namur at the southwest end of the runway and contact our security contractor and the company from the 65th that has been building the Known Distance Range there. A fourth will HALO on Majuro and ensure the international airfield and tower are secure, and the fifth will HALO onto the western end of Kwaj tonight. They will link up with us. The Special Forces Battalion headquarters and a sixth ODA will land early tomorrow morning at our airfield on Kwaj.[1]

"Each ODA has a specific mission to quietly secure the airfields and towers and ensure they are open and operational for the 1/27th Infantry Battalion, which will fly in tomorrow night to add to our forces. We will make it clear to the PRC and their soldiers that they must leave by the force of the Wolfhounds from the 1/27th if necessary. After linking up with the company commander from the 65th, the ODA on Aur will take rigid rubber Zodiac boats from that island to Tabal. The PRC has completed the launch complex with a rail launcher site on Tabal, but the ODA will render it inoperable. The ODA on Roi also has the task of preventing the KREMS complex from falling into the hands of the Chinese military.

"Alpha Company 1/27th will fly into Wake, Bravo

Company will fly into Majuro, and Charlie Company will fly into Kwaj tomorrow night at 2300 hours (11 PM).

"Ron, I want you to head to Roi via DASH 7 today. Be prepared to remain there for a few days as my eyes and ears on the ground. Link up with the company commander from the 65th at that site. Eli, take a Huey to Ebadon, where the third company of the 65th is doing their CAT mission, and tell them what is going on. They are seemingly not in harm's way, but they need to let us know if they see or hear anything suspicious. I prefer to fly one of you, Lieutenant Colonels, to Aur Atoll via Huey, but that would raise too many questions and might tip off the Chinese to our intent. Lieutenant Colonel Smith, the commander of the 65th, will remain here on Kwaj with me and keep his company commanders on Roi, Aur, and Ebadon informed.

"Remember, we have a peaceful escort mission. You will carry your individual weapons, locked and loaded, but do not use them unless fired on by the PRC soldiers," said Seth.

To the head of the base operations contractor, Colonel Grayson requested their voluntary assistance to continue blocking the passes into the lagoon with the large safety ship and cargo ships and use the minisub to disable the Chinese frigate at Echo Pier clandestinely. As the safety ship was already in place and commanded by a retired Coast Guard officer, that was a no-brainer. The cargo ships commanded by former Army warrant officers began to surreptitiously move back into place within the hour, having been temporarily pulled for unavoidable cargo duties. After all that, it took a couple of hours to find the minisub crew and get their buy-in to the mission. The two former Navy petty officers did not hesitate once they got the facts and understood the urgency.

Initially, preparatory actions seemed to be going well. But shortly after 1500 hours (3 PM) that day, things spun out of control. The Chinese captain and twenty-five of his soldiers commandeered the Jera, one of the two, two-hundred-passenger, high-speed catamarans, and headed toward Roi-Namur. Then the Chinese major, with two armed soldiers, broke into Seth's office and took him and Lieutenant Colonel Smith, the 65th Engineer Battalion commander, hostage. At the same time, an additional twenty-five Chinese soldiers opened the door of the Antonov cargo aircraft. They began firing randomly in the air, apparently trying to scare onlookers back into their offices and quarters as they exited the plane.

This new group of soldiers stormed the control tower and shot the two FAA controllers and the security contractor in the head. They were dead before they hit the ground. What had been a tense standoff suddenly became a hot and hostile takeover of an American military installation and parts of a world-class missile range.

The Kwajalein Garrison operations officer saw and heard part of what was going on and had time to send a quick email to Pacific Command J3 Operations section before he was found and shot in the back by the advancing twenty-five Chinese soldiers. At Quarters 241, Sara heard the noise and called on the unsecured landline to Colonel Will Bishop at the National Military Command Center J3 Operations. She had just mentioned shooting when that line went dead.

———

ON OAHU, the first of the Operational Detachment Alpha (ODA) was wheels up for their long 10 hour flight. The other ODAs were on their heels, winging westward. The three HALO ODA units flew in C17 Globemaster aircraft while the two low-level static line ODAs flew in MC130J Command II aircraft.[2] The speed of these two different types of aircraft were adjusted to arrive on station in accordance with the plan of action. The 1/27th Infantry Battalion was in the final stages of their deployment preparation timeline for their departure the next day from Hickam Air Force Base near Pearl Harbor. They would fly in C17 aircraft, one bound for Kwaj, one for Majuro, and one for Wake Island. All the aircraft would be met in the air by aging KC-135 and KC-10 Stratotankers for refueling on their way out and on the return trip if required. The MC130J Special Operations aircraft for the low-level drops departed earlier than the C17s flying the HALO ODAs, since they were a bit slower, as were the AC130 gunships which had the mission to support the ODAs with highly accurate aerial fire support. The AC130 aircraft would top off en route and then loiter around Wake Island, Aur, and Kwajalein Atolls, to engage specific targets as lased by the ODAs. One preplanned target was the PRC frigate west of Wake. Another was the launcher/rail launch site on Aur Atoll if the ODA could not take it from the ground.

1600h (4 PM)

The situation on the ground continued to deteriorate and was suddenly very different. While the minisub crew had successfully damaged the propeller and rudder of the PRC frigate at Echo Pier on Kwaj, the catamaran Jera landed at Roi-Namur, and the twenty-five Chinese soldiers came out guns blazing and headed directly toward the KREMS complex on the Namur side. The company commander of the engineer company that was working on the Known Distance range heard the commotion, as did the security contractor and Lieutenant Colonel Ron Bakerson. Ron tried to call Seth but got a busy signal. Quickly, Ron told the security contractor to lock up the radar control buildings of the KREMS complex and guard them and the sensors themselves from the Chinese. He told the 65th captain to alert his company, grab their small arms, and set up a semicircle perimeter around the KREMS complex using the ocean to cover their backside. He told them to set up their SAWs (M249 Squad Automatic Weapon, a small machine gun). Fortunately, as they were building the Known Distance range on the Namur side, they were already very close to the KREMS complex. The largest sensor, ALTAIR, was separated from the other three KREMS sensors (TRADEX, ALCOR, and MMW), being closer to the lagoon-side pier than the other three on the north side of Namur, essentially on the Pacific. ALTAIR fell into the hands of the Chinese as they killed the security contractor personnel before they could get situated.

A quick call from the National Military Command Center in the Pentagon to Pacific Command headquarters in Oahu apprised them of the situation. Pacific Command J3 Operations contacted Special Operations Command-Pacific and the 1st Special Operations Group elements in the air via satellite communications to make sure they knew. They would be arriving in a hot and hostile situation.

Major Jones, the Executive Officer of the 65th Engineer Battalion, after hearing the commotion in Colonel Grayson's office, rounded up some of the battalion staff, locked and loaded their 9MM and M16s, and assembled behind the Kwaj Lodge to assess the situation. It took only a few minutes for Major Jones to realize the gravity of the situation and that his window of opportunity for action was closing rapidly. First, he called the company commanders of CAT teams of the 65th Engineer Battalion on Aur, Wake, and Roi on their secure radios and brought them up to speed. The captain on Roi explained his status and the orders that Ron Bakerson had given him. He could hear Chinese soldiers at ALTAIR but could not see them. The rest of the KREMS complex was inside his perimeter. The captain on Aur was ready to receive the ODA that would jump in later that night and had heard nothing from Aur Atoll's Tabal Island yet, the island where the PRC built their launch facility. The captain on Ebadon reported that Lieutenant Colonel Eli Shan had arrived via helicopter and that all was calm.

Back on Kwaj, Major Yeng of the Chinese Army slapped Seth with his bare hand. "What happened to the rudder on our frigate?" he demanded to know. Then he shot Lieutenant Colonel Smith in the leg. "Tell me now, or the next round is thru his right eye," yelled Major Yeng.

"We have a very shallow anchorage at Echo Pier, in addition to several large turtles that play in and around the area. It is probable that your rudder either hit the wrong spot or got fouled up by the large turtles," screamed Seth. Incredibly, Major Yeng bought it, or at least it gave him reason to stop and think for just a second.

At that moment, Major Jones, two of his Non-Commissioned Officers, and Amata burst into the room, shot Major Yeng, and then aimed at the other two Chinese soldiers. One of the Chinese soldiers hit Major Jones in the gut, and the other hit one of the Non-Commissioned Officers. Amata grabbed that Sergeant's M16 and got off two rapid and well-aimed shots with it. They found home in the chest of one of the Chinese and the neck of the other. Seth looked at Amata, who just grinned back.

Chaos reigned on Kwaj. Of the seventy or so Chinese soldiers remaining on Kwaj (five of the seventy-five were dead, twenty-five took the Jera to Roi, but were replaced by the twenty-five that appeared out of the Antonov cargo plane), they were equally divided into three groups. One spread out near the Kwajalein Missile Control Center and seemed unaware of what had happened at the Kwajalein Garrison headquarters building as the sound of the 1000-kW generators that powered the island masked the gunshots that far away. Another group was guarding the Echo Pier area and also unaware, while the third was in and around the headquarters building and FAA tower. They were very much aware of the resistance and were a bit leaderless as their major was unaccounted for, one of their captains went to Roi, and the other captain was at the Kwajalein Mission Control Center.

Seth heard the Chinese captain, or someone who spoke only Chinese, call Major Yeng's radio. He called three or four times before it stopped. It would only be a matter of time before they sent someone to check on the Major and discover their loss. Fortunately, the Chinese did not seem focused on the civilians on Kwaj, other than those at the mission control center and Echo Pier. Seth called Sara but could not get through, getting only a busy signal. He tried to call Will Bishop at the Pentagon and the Pacific Command J3 Operations and J5 Plans Sections in Oahu but could not get a line off the island. Apparently, people had heard the firing and were calling home, or the lines were cut.

While bandaging his injured leg, Lieutenant Colonel Smith pulled out his satellite phone that the 25th Division issued him for the CAT mission and offered it to Seth. Seth immediately called the Pacific Command J3 and J5 and asked about the status of the ODAs and follow-on 1/27th Infantry Battalion. They were in the air, with the ODAs scheduled to arrive around 2100 hours (9 PM) on this moonless night.

"Sir," said the Non-Com from the 65th who had accompanied Major Jones to Seth's office. "We need to get out of here ASAP. The rest of our battalion staff is behind the Kwaj Lodge. I suggest we move there and decide what we do next."

Meanwhile, as the Chinese on Roi-Namur probed the semicircle set up by the 65th at the KREMS complex, they realized they were outnumbered and outgunned. Their small arms were no match for the machine guns, and their casualties were mounting. As dusk began to roll in, the Chinese captain began thinking about taking the catamaran to their rally point on Ebadon Island.

2100h (9 PM)

The ODA team leaders received the latest intel and update from the Marshall Islands, courtesy of the Pacific Command J3.

Surprise was compromised, and the Chinese were actively engaging anything that moved on Kwaj and Roi-Namur. Majuro, Wake, and Aur seemed quiet—not sure if they knew about the action on Kwaj and Roi, but the assumption had to be yes.

2110h (9:10 PM)

The doors opened on their aircraft, and the three HALO ODAs left their aircraft at twenty-five thousand feet in their pressurized suits, with individual jumper helmet night tracking lights turned on and night vision goggles ready for under canopy tracking. They would plummet toward the earth reaching terminal velocity of 120 mph within seconds and then pull their high lift, low drag gliding canopy at five thousand feet, landing quietly on Roi, Kwajalein and Majuro. At least that was the plan. At Roi and Majuro, the plan worked. The two low-level ODA jumps at Wake and Aur Atoll were timed to land simultaneously with the HALO jumpers at Roi, Kwajalein, and Majuro.[3] The ODA on Majuro landed on the far end of the runway and silently made their way to the control tower. After sizing up the situation, they stealthily and ruthlessly attacked the Chinese soldiers at critical locations. They controlled the towers and patrolled the runways for other Chinese within an hour. When they found them, they took them out.

On Aur Atoll, the ODA landed on the southernmost island and linked up with the company commander from the 65th. After a brief rest, they opened the supply package that also dropped in (steered by some Special Forces soldiers), inflated their rubber Zodiac rafts, and started their small outboard engines. Since the engines' exhausts were muffled, they could move quickly and quietly to Tabal Island, the northernmost island in Aur Atoll. That was the location of the test site with the rail launcher and suspicious range fans.

By 2300 hours (11 PM), the ODA was on Tabal Island and could hear some activity and a lot of excited discussions. A Senior Non-Commissioned Officer on the ODA translated. "They know something has gone wrong on Kwaj and heard a rumor about Wake. They are alert," said the Sergeant First Class. The team leader, the young Special Forces captain, huddled them up for a quick review and adjustment of the plan. "OK, there are twelve of us. We will divide into three fire teams. Sergeant First Class Welsh will take his team and secure the control building. Sergeant First Class Johnson will take the buildings that look like ammo bunkers. I will take the rest to the launch facility. Remember, be quiet and quick. Use your knives until we are discovered, and then you can use your weapons. We do not want the PRC frigate parked about two miles off the northern coastline to use us for target practice. We start at 2315 hours (11:15 PM)

2330h (11:30 PM)

It was over in 15 minutes as the ODA still had the element of surprise when they arrived from the dense jungle behind the launcher, and it was pitch black dark. They killed five of the ten

PRC armed guards on Aur and locked up the twenty or so technicians in a sleeping facility. Then, the Special Forces soldiers set explosive charges on the launcher site, the control building, and the ammo bunker, all with remote-controlled Radio Frequency detonators. They also took video and hundreds of still shots of the armed PRC soldiers, and all the structures including the swivel launch facility as evidence of the PRC efforts and placed a closed-circuit TV camera to watch the facilities. Finally, they returned to the other island in their rubber boat. The plan was to blow the facility (less the technicians) to kingdom come when the AC130 gunships arrived in the area. The gunships would keep it occupied if the PRC frigate decided to investigate their island.

———

2400h (midnight) on Roi-Namur

The ODA that landed on Roi-Namur did so at the western end of Roi, near the southwest end of the runway, and quietly retook the Roi airfield control tower. Soon after that, they received a call from Lieutenant Colonel Ron Bakerson, who was able to contact them using the landline from the KREMS complex on Namur to the control tower on Roi. It was a chancy call, but one that Ron made after he figured the ODA had had time to get there. The ODA then began advancing to the east, across the runway, then across the areas that used to be a causeway to Namur, and began engaging the Chinese platoon from their rear, making good use of their night vision goggles. A fierce firefight ensued at ALTAIR, killing one of the ODA members and three of the Chinese before they broke off the action and headed toward the pier.

After midnight, the Chinese captain and the Jera finally

pulled away from the pier on Namur and headed toward Ebadon with only ten of his men. The ODA and the 65th had picked off the others. The PRC frigate west of Wake, not knowing that the ODA had retaken Wake, pulled off to sail for Ebadon and rescue the remnant of the Chinese platoon that escaped from Roi. But that would take hours of steaming before they arrived.

2100h (9 PM) on Kwajalein

On Kwajalein, with their major out of action and most of his command dead or missing, the Chinese captain near the Kwajalein Mission Control Center was on high alert. He called his two men in the tower but did not get an answer, so he sent two more men there and set up several observation posts around the perimeter of Bucholz Field. The ODA landed after their HALO jump on the western end of the runway. The Chinese observation post in that area spotted their parachutes and immediately engaged with machine guns. The night sky lit up with green tracer rounds. Three of the Special Forces soldiers were killed before they hit the ground, and a fourth was seriously wounded by the pounding and crushing wave action and razor-sharp reefs when he landed in the Shark Pit area of surf at the far western end of Kwajalein. The remaining eight hit the ground running, literally, as they hit the quick release on their paragliders and returned fire. The action was intense as those eight momentarily confused the PRC soldiers with their audacity. Then, one of the ODA members was hit in the arm and another grazed in the leg. The team leader fired his grenade launcher at the source of Chinese firing which silenced them for a moment. This allowed them to assemble near the

Japanese cemetery to get reorganized and understand the situation on the ground—situational awareness.

Suddenly, the ODA team leader received a satellite call from Colonel Seth Grayson, patched through via the Pacific Command J6 Communications section. "We are holed up behind the Kwaj Lodge, just east of the airfield, oceanside," said Seth. "The Chinese major leading everything is dead, as are several of his men, but there are still probably more than sixty Chinese soldiers on Kwaj, armed and waiting. I think there is a captain on the island, who is now in charge, but I am not sure where he is."

"Un-huh," mused the ODA team leader. "Given their well-organized opposition on the runway, I would say he is in our area."

"There is another large group of Chinese near Echo Pier, and still some more near the Kwajalein headquarters building and the control tower. Earlier today, another group of Chinese took one of my catamarans to Roi-Namur, " whispered Seth. "I have about fifteen men here, all with small arms. We can create a diversion if you need it."

"Great. Give me until 2130 hours (9:30 PM), and then start that diversion," said the team leader. "Keep yourselves out of harm's way, but a few well-placed shots in the center of the island will certainly help us move toward the tower and distract the Chinese from the other ODA and the Special Forces Battalion headquarters that will start landing around 2145 hours (9:45 PM). Any ideas on clearing the planes off the runway to allow the C17 with the 1/27th on board? They will land around 2300 hours (11 PM) tomorrow."

"We have two D6 dozers near Echo Pier," said Lieutenant Colonel Smith. "They arrived by barge yesterday and are awaiting transport by landing craft to Aur for the airstrip improvement project. The 65th has equipment operators here if the Special Forces can get them started and moved down to the runway."

Seth relayed this info to the ODA team leader.

2130h (9:30 PM)

Shots rang out in the center of the island. Seth and the men with him had spread out to several places along the eastern shoreline and began sporadic fire aimed only at the Chinese or buildings nearby to ensure they hit no friendlies. This effort seemed to have the intended effect until the bullet slammed into Seth's right arm. It hurt like the devil, but he still got off a few more shots and then moved back to the rear of Kwaj Lodge.

"Eli," called Seth on the sat phone to Lieutenant Colonel Shan on Ebadon. "Things are not going so well here, but the Special Forces ODAs have arrived, and the 1/27th Battalion headquarters is supposed to land here at 2300 hours (11 PM) tomorrow. Keep your eyes and ears open. Have you heard from Ron on Roi-Namur?"

"Not a peep," said Eli. "All quiet on this western front."

At that moment, the AC130 gunship that had been loitering at 7000' above Kwajalein engaged a squad of PRC soldiers near the control tower and then another cluster of PRC near Echo Pier. The deadly accurate 105mm airborne howitzer aboard the gunship had a chilling and devastating effect on the remaining opposition on Kwajalein,[4] as the 105 rounds landed among the PRC soldiers and blew them up, with limbs flying in all directions. War is ugly.

August 30, 0100h (1 AM)

After the second ODA arrived along with the Special Forces Battalion headquarters, the two ODAs killed or rounded up the remaining Chinese soldiers on Kwaj. In addition, the ODAs that airdropped on Kwaj, Roi, Wake, and Majuro also had with them Air Force Combat Controllers to provide air traffic control since the FAA controllers had been killed. This allowed the arrival of the C17 cargo aircraft with the 1/27th Infantry Battalion forces at those locations.[5]

Seth tried to call Ron Bakerson again, using the satellite phone, and this time he got through. "Ron, what is happening on Roi-Namur?"

Ron responded, "Well, it appears we prevented the Chinese from getting their hands on the KREMS complex, although they took ALTAIR temporarily. Now it seems they took off in the Jera, headed west toward Ebadon. I tried to call Eli but couldn't get through."

Seth brought him up to speed. "I spoke to him a little while ago and told him to be on alert. I'll call him again. As I understand it, the ODAs have things under control here and on Wake and Majuro. Not sure about Aur Atoll."

———

August 30, 0200h (2 AM)

As the Jera approached Ebadon inside the lagoon, so did the PRC frigate that departed Wake hours earlier, oceanside. The Chinese captain contacted the frigate and coordinated a pick-up on the ocean side through the surf. It wasn't smart to do, as the surf was enormous, and the coral reef was sharp and everywhere. But that was their plan after they saw the large cargo ship blocking Tabik Chan Pass and docked the catamaran at Ebadon, lagoon side. Little did they know that an engineer company armed with small arms was on the island. While Eli had not expected to see Chinese soldiers on Ebadon, he was prepared as were the members of the 65th. The observation post near the dock called Eli when they first spotted the catamaran. More than thirty soldiers from the 65th stood ready where the dock connected to the land, hidden in the vegetation. When the Chinese captain and his band of ten finally reached firm ground, Eli called out in Chinese to surrender or die. At nearly the same time, F/A 18 fighters from the US Navy carrier battle group intercepted and engaged the PRC frigate, severely damaging its ability to fire upon Ebadon.

August 30, 0700h (7 AM)

When the PRC frigate positioned near Aur Atoll began to move in closer and sent its launch to investigate the inactivity at the site and failed radio contacts, the ODA team leader detonated the explosives. It was louder than anticipated since the ammo bunker held anti-ship missiles, which the PRC could have used against US Navy vessels between Aur and Wake. Not only were there hundreds of anti-ship missiles in the bunker but buried beneath that level was an underground facility that housed cruise missiles tipped with conventional payloads, adapted to fit the rail launcher. They were capable of reaching Hawaii, Guam, and Japan. The shockwaves from the sympathetic blast were felt on the other islands in Aur Atoll, causing several injuries among the ODA and members of the 65th. The resulting black cloud rose several thousand feet into the air, visible from Kwajalein. Shades of the 1944 incident when the Marines blew up the Japanese torpedo warehouse during Operation Flintlock! Fortunately, none of the cruise missiles had received their nuclear warheads yet.

———

August 30, 2300h (11 PM)

Elements of the 1/27th Infantry Battalion from Schofield Barracks began arriving at Wake Island, Kwajalein, and Majuro to reinforce the ODAs that had taken those runways and towers. By 0600 hours (6 AM) the following day, August 31, the airfields, the towers, and surrounding facilities were secure, and all of the remaining Chinese soldiers had been rounded up and accounted for.

By 0800 hours (8 AM) on August 31, it was apparent that the PRC had reached its operational culminating point in the Central Pacific. They had gone beyond the point where they could hold the ground they had taken, i.e., the Marshall Islands, with the forces they had allocated to the task. Trying to take over US Army Garrison – Kwajalein Atoll and the Reagan Test Site had been a massive miscalculation on their part, fueled in part by the political firestorms in the US. Nor had they figured on the honor and resolve of the American military.

South China Sea – Competing Claims

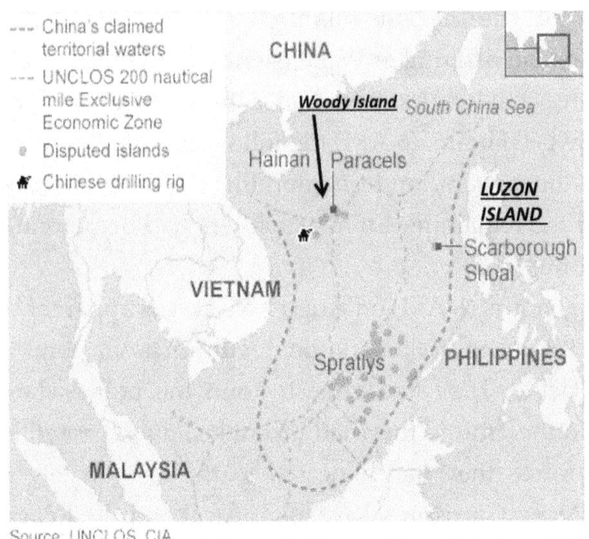

Author added items are in **_Italics_**

UNCLASSIFIED

CHAPTER 34
THE SOUTH CHINA SEA NAVAL ACTION

South China Sea, September 3

ANOTHER MOONLESS NIGHT IN THE SOUTH CHINA SEA HAD everyone on edge. The news of the Kwajalein debacle had reached Beijing and, to a certain degree, filtered down to the rank and file aboard the Chinese carrier, the *Liaoning*. Along with several frigates, one of their newest guided-missile cruisers, and several Kilo and Yuan class submarines, the PRC Navy was still a potent force in the South China Sea,[1] but one whose confidence had been shaken.

The US carrier battle group led the coalition against the PRC Navy. That alone should have given the Chinese a pause to reflect. But also arrayed against the PRC were the considerable naval forces of the UK, Australia, New Zealand, the Philippines, South Korea, Japan, Malaysia, and the Republic of the Marshall Islands. At least those that had had time to steam from their home ports or their RIMPAC exercise locations to the South China Sea.

The plan had been to merely intimidate the PRC into departing from the eastern part of the South China Sea, specifically from anywhere near Scarborough Shoals. The US

Navy put up a sizeable electronic signal, not trying to hide in any way that it was coming, and with a few of its closest friends. That signal included direct messages to the PRC Navy admiral in charge of their fleet. When that had no effect, they began to run sorties around the clock, buzzing the Chinese ships with some of them coming close to the *Liaoning*.

Nerves were tight as one of the PRC subs began to ping one of the British destroyers. Then some Australian destroyers placed depth charges near the PRC subs, but not really near, so as not to cause a panic in the Chinese submariners' minds, but close enough to get their attention.

But it was too late. The Kilo-class sub fired two torpedoes at the Australian ship, both of which missed. However, one of them found a home in the rear of a Philippine frigate and blew it to bits, sinking it in a matter of minutes with all hands on board.

All bets were off as the *Liaoning* scrambled her SUMK2 and J-15 fighters as fast as she could, not wanting to lose face to the Americans. But they were no match for the F/A 18 Super Hornets and the F-35 Joint Strike Fighters that had already established air superiority, knocking ten of the PRC fighters out of the air in a matter of minutes. In a last-ditch effort, the PRCs guided-missile cruiser fired one of its "carrier killer" anti-ship missiles at the American carrier. However, the US Navy carrier had recently been outfitted with the newest version of the "sea whiz" close-in protection system and was able to hit the anti-ship missile before it could impact the ship. Unfortunately, shrapnel from the explosion collided with the carrier's bridge, killing three and wounding four more.

At the same time, the UK and Australian ships began launching their guided missiles at the smaller PRC frigates and destroyers, while a US Navy cruiser homed in on the PRC cruiser. After four hours of intense aerial and naval combat, during which time two PRC ships were destroyed, another was severely damaged and listing, and the *Liaoning* had also been hit, it appeared that both sides decided to take an operational pause.

One Malaysian and one South Korean ship had been damaged, in addition to the sunk Philippine ship. But the US-led coalition still had a great deal of firepower and fight left in it and was preparing a second wave when the PRC admiral called the US admiral on the carrier.

"We have just received word that the RIMPAC exercise is now over, and we are to reposition our forces farther to the west, somewhere near the Spratly Islands. Please know that we will be moving that way in fifteen minutes," said the Chinese Admiral.

While it was not an admission of defeat, it was a startling announcement and a way for the Chinese to retreat while maintaining much of its naval strength and face. As far as the US Navy admiral was concerned, his forces had accomplished one of the operation's primary objectives— removing the PRC Navy from the eastern part of the South China Sea and from the vicinity of Scarborough Shoals.

"I received your transmission, Admiral," said the American Admiral. "We understand you are moving your forces back toward the Spratly Islands. That is a great idea, and we agree with it. Be advised that we will shadow your relocation just in case you all need some assistance with your move and will also help you with the cleanup of those small islands that appeared out of nowhere near the Spratlys and the Paracels. Those must wreak havoc on proper navigation."

"That will not be necessary," retorted the Chinese admiral.

"Oh, but I insist," yelled the American admiral, as a F/A18 fighter streaked over the deck of the *Liaoning*.

EPILOGUE

NOVEMBER 13

The Battle of the South China Sea was hailed as a great victory for the US Navy and its allies. The President of the Philippines came to visit the new President-elect, Ted Wilson, and the interim president, the former Vice President (installed after the senate guilty verdict against President Justice), in the Naval Observatory. Slowly, former and fading President Roland Justice was beginning to see the light, as few members of Congress would return his calls. Only the governors of California, Oregon, and Washington still referred to him as the President, and no foreign leaders would contact him at all. All of his department heads had resigned except the Secretary of Defense, and she was off to another global climate change conference, this one in Venezuela, and poorly attended.

Russian forces, inside the borders of Latvia but not yet in control of Riga, were put into a quandary when a large NATO force led by the UK docked at the port of Riga for a six-month exercise. Another NATO force led by Germany flew into Poland, adjacent to the Belarus border, and began its six-month training.

Carlos De Von Heim's operation was still going strong and

making money fast. The Border Patrol was doing its best to stop the flow of goods and making some headway. The President, i.e., the former VP did what he could to enforce existing immigration laws. He also allowed the states to assist in the construction of border walls at the most sensitive locations. The Drug Enforcement Agency (DEA) worked hand in hand with the Border Patrol, but this is a huge problem.

The AJL was officially declared an international terrorist organization by the Department of State. Sharia law was not allowed in the US, and the Pentagon began to implement its plan to dismantle the caliphate. But it would be a long road. The recovery operations in San Diego, Minneapolis and Orlando are far from over.

———

ADMIRAL HALSEY BURKE finally submitted his retirement papers, but not before receiving a letter of reprimand from the outgoing Secretary of Defense Amanda Carson, and the Defense Distinguished Service Medal from the new President for his performance under extreme prejudice and political pressure to ignore his oath of office. He was replaced by General Adam Abrams, US Air Force, as the new Chairman of the Joint Chiefs of Staff.

After recovering from the gunshot wound to his arm, Colonel Seth Grayson received a Purple Heart and completed his tour of duty on Kwajalein the following summer. He and Sara were moving on to their next assignment at US Northern Command at Peterson AFB in Colorado Springs, Colorado.

Seth and Sara were excited to return to the US, closer to family, their friends, and their new assignment. Sara's Aunt Sally finally called from Jacksonville and assured her that she was alright and would visit her soon.

Sara had hoped for a little respite when they moved to the northern end of Colorado Springs. They bought a house in Briargate Subdivision, about twenty minutes from Peterson Air Force Base. She and Seth attended church services at the Protestant Chapel on the US Air Force Academy until they could find a church to plug into closer to their house. Life was good for a while until the mammoth tunnels were revealed under the US-Mexican border between Mexicali and Calexico, with evidence that Al Jihadi Levant and certain drug cartels were involved.

While the fact that a huge tunnel existed under the US-Mexican border was not a big surprise, it was very surprising and unnerving to discover that some specific PRC, Mexican, and US contractors had also secretly participated in the design and construction of the tunnel. It could accommodate large armored and mechanized equipment, was well-lit, had reinforced ceilings and walls, and extended many miles back on both sides of the border. The US exit was located and well hidden in a very large barn east of Calexico, near I-8, that had been purchased by the US contractor.

So, two months after Seth arrived in Colorado Springs and signed into the Northern Command Headquarters at Peterson Air Force Base, his boss sent him on TDY (temporary duty) to the southern border in California to assess the newly found tunnels.

AFTERWORD

As stated before, this was a fictional story with some elements of history and current factual information. The story's purpose was to highlight several real-world constitutional issues as they relate to the American military and other Americans. Hopefully, the storyline suggested a few constitutional amendments or laws, such as:

1.   Term limits for Congress, such as eighteen years (three Senate terms, nine House terms, or some combination of Senate and House terms, not to exceed eighteen years), to ensure fresh members and ideas are injected into the Congress. This would provide a more rapid turnover of the members than the current situation, which seems to result in the professional politician whose number one priority (even if subconscious) defaults to re-election instead of doing what is best for the nation, and their state or district.

2.   A balanced budget amendment to put the nation's financial house in order where Congress and the President have failed. Spending limits go hand in hand with number one above, term limits. One method current members use to stay in office is the "pork barrel" line item, AKA earmark, intended mainly to ensure their re-election, but it does not help balance

the budget. A balanced budget amendment could also include a provision that withholds Congress' pay until a balanced budget is passed and signed each year. A limited line-item veto authority for the President could be considered.

3. Clarifying executive authority, one of the most abused and ill-defined duties in the constitution. It would constrain the President's ability to pass "legislation and laws" or govern by executive authority. It would provide: a. Executive actions definition and purpose, and limitations; b. Executive orders definition and purpose, and limitations; c. Executive agreements definition and purpose; and limitations (see #5 below)

4. Clarify and strengthen existing laws on signing statements to preclude future presidents from failing to carry out their constitutional duties, which is the complete execution (implementation) of the laws that Congress passes and he or she signs.

5. Clarification and strengthening of the Senate's advise and consent role as it relates to treaties versus executive agreements, which may or may not have any Congressional involvement and have been used to bypass the constitutionally prescribed duty of the Senate.

6. Clarification and formalization of the 1973 War Powers Resolution as it relates to the use of military force and declaring war to bring the constitution up to date on the nature of conflict in the 21st Century.

7. Clarification of roles involved in controlling our international borders. The need for comprehensive immigration reform may or may not be necessary. First, lawmakers, governors, and voters must be thoroughly informed of the laws already in place. If enforced, that may be sufficient. This effort should also include eliminating sanctuary cities and the practice/provision that designates any baby born in the United

States as a US citizen, even if both parents are here illegally and only crossed the border to have their child. A well-constructed border wall is also highly recommended, adequately manned, and monitored with the latest equipment. The Israeli wall around the West Bank is a testament to this.

8. A law must be passed that requires senior military officers (colonel and above), and Department of Defense Officials, to take Constitutional courses which ensure they understand their role in constitutional issues between the military and the President. Simply yielding to the Commander in Chief, is sometimes not appropriate when that Commander in Chief acts unconstitutionally.

ACKNOWLEDGMENTS

First, I must acknowledge my wife, Peggy, for her support in the time-consuming effort to write a book of this nature. She has been a rock and an excellent sounding board.

Next, I would like to acknowledge my old West Point classmate, JM (Mike) Patton, author of "A Full Measure" trilogy, for his support and advice. Also, SGM Stan Parker, a long-time friend, for his insights into the action and the use of the Special Forces.

I am thankful to have had 29 years in the Army. I have been to so many places, seen such things, and learned countless lessons, some the hard way and some repetitively, as a result of my military career.

Finally, I must mention my publisher, Frank Eastland, my editors, Nancy and Bob Laning, and the rest of the team at Publish Authority. Their professionalism and advice have been the cornerstone of this novel's success.

ABOUT THE AUTHOR

Scott Cottrell is a retired US Army Colonel. A graduate of the United States Military Academy at West Point, he served for 29+ years in various locations, including as Commander of the US Army Kwajalein Atoll/Kwajalein Missile Range. Scott has three master's degrees, including a Master's in Military Art and Science from the Army's School of Advanced Military Studies; and a Master's in National Security and Strategic Studies from the US Naval War College. Scott's other military assignments included the 25th Infantry Division in Hawaii; the Near East Project Office in Ovda, Israel with the US Army Corps of Engineers; US Southern Command's Engineer Directorate in Panama; XVIII Airborne Corps G3 Plans section in Fort Bragg, NC; US Space Command J5 Plans Section; and the US Central Command's Engineer, which involved many trips to the Middle East. He is married to Peggy, with two children and eight grandchildren.

For more about the author, you are invited to visit his website at ScottCottrell.com

ENDNOTES

Below websites Accessed 23 April 2023.

Note: Some websites might not be able to be accessed when using a VPN.

Chapter 1

1. Over the Edge of the World: Magellan's Terrifying Circumnavigation of the World. Laurence Burgeen, First Harper Perennial Edition, 2004; and Brand, Donald D. The Pacific Basin: A History of its Geographical Explorations, The American Geographical Society, New York, 1967, p.39.
2. https://marshall.csu.edu.au/Marshalls/html/atolls/bokak.html; and The Eastern Mandate Campaign: Roi-Namur and Kwajalein Staff Ride, US Army Space and Strategic Defense Command, November 1996, p. 4.
3. https://www.infomarshallislands.com/captain-john-marshall/
4. https://marshall.csu.edu.au/Marshalls/html/atolls/kwajalein.html; and http://marshall.csu.edu.au/Marshalls/html/japanese/bouj.html
5. Seizure of the Gilberts and Marshalls, Philip A. Crowl and Edmund C. Love, US Army in WORLD WAR II, Center of Military History, Wash. DC, 1993 (50th Anniversary edition), p. 167.
6. The Eastern Mandate Campaign: Roi-Namur and Kwajalein Staff Ride, US Army Space and Strategic Defense Command, November 1996, p. 5.
7. Seizure of the Gilberts and Marshalls, Philip A. Crowl and Edmund C. Love, US Army in WORLD WAR II, Center of Military History, Wash. DC, 1993 (50th Anniversary edition), pp. 206–207.
8. https://www.cia.gov/the-world-factbook/countries (Spratly and Paracels)
9. https://www.cia.gov/readingroom/docs/DOC_0000710366.pdf

Chapter 2

1. The Battles for Kwajalein and Roi-Namur, pamphlet, Bell Telephone Laboratories, 1974, Kwajalein, p. 4.
2. The Battles for Kwajalein and Roi-Namur, pamphlet, Bell Telephone Laboratories, 1974, Kwajalein, pp. 5, 33
3. Ibid., p. 5.

4. Seizure of the Gilberts and Marshalls, Philip A. Crowl and Edmund C. Love, US Army in WORLD WAR II, Center of Military History, Wash. DC, 1993 (50th Anniversary edition), p. 217.

5. The Battles for Kwajalein and Roi-Namur, pamphlet, Bell Telephone Laboratories, 1974, Kwajalein, p. 6.

6. Ibid., pp. 7, 25.

7. Ibid., p. 8.

8. Ibid., pp. 9–10, and History of the 7th Infantry Division in World War II, Edmund G. Love, The Battery Press, Nashville, 1988, pp. 121–127; and Seizure of the Gilberts and Marshalls, Philip A. Crowl and Edmund C. Love, US Army in WORLD WAR II, Center of Military History, Wash. DC, 1993 (50th Anniversary edition), pp. 232–236

9. The Battles for Kwajalein and Roi-Namur, pamphlet, Bell Telephone Laboratories, 1974, Kwajalein, pp. 44–45.

10. Seizure of the Gilberts and Marshalls, Philip A. Crowl and Edmund C. Love, US Army in WORLD WAR II, Center of Military History, Wash. DC, 1993 (50th Anniversary edition), map V.

11. The Battles for Kwajalein and Roi-Namur, pamphlet, Bell Telephone Laboratories, 1974, Kwajalein, p. 17.

Chapter 3

1. https://www.smdc.army.mil/ORGANIZATION/TC/

2. https://www.army.mil/article/112881/army_installation_management_command_welcomes_new_teammate_u_s_army_garrison_kwajalein_atoll

3. US Army Kwajalein Atoll Kwajalein Missile Range: Yokwe and Welcome, pamphlet, Raytheon Range Systems Engineering, August 1999, Kwajalein, p. 4.

4. Strategic Defense: Four Decades of Progress, Historical Office, US Army Space and Strategic Defense Command, 1995, pp 61-62

Chapter 4

1. Ebeye 2023: Comprehensive Capacity Development Master Plan, CENTER FOR NATION RECONSTRUCTION AND CAPACITY DEVELOPMENT United States Military Academy West Point, New York 10996, July 2012

2. Summary USAKA/KMR Instrumentation, pamphlet from USAKA/KMR, ~1998

3. Ibid.

4. https://www.smdc.army.mil/ORGANIZATION/TC/ and Summary USAKA/KMR Instrumentation, pamphlet from USAKA/KMR, ~1998

5. Ibid.

6. https://www.smdc.army.mil/ORGANIZATION/TC/

Chapter 5

1. http://www.un.org/en/sc/members/

Chapter 6

1. http://www.tonation-nsn.gov/nowall/

2. http://www.tonation-nsn.gov/84th-annual-rodeo/event-information/

3. https://www.state.gov/wp-content/uploads/2019/02/14-625-Philippines-Defense-Cooperation.pdf

Chapter 7

1. https://www.whitehouse.gov/the-press-office/2014/11/20/fact-sheet-immigration-accountability-executive-action

2. https://www.gsa.gov/about-us/regions/welcome-to-the-pacific-rim-region-9/land-ports-of-entry/san-ysidro-land-port-of-entry

3. https://www.state.gov/wp-content/uploads/2019/02/14-625-Philippines-Defense-Cooperation.pdf

4. https://www.state.gov/wp-content/uploads/2019/02/14-625-Philippines-Defense-Cooperation.pdf

Chapter 8

1 "Catch a Falling Missile," Smithsonian Air and Space Magazine, Dec 97/Jan 98, p. 37

. . .

Chapter 9

1. https://www.smdc.army.mil/ORGANIZATION/TC/ , and Kwajalein Missile Range – A Vital National Asset, pamphlet from USAKA/KMR, ~1998; and Summary USAKA/ KMR Instrumentation, pamphlet from USAKA/ KMR, ~1998

Chapter 10

1. https://crsreports.congress.gov/product/pdf/IF/IF10607
2. http://www.usap.gov/usapgov/
3. http://www.archives.gov/exhibits/charters/constitution_transcript.html
4. http://www.presidency.ucsb.edu/data/orders.php
5. https://guides.loc.gov/federalist-papers
6. Op cit.

Chapter 12

1.   https://www.epw.senate.gov/public/_cache/files/7/d/7db3fbd8-f1b4-4fdf-bd15-12b7df1a0b63/01AFD79733D77F24A71FEF9DAFCCB056. crufinal.pdf
2. http://www.ncdc.noaa.gov/sotc/
3. http://www.friendsofscience.org/index.php?id=3

Chapter 13

1. https://www.smdc.army.mil/ORGANIZATION/TC/ , and Kwajalein Missile Range – A Vital National Asset, pamphlet from USAKA/KMR, ~1998; and Summary USAKA/ KMR Instrumentation, pamphlet from USAKA/ KMR, ~1998
2. Ibid.
3. http://www.military-today.com/aircraft/an_22.htm

Chapter 14

1. https://www.cia.gov/the-world-factbook/countries/angola/summaries/ #people-and-society

Chapter 15

1.   https://cnrse.cnic.navy.mil/Installations/NS-Guantanamo-Bay/About/History/

Chapter 16

1. https://www.archives.gov/milestone-documents/monroe-doctrine

Chapter 17

1. http://www.astronautix.com/t/taiyuan.html
2. Joint Space Fundamentals Course, Student Reference Text, Chapter 3, Orbital Mechanics, Fifth Edition, 1994.
3. Op Cit.
4. Op Cit.

Chapter 18

1.   https://www.smdc.army.mil/ORGANIZATION/TC/ , and Kwajalein Missile Range – A Vital National Asset, pamphlet from USAKA/KMR, ~1998; and Summary USAKA/ KMR Instrumentation, pamphlet from USAKA/ KMR, ~1998

Chapter 19

1. Iraq Culture Smart Card, Guide for Communication and Cultural Awareness, USMC, MCIA-2630-IRQ-003-04
2. https://www.osti.gov/opennet/manhattan-project-history/Events/1945/hiroshima.htm

. . .

Chapter 20

1. http://water.usgs.gov/ogw/aquiferbasics/ext_floridan.html
2. https://maps.conservation.ca.gov/cgs/fam/
3.http://www.northcom.mil/Newsroom/FactSheets/ArticleView/tabid/3999/Article/563999/joint- task-force-civil-support.aspx

Chapter 21

1.	https://news.usni.org/2022/12/19/chinese-liaoning-carrier-strike-group-now-operating-in-the-philippine-sea
2.	https://www.cia.gov/the-world-factbook/countries/moldova/#military-and-security

Chapter 22

1. http://www.philstar.com/headlines/2014/11/27/1396451/
2. Ibid.

Chapter 23

1.	https://www.nps.gov/parkhistory/online_books/npswapa/extcontent/usmc/pcn-190-003119-00/sec1.htm
2. https://www.loc.gov/search/?in=&q=signing+statements&new=true&st=

Chapter 25

1. https://www.worlddata.info/oceania/marshall-islands/airports.php
2. https://home.army.mil/hawaii/index.php/25thID/units/2ndIBCT
3.http://www.army.mil/article/98088/
   Civil_Action_Team_helps_Palau_community/
4. https://www.military.com/equipment/army-weapons
5. http://www.84thengineers.com/pictures/history/history.htm

Chapter 26

1. https://www.nps.gov/people/andrew-johnson.htm
2. https://guides.loc.gov/federal-impeachment/bill-clinton
3. http://www.heritage.org/constitution/#!/articles/2/essays/85/oath-of-office

Chapter 29

1. https://www.fema.gov/txt/nims/nims_ics_position_paper.txt
2. https://cis.org/Map-Sanctuary-Cities-Counties-and-States

Chapter 30

1. https://11thairbornedivision.army.mil
2. https://www.mcbblaz.marines.mil/
3. Communication with SGM Stan Parker, SF, US Army (Ret)

Chapter 32

1. Communication with SGM Stan Parker, SF, US Army (Ret)
2. Ibid.
3. Ibid.
4. Ibid.
5. bid.

Chapter 34

1. https://news.usni.org/2022/12/19/chinese-liaoning-carrier-strike-group-now-operating-in-the-philippine-sea

GLOSSARY

Named Characters

(An asterisk (*) indicates a historical figure)

* Spanish explorer Captain Alonso de Salazar

* English Captain John Marshall

- Amata—a common Marshallese name. Various iterations are in several chapters throughout the centuries. Different man, the same name
- Hans Wilhelm, a German businessman in the Marshall Islands
- Ensign Fujiyama, Imperial Japanese Navy

* Lieutenant Colonel (Lt Col) Pete Ellis, US Marine Corps Planner in 1923

* Captain Hidemi Yoshida, Imperial Japanese Navy

- Isao Akisao, Japanese engineer intern in the South China Sea, Scarborough Shoals, and then Japanese soldier on Kwajalein

* Rear Admiral Monzo Akiyama, Commanding Officer, 6th Base Force, Imperial Japanese Navy (IJN)

* Rear Admiral Michiyuki Yamada, Commanding Officer, 4th Combined Air Group, Roi-Namur, IJN

- Corporal (CPL) Ralph Grayson, 184th Regimental Combat Team, 7th Infantry Division
- Colonel (COL) Seth Grayson, grandson of CPL Grayson, Commander, US Army Garrison-Kwajalein Atoll (USAG-KA), graduate of the United States Military Academy (USMA)
- Sara Grayson, wife of COL Grayson and leader of the Yokwe Yuk Women's Club of Kwajalein
- Lieutenant Colonel (LTC) Eli Shan, Deputy Commander, USAG-KA, graduate of the University of Oregon
- Lieutenant Colonel (LTC) Ron Bakerson, Director, Reagan Test Site (RTS), graduate of Virginia Military Institute (VMI)
- Colonel (COL) Will Bishop, assigned to Joint Staff J3 Operations in the Pentagon, a graduate of The Citadel
- Jill Bishop, wife of COL Bishop and interpreter at the UN
- Ambassador Jane Taylor, US Ambassador to the Republic of the Marshall Islands (RMI)

- President Markus Kabua, President of the RMI
- President Roland Justice, President of the United States (POTUS)
- Secretary of State (Sec State) James Aranson
- Secretary of Homeland Security Jack Ruiz
- Secretary of the Interior Janey Mills
- Deputy Assistant Secretary of State (DASS) for Eastern Asia and the Pacific, Marsha Eckerd
- Secretary of Defense (Sec Def) Amanda Carson
- Chairman of the Joint Chiefs of Staff (CJCS), Admiral Halsey Burke, US Naval Academy graduate
- General Shin Yao, Peoples Republic of China (PRC) rep to the Trilateral Agreement with Russia and the Drug Cartel
- General Valeri Borzovich, Russian rep to the Trilateral Agreement
- Carlos de Von Heim, Drug Cartel rep to the Trilateral Agreement
- Abdul bin Rastafa, Al Jihadi Levant (AJL) rep working with the Cartel to gain access to the Southwest US
- Clausewitz – Carl von Clausewitz, a Prussian military theorist whose primary work was "On War."

Abbreviations & Speciality Terms

AFB – Air Force Base

AJL Al Jihadi Levant terrorist organization

AUMF – Authorization for use of military force

BOS – Base Operations Support, or base ops

CG – Commanding General

CENTCOM – US Central Command

CJCS – Chairman, Joint Chiefs of Staff

CNO – Chief of Naval Operations

CSA – Chief of Staff of the Army

CSAF – Chief of Staff of the Air Force

CMDT – Marine Corps Commandant

CVBG – Carrier Battle Group

DCG – Deputy Commanding General

DHS – Department of Homeland Security

EOC – Emergency Operation Center

FEMA – Federal Emergency Management Agency

HALO – High Altitude Low Opening parachute jump

ICBM – Intercontinental ballistic missile

IMCOM – Installation Management Command

J2 – Joint headquarters intelligence section

J3 – Joint headquarters operations section

J5 – Joint headquarters plans sections

J6 – Joint headquarters communications and computers section

KALGOV – Kwajalein Atoll Local Government

KMISS – Kwajalein Missile Impact Scoring System

KMR – Kwajalein Missile Range, a.k.a. Reagan Test Site

KMRSS – Kwajalein Missile Range Safety Ship

KREMS – Kiernan Re-entry Measurement System

LCM – Landing craft mechanized

LCU – Landing craft utility

MAGTF – Marine Air-Ground Task Force

MARFORPAC – Marine Forces Pacific

MEF – Marine Expeditionary Force

NATO – North Atlantic Treaty Organization

NORTHCOM – Northern Command

NSA – National Security Agency

PACFLT – Pacific Fleet

PACOM – US Pacific Command

PLA – Peoples Liberation Army

POTUS – President of the United States

PRC – People's Republic of China

RIMPAC – Rim of the Pacific naval exercise

RMI – Republic of the Marshall Islands

RTS – Reagan Test Site, a.k.a. Kwajalein Missile Range

SAM – Surface-to Air Missile

SAMS – School of Advanced Military Studies

SCOTUS – Supreme Court of the United States

SCS – South China Sea

SES – Senior Executive Service

SMDC – Space and Missile Defense Command

SOCOM – Special Operations Command

TAGOS – Tactical Auxiliary General Ocean Surveillance (type of ship used for
    the Kwajalein safety ship)

USAG-KA – US Army Garrison-Kwajalein Atoll

USAKA – US Army Kwajalein Atoll

USARHAW – United States Army Hawaii

USCG – United States Coast Guard

USMA – United State Military Academy at West Point

USNA – United States Naval Academy at Annapolis

Military Ranks

ADM – Admiral (Navy)

LTG – Lieutenant General (Army)

BG – Brigadier General (Army)

COL – Colonel (Army)

LTC – Lieutenant Colonel (Army)

MAJ – Major (Army)

CPT – Captain (Army)

1LT – First Lieutenant (Army)

2LT – Second Lieutenant (Army)

CSM – Command Sergeant Major (US Army)

SGM – Sergeant Major (US Army)

1SG – First Sergeant (US Army)

SFC – Sergeant First Class (US Army)

SSG – Staff Sergeant (US Army)

SGT – Sergeant (US Army)

CPL – Corporal (US Army)

A NOTE OF THANKS

If you enjoyed *When Chaos Reigns*, we invite you to leave a review online and share your thoughts and reactions with friends and family.

Publish Authority

www.ingramcontent.com/pod-product-compliance
Lightning Source LLC
Chambersburg PA
CBHW060904210726
48293CB00006B/1955